Praise for Commissaire Georges Dupin
and the Brittany Mysteries

"Delicious Brittany mysteries . . . If this isn't heaven, it's close enough."
—*The New York Times*

"[Bannalec] lets his love and knowledge of Brittany shine through in his books."
—*The Washington Post*

"Roll over, Maigret. Commissaire Dupin has arrived."
—M. C. Beaton

"Perfect for fans of Louise Penny or Mark Pryor."
—*Shelf Awareness*

"The descriptions of the Brittany coast will have readers booking flights to France—murder notwithstanding—and Bannalec's plots, no-frills but clever, with satisfying misdirection and good solid police work, never fail to satisfy."
—*Amazon Book Review*

"The descriptions of Brittany are mesmerizing. It has been elevated into my top ten places I need to visit, all thanks to Bannalec."
—*BookPage*

"A healthy chunk of Brittany with a bracing dash of murder."
—*Kirkus Reviews*

"[Bannalec's] mysteries are both well-crafted and impossible to read without wanting to use them as guides for future trips to the region."
—*Booklist*

T0038731

The Granite Coast Murders

The Killing Tide

The
Body
by the
Sea

—⊹ **A BRITTANY MYSTERY** ⊹—

Jean-Luc Bannalec

Translated by Sorcha McDonagh

MINOTAUR BOOKS
NEW YORK

Published in the United States by Minotaur Books, an imprint of St. Martin's Publishing Group

THE BODY BY THE SEA. Copyright © 2019 by Verlag Kiepenheuer & Witsch. Translation copyright © 2023 by Sorcha McDonagh. All rights reserved. Printed in the United States of America. For information, address St. Martin's Publishing Group, 120 Broadway, New York, NY 10271.

www.minotaurbooks.com

Designed by Devan Norman

The Library of Congress has cataloged the hardcover edition as follows:

Names: Bannalec, Jean-Luc, 1966– author. | McDonagh, Sorcha, 1988– translator.
Title: The body by the sea / Jean-Luc Bannalec ; translated by Sorcha McDonagh.
Other titles: Bretonisches Vermächtnis. English
Description: First U.S. edition. | New York : Minotaur Books, 2023. | Series: Brittany mystery series ; 8 |
Identifiers: LCCN 2022052662 | ISBN 9781250840974 (hardcover) | ISBN 9781250840981 (ebook)
Subjects: LCGFT: Detective and mystery fiction. | Novels.
Classification: LCC PT2662.A565 B74613 2023 | DDC 833/.92—dc23/eng/20221031
LC record available at https://lccn.loc.gov/2022052662

ISBN 978-1-250-32235-7 (trade paperback)

Our books may be purchased in bulk for promotional, educational, or business use. Please contact your local bookseller or the Macmillan Corporate and Premium Sales Department at 1-800-221-7945, extension 5442, or by email at MacmillanSpecialMarkets@macmillan.com.

Originally published in Germany under the title
Bretonisches Vermächtnis by Verlag Kiepenheuer & Witsch

First Minotaur Books Trade Paperback Edition: 2024

10 9 8 7 6 5 4 3 2 1

À L.

À Sandra, much like every book

Ret eo terriñ are graoñenn
Evit kaout ar vouedenn.
There is only one way to do it:
You need to crack the nut
to get the kernel.

—BRETON SAYING

The

Body

by the

Sea

The First Day

There were days when the world was one thing above all else: sky.

May 24 was one of those days. Glorious, bathed in light, clear, bright, with a freshly washed feel.

The heavens looked wider and higher than usual. It seemed like space was expanding, as if the earth's atmosphere were reaching farther into the universe. The sky was a radiant, celestial blue that gradually paled only at the horizon. A curious, oddly pulsating blue, it might be mistaken for a kind of energy or substance in and of itself. The earth appeared to contract underneath this expanse of blue, becoming flatter and smaller.

Commissaire Georges Dupin from Concarneau was lying on his back in the grass. He had stretched himself right out on a summit high above the sea. It was a green hilltop that soared into the sky before the steep cliffs, an impressive seventy-two meters above sea level—according to a sign in the parking lot. The hilltop was covered in heather, bright yellow gorse, bushy grasses and mosses in all kinds of colors: green, rust-red, yellow.

The outermost headland in the very west of Finistère was called the Pointe du Raz, its towering cliffs jutting far out into the Atlantic in the shape of a rough, jagged wedge. The northern end of the Bay of Biscay, the legendary *pointe*, was battered by powerful, turbulent currents, while the other end extended as far as the west coast of Spain. Riddled with sandbanks, it was one of the most dangerous parts of the whole Atlantic, with huge amounts of water gushing around Brittany and into the English Channel where it turned into the North Sea.

The view from up here was breathtaking: the majestic Atlantic, the strange cliffs (they looked like a dragon's tail), two intrepid lighthouses on inhospitable rocks and, in the distance, the stunning Île de Sein. If you truly wanted to experience the End of the World, there was perhaps no more impressive a place to do so than the Pointe du Raz. You could see it, you could feel it: finis terrae. The last stronghold defying the wild, seemingly endless ocean. All of a sudden, solid ground felt dizzyingly fragile.

There's another of Brittany's mysteries you can see particularly well in this spot: the unique interplay of light and color. It seemed to Dupin there was more light in Brittany than there was in other places. Its extraordinary luminosity made the colors there extraordinary too, being simply refractions of this light. It made it seem like the spectrum of color visible to the human eye—the spectrum from red to orange, yellow, green, blue, indigo, and violet—was much wider ranging here. As if the light endlessly refracted on the surface of the water around the Breton peninsula was more finely nuanced. This intensity of light and color had beguiled even the greatest of fans: Monet, Gauguin, Picasso, and many other painters had fallen under Brittany's spell.

Ever since Dupin's first visit to it, the Pointe du Raz had been on his list of favorite places. Outside of tourist season. There were two reasons for today's trip: the first was Le Fumoir de la Pointe du Raz, a new fish smokehouse nearby that Riwal had raved about. They smoked the finest fish from the dangerous strait there, most notably *lieus jaunes,* a particular kind of cod. They were generally smoked with the "incomparable flavors of the smoke from Breton oaks and with a secret mixture of various types of pepper and spices." The smokehouse belonged to the cousin of a cousin of Riwal's. Dupin hadn't been listening properly at the time. Riwal's distant family relationships—which included friends he considered family—always baffled the commissaire. In any case, Riwal's glowing report had persuaded Dupin to visit the fish smokehouse. And he and Claire were having their first evening off together in weeks, because Claire had been working at the hospital more or less without a break. *Lieu jaune* was her favorite kind of fish and she liked smoked fish in general. Dupin wanted to surprise her.

The second reason for the trip was the renovation work at the police station. It had been going on for four weeks now and was an absolute nightmare. The company they had hired had promised the running of the station would be "completely unaffected," which was nonsense, even in theory. And, of course, that wasn't how it had turned out in practice either. Utter chaos had broken out on the very first day. *Everything* affected the running of the station, not to mention the added noise, dust, and dirt. And of course—the painter having assured them "the whole thing will be totally odorless"—there was an immediate, unbearable stench of paint. Even throwing open all the windows and doors hadn't made any difference. The only good thing about it was that the stench of paint and solvents masked the hideous underlying smell of the building that had been driving Dupin mad since his first day of work—although he was the only person who noticed it. Dupin hoped the smell might even be completely gone by the end of the renovation.

All of the staff at the station had made a break for it in the last few weeks. Only an ever-changing skeleton crew held down the fort. Everyone had constantly been looking for new and increasingly imaginative excuses for avoiding the office. Outrageous incidents such as a raided carrot patch or unauthorized mussel-harvesting on the beach suddenly had to be investigated at the scene. Sometimes they went out in threes or fours. They had taken up ancient "open cases" again: the theft of three surfboards last October and the disappearance of a pink dinghy in the harbor. Everyone had been glad when there really had been a crime: during the demolition of an old house in Pont-Aven, six hundred Belgian gold coins from 1870 had been found. A real treasure trove; it was valued at a few hundred thousand euro and the find sparked wild speculation.

At the beginning of the week, even Dupin's assistant, Nolwenn, had reached the end of her rope. A bucket of thick paint had leaked outside her door and she had stepped right in it. For weeks beforehand she had been gamely trying to remain calm, but after this incident she had promptly taken several days off. This had instantly made Dupin nervous, all the more so because she had given no details whatsoever about when she planned to return to the office. Over the years—through vast amounts of overtime—Nolwenn must have saved up several months' worth of holiday. Dupin didn't dare check. Nolwenn being absent for quite a long time—especially in protest—would, and there was no doubt about this, end in disaster sooner or later. She and her husband had lost no time setting off on a cycling tour that had originally been scheduled for September. A very special cycling tour, inspired by the Breton bestseller *Bistrot Breizh: Le tour de Bretagne des vieux cafés à vélo*, which was a guide to the oldest, most authentic pubs that Brittany had to offer. The pubs were expertly handpicked. The tour literally went from village to village. More for pleasure than exercise by the sound of it, Nolwenn had chosen the inland route through gorgeous, secluded scenery. She had suggested Riwal and Dupin take time off too, and so Riwal had promptly decamped to Belle-Île with his wife and their two children for a few days. One of his sisters owned a house there that had been empty since she had moved to her husband's hometown on Cape Cod on the American East Coast. The commissaire had had no interest in taking time off. For a start, there was no way Claire could get away from the hospital at the moment, but on top of that, holidays were not Dupin's thing. Kadeg, Dupin's other inspector, was sitting pretty. He had been on parental leave for two and a half months and he wouldn't be back till July. His wife had given birth to twins in March. Anne and Conan. The inspector had bought himself one of those double prams—a monstrous contraption—and turned up at the station with it from time to time. It wasn't unusual for him to be on his own with the children for days at a time. His wife—a martial arts teacher of *kyokushin* karate in Lorient, the "toughest contact martial art in the world" as Kadeg proudly pointed out every time—did a lot of traveling for classes and tournaments.

Dupin had set out at noon, bought the fish for dinner, and had a long chat with the friendly owner of the *fumerie*. From the car park, he had walked to the end of the *pointe*. Later, after this little break he was currently enjoying, he would drink a cold beer in the sun on the gorgeous terrace of Relais de la Pointe by the stunning beach at the Baie des Trépassés. This was another of his rituals; he loved sitting there. He would eat a few *galettes apéritives au jambon*, little rectangles of crispy, buttery pancake batter with succulent ham. He would be back home by around seven or half past seven. Claire had promised to make it back by half past eight, so he would have plenty of time to get everything ready.

He was lucky with the weather. It felt like spring was giving way to summer today. The long Breton summer that would stretch into the beginning of October, maybe even a little later. The year before, Dupin and Claire had their last swim on the thirty-first of October. It was more than twenty degrees today, a slightly salty, iodine note on the gentle breeze. The taste of the summer sea. The sun warmed your skin but didn't burn it. *"Beau et chaud,"* was *Le Télégramme*'s forecast for the next few days. Did it get any more promising than that?

Instead of the fifteen minutes he had planned, Dupin had been lying in the grass for forty-five minutes now. He was finding it difficult to move. And this wasn't just because of the comfortable place he was lying and the vast, spellbinding sky, it was mainly the meditative lapping of the waves breaking steadily and languidly against the cliffs beneath the hilltop. Usually so restless, the commissaire had drifted off into a blissful doze.

Suddenly he heard the insistent sound of his cell phone.

Dupin sat up and looked for his cell. It fell silent. By the time he had finally pulled it out of his trouser pocket, it was ringing again.

"Yes?" growled the commissaire.

"It's me, boss."

Inspector Riwal.

"What is it?"

"Nothing, boss. I just wanted to check in."

Riwal had already checked in the day before and the day before that. And even then Dupin had thought he could hear something like a guilty conscience in his voice. Must have been because of the speed with which the inspector had hightailed it off the sinking ship.

"Everything is okay here, Riwal. How are things on the island?"

"Lovely. But I'll come straightaway if there's anything, please just . . ."

"Enjoy yourself!"

"All right, boss. Just so you know, we usually don't get reception in the house, my sister had the landline disconnected. I'm in a pub right now, but . . ."

"It's okay, Riwal. Relax. Did you try my phone just then?"

"No, why?"

"Doesn't matter. Happy Pentecost."

Dupin hung up. His gaze swept across the ocean. A never-ending, sparkling, shimmering expanse.

Last summer he had gone to Le Conquet with his friend Henri, the owner of Café du Port in Sainte-Marine. Henri had bought one of the famous rustic sausages that were a specialty of the nearby Île Molène, as well as *pétoncles,* small, nutty-flavored scallops, to make into an incredible ragout. They parked the car at the Pointe de Corsen close by and went for a stroll. They enjoyed the view: the deep blue sea, the fabled maze of islands around the Île Molène in the distance. Dupin said: "All we're missing is a few dolphins." "Well, there they are," Henri replied in the most airily casual way you can imagine, pointing to the water. There were ten or fifteen dolphins. For several minutes they performed daredevil leaps and high-speed tricks. A real show. Then all of a sudden they disappeared. Dupin knew it was ridiculous, but ever since that day he always kept a particularly keen eye on the sea.

The phone was ringing again.

Within moments, the commissaire had risen to his feet with a sigh.

"Yes?"

"Georges! So glad we've got hold of you."

A serious, female voice.

"We're going to keep driving without stopping, we've just decided. We're already at Laval. But we can't get through to Claire."

Dupin recognized the voice now. It was Claire's mother.

"We'll be there around nine." There was a rustling sound. "Isn't that right, Gustave?"

From the background there quickly came a loud "Absolutely! At the latest. If not earlier." Dupin could hear the noise of the engine now too.

"That's fantastic, isn't it?" Claire's mother said enthusiastically. "This way we'll have the whole evening together. We're so pleased, Georges. Can you let Claire know?"

"I'm . . . sure she'll be beside herself. With absolute delight."

"I think so too! See you soon, then, Georges."

The conversation was over.

It took Dupin some time to compose himself.

So much for the two of them spending a quiet evening together. It would all begin today, then. Not tomorrow, Saturday, as per the original plan. Dupin had been studiously ignoring all of this. Claire's parents were coming for a visit, his parents-in-law, effectively. For the entire Pentecost long weekend. Gustave and Hélène Lannoy. From near Fécamp in Normandy. Dupin had seen them only a handful of times since he and Claire had got back together. They would be staying with them. For three days. Dupin was pleased with the house he and Claire had moved into the year before, but a house with plenty of room came with—as it now turned out—disadvantages too. Claire's parents were as different from each other as it is possible to be. Hélène was a yoga teacher and Claire's father was the head of a successful law firm that he had, officially speaking, already handed over to a senior partner. It was impossible for him to let go, though. Among the few things they had in common, along with a fondness for food and drink and a profound love for Claire, was an enthusiasm for debate, with a speaking ratio of nine to one in favor of Claire's mother. There was always plenty to talk about because of their different viewpoints, enough for several shared lifetimes together. An intriguing basis for a marriage, Dupin thought. Nevertheless, anyone would describe their marriage, without hesitation, as "extremely happy." "That's just how they are," Claire had chided him. "I'm sure it'll be lovely!"

"Damn it!" he blurted out. He'd really been looking forward to this evening. To their time alone together. "This is—"

The phone. A fourth time.

He answered again, curtly this time.

"Yes?"

"Is that Commissaire Georges Dupin?"

The voice belonged to an elderly woman. Dupin pulled himself together. The caller wasn't to blame for the unfortunate turn his evening had taken.

"Speaking. And whom am I talking to?"

"It's Madame Chaboseau. The wife of Docteur Pierre Chaboseau."

Docteur Chaboseau, the doctor with the most modern practice in Concarneau. It was in a villa on Boulevard Katerine Wylie, right on the seafront. Not far from Claire and Dupin's house. Chaboseau was a cardiologist and general practitioner and he cared a lot about social status, as did his wife. They were some of the town's "notables," people from long-established, well-to-do families who had shaped the fortunes of Concarneau over generations and had a network of influential contacts. Another reason Dupin knew of them was that they did not live in the villa where the practice was, they lived in the same building as Dupin's favorite restaurant, the Amiral. Another marvelous piece of real estate in a sought-after location; the Chaboseaus owned the second and third floors of the building as well as the deluxe loft conversion.

"What is this about, madame?"

"He's dead."

"Excuse me?"

Had he misheard?

"My husband"—there was a clear note of disapproval in her voice—"he's dead. I found him a few minutes ago, down in the courtyard. He fell out of his study on the top floor."

She was speaking in a way that was almost robotic, making an effort to give precise details.

Dupin stood rooted to the spot.

"Your husband is dead?"

"Yes."

"He fell out a window?"

"He's lying mangled on the ground."

A pause.

"I . . ." Dupin broke off. And tried again: "Have you notified the police?"

A strange question, he had to admit.

"I had them give me your number at the station. I said it was urgent."

"And you didn't report the incident *then*?"

"I think this is a matter that the most senior commissaire should deal with personally."

Dupin had already started walking. He came to a small path.

"Are you certain your husband is dead?"

"There's a large pool of blood. He's lying there very . . ." She searched for the right words. "Very *oddly*."

"Call an ambulance immediately, madame. I'm leaving right now but it will take me forty-five minutes to get to you." At the very least, in fact. If he drove flat-out.

"I'll let my colleagues know so that someone can drive out to you straightaway."

He slowed his pace.

"So do you think it was murder, then?"

Madame Chaboseau hesitated.

"Madame? Are you still there?"

"You must try and get here as quickly as you can, Commissaire."

It was a gruesome sight. And a peculiar one too. The remarkably large pool of blood had spread out around the entire torso. Almost circular and a deep red. Fragments of glass flashed in the sunlight like decorations. They were scattered across the little enclosed courtyard: the remains of the large picture window that Docteur Chaboseau had fallen through. He had landed on his front, on his right side. His shoulder stuck out in an unnatural way. And his hips were at a strange angle to his slack legs. Dupin estimated the doctor fell from a height of about fifteen meters. The dead man was wearing dark cord trousers, a beige shirt and a waistcoat in the same color, as well as what looked like good-quality black leather slippers that had, absurdly, stayed on his feet. His reddish hair looked as though it had just been combed. Only the left side of his face was visible, his left eye open a crack.

After Dupin spent some time examining the body, he made his way straight into the Chaboseaus' apartment via one of those elevators that lots of old buildings get retrofitted with. The elevator was like a sardine tin hanging from a wire cable.

The medical examiner—old Docteur Lafond, still the most tolerable of all the people in his profession—had, of course, long been on the scene, along with the crime scene investigators. Dupin was by far the last to arrive at the crime scene. Docteur Lafond had been waiting for him to arrive before having the body brought to the lab in Quimper.

During the hair-raising journey back to Concarneau from the Pointe du Raz, Dupin had tried to get ahold of Nolwenn and Riwal numerous times. But no luck. He had left a message on every second phone call. It was no use—he would have to get by without them for now. Of the four members of the staff who had actually stayed at the station, two had gotten to the scene very quickly. Rosa Le Menn and Iris Nevou. The station had been allowed to hire two more people at the beginning of the year. This was mainly down to Nolwenn's perseverance—they had been notoriously understaffed for some time now. The team had now been reinforced by two policewomen, a development Nolwenn considered "badly needed." Le Menn was straight out of the police academy, in her early twenties, tall, with broad shoulders like a swimmer, and wore her dark blond hair in a braid. She was self-confident and full of energy. Iris Nevou was more petite— she always looked a little forlorn in her uniform—very pale skin, dark pageboy haircut, with a remarkably deep, penetrating voice. She had twice won the award for best police markswoman in Brittany without even doing much training. She had worked in the gendarmerie in Le Conquet for fifteen years. At the end of last year, she had left her husband and her former life behind and moved from the most northwestern part of Brittany to "the south."

Le Menn and Nevou had done an initial examination of the body. And now that Dupin had seen the body too, Madame Chaboseau's assumption that her husband was already dead when she called Dupin seemed extremely plausible. She obviously should've called an ambulance, but she hadn't, even after Dupin explicitly told her to do so.

By this point they were in the loft, Dupin having cast just a quick glance at the living quarters on the second and third floors. The loft conversion was "monsieur's domain," as Madame Chaboseau had put it. They were standing in the spacious private study. Dupin guessed it was at least fifty square meters. Three small windows onto the harbor, and then on the other side there were two large picture windows. They gave a superb view of the town over the roofs of the surrounding houses. The window on the right-hand side was broken. It was more than three meters wide and almost reached to the wooden floor—this was where it had happened.

The way the loft had been converted suggested a 1970s renovation. The furnishings were all antiques: old floor lamps; two narrow, elegant bureaus with coffee-table books about art on them; Persian rugs on well-kept, dark parquet; a chaise longue covered in red velvet in one corner and a black leather armchair with an upholstered footstool in front of it in another. Paintings hung on the walls in old, gold-painted wooden frames. There must have been two dozen of them. An enormous desk with an uncomfortable-looking, high-backed chair behind it. Everything was in meticulously well-cared-for condition, almost obsessively neat. It reminded Dupin of his childhood home in Paris. His mother's motto was: if you allow even one speck of dust, universal decline will inevitably follow.

"And just in case you're thinking it, Monsieur le Commissaire," said Madame Chaboseau, absolutely indignant, "my husband was definitely not unsteady on his legs! Even though he turned seventy-four this year. His hip was giving him a bit of trouble, but it was nowhere near making him lose his balance and fall out a window!"

She jutted her pointy chin out.

"And much less—frankly it doesn't bear thinking about even for a moment—" She breathed out with a hissing noise. "Much less was it suicide! The very idea of it is disgraceful."

Le Menn, Nevou, and the crime scene investigation team had searched for a letter or note, a message from Monsieur Chaboseau, and hadn't found anything. Nothing downstairs either. But this didn't mean very much; most people who took their own lives didn't leave a farewell letter behind. However, for the moment there was nothing to indicate suicide.

Dupin would have put Madame Chaboseau in her early seventies. Chin-length hair dyed chestnut brown, an elegant hairdo with plenty of volume that—Dupin suspected—required daily visits to the hairdresser. Her makeup was discreet and she wore expensive-looking glasses in a Bordeaux red. She had on a dark green blouse and loose-fitting black trousers. Even now, perhaps two hours after she had found her husband dead, she wasn't letting much emotion show. Dupin knew that a state of shock manifested itself differently in every person. He was careful not to infer anything about what was going on in her head from her outward appearance. Just as he was firmly opposed to jumping to conclusions and assumptions in general.

"First of all, Docteur Lafond will examine the body at the medical examiner's office for hematomas, scratches, and contusions," Rosa Le Menn explained clearly and calmly but without mincing her words, "to see if there are any signs of a physical struggle."

There were no indications of a struggle anywhere in the study. However, it wouldn't have taken more than one powerful, well-aimed shove to make the doctor fall through the window.

In the meantime, Dupin had been inspecting the second, intact picture window, which was built exactly like the broken one. There was no double glazing or safety glass. The kind of building regulations that would probably have prevented what happened most likely didn't exist when the attic was being converted. If a grown man fell onto such a simply glazed pane head-on, possibly helped by a shove or by deliberately throwing himself against it, it would give way immediately.

"They will also examine him for signs of a heart attack or stroke," added Le Menn, now facing Madame Chaboseau. "These could also have caused a fall against the window."

Of course, such unfortunate accidents did happen. But Dupin considered it extremely unlikely.

"That's the procedure, Madame Chaboseau. We'll know more soon," finished Le Menn. Dupin had noticed this before in recent weeks: she was meticulous about presenting the police regulations, but the way she did it, her expressions, her voice, her demeanor, told a different story. They revealed that Le Menn was occasionally skeptical of "official procedure," which made Dupin take a liking to her from the beginning.

The commissaire was walking around the large room, stopping now and again, murmuring to himself.

Madame Chaboseau was standing next to her husband's massive desk. Made from dark, polished wood, it had a big felt inlay with a computer screen on it. Dupin turned to the paintings on the walls, which were hanging close together. Just like on the other two floors when they had taken a quick look around earlier. Up here the artworks were mainly on paper. Pastels, watercolors, pencil. Dupin managed to make out signatures by Gauguin, Berthe Morisot, Signac, and Monet. Two Monet-style watercolors of Belle-Île hung directly above the desk. Almost all of them were of Brittany. Dupin was no expert, but he knew enough to know there was a lot of money hanging on these walls. There was presumably even more money downstairs, where there were mainly oil paintings. The commissaire also noticed the ultramodern air-conditioning system, the well-secured door, the alarm system. As soon as he'd come in, before he could even ask a question about the paintings, Madame Chaboseau had volunteered that none of the pieces were missing, and none of the other valuables were either. Clearly they weren't dealing with a robbery.

Dupin turned to Madame Chaboseau: "And you have no idea who might have . . . called to see your husband? Think carefully."

"I've thought carefully already." Madame Chaboseau made no effort to suppress any of the frustration in her voice. "There's nothing marked in his calendar. There's nothing all day. And that's the third time you've asked me."

The pristine condition of the door and lock proved that nobody had got in by brute force. If it had been neither an accident nor suicide, there was currently reason to believe Chaboseau himself had opened the door to the person who had killed him. Which meant that he had probably known this person, or at least expected them. Perhaps they had arranged to meet. But there were many other possible scenarios: for instance, that he had left the house, then someone secretly followed him home and didn't make themselves known until the moment the doctor unlocked the apartment. Or somebody had done a convincing job of pretending to be someone else. But Dupin thought Docteur Chaboseau would definitely not have been that easy to fool.

Iris Nevou left to try to find out which of the other residents had been at home that afternoon and whether they had noticed anything out of the ordinary. The Chaboseaus' living quarters in the upper stories took up two-thirds of the tall old building. It was also home to the Amiral. Three residents lived in the other third, on the side facing away from Place Jean Jaurès. The Amiral had an extra room on the first floor—generally reserved for quite large parties—and there was also another apartment there where a family with two children lived.

Dupin went back over to the broken window. He didn't stop until just before the drop, then looked down. An involuntary shudder ran the length of his spine.

"And what about yourself, Madame Chaboseau, you said earlier that you were busy in town between two and four o'clock?"

Her phone call had come through to Dupin at the Pointe du Raz at 4:07.

"I had a hair appointment at two. Until about three fifteen. After that, I had a few things I needed to do."

"If you wouldn't mind telling us about that in more detail?"

Dupin walked around the room again during this last exchange and stopped at the broken window once more. He looked down and suddenly recalled the ten-meter diving board in a Paris swimming pool that he'd been forced onto by a bet with his friends when he was twelve years old. He took a firm step backward and turned back to Madame Chaboseau.

"I was in Galerie Gloux. About a painting. And then I went to Maurite's."

Maurite was the owner of a Moroccan deli in the legendary covered market. Dupin loved his stall. Maurite was wonderful and sold the most delicious things. And of course, the commissaire knew Galerie Gloux too. Françoise and Jean-Michel Gloux had become friends of his over the years.

"The maid has the day off today. I bought a splendid *poulet noir*."

These words sounded like something from fifty years ago. A hundred years ago.

"That was it? Nothing else?"

"I also went to Hops briefly. To buy some Black Angus sausages."

Another place where Dupin and Claire liked to shop. The owner, Katell Cadic, sold amazing salami and fantastic cheeses.

"We will be checking that," Dupin said, aware of how distracted he was getting at the thought of the salami. He pulled himself together. "Has anything happened in your husband's life recently that you suspect could be linked to the murder?"

"Of course not!" Madame Chaboseau was beside herself. "Nobody had any reason to kill my husband. A hideous thought."

"An incident at the surgery?" Dupin kept probing, undeterred. "A misdiagnosis, perhaps? That kind of thing happens." As far as Dupin knew, the doctor had, in fact, had an impeccable reputation, but purely statistically, even he must surely have made these kinds of mistakes during his long career.

Madame Chaboseau said nothing, fixing Dupin with a hard look.

"Or some other dispute? An argument that escalated? Please think, madame. This is crucial."

She shook her head firmly.

"Rivalries? He couldn't have been friends with everyone."

The power and status possessed by families such as the Chaboseaus were sometimes won and retained at other people's expense. Which these families called "collateral damage." They generally weren't even aware of it because they were busy with "more important things."

"My husband is highly regarded." She may have lowered her

voice but there was a latent aggression in her tone. "He enjoys an impeccable reputation. In his career as a doctor but also as a philanthropic donor and patron of the arts. He's involved in all kinds of projects."

"So you have absolutely no idea who might have had it in for your husband? And why?" Dupin was speaking quietly and sharply now too. "If you keep information from us, you are obstructing our investigation."

"Ridiculous."

Dupin turned away and began to walk around again. He was feeling quite agitated. It was only partly to do with Madame Chaboseau and her arrogant, infuriatingly frosty manner. Dupin was in a strange mood. A mixture of horror at the possible—his intuition told him probable—murder, and utter indignation. Although it was not yet confirmed as such, there was a brazenness to committing this kind of crime right under their noses, right on the police station's doorstep.

"How come," Le Menn interjected, taking care to adopt a matter-of-fact, friendly tone, "it was you of all people who found your husband? Or, to put it another way, why did you come in through the courtyard entrance?"

The smarter apartments in town often had little courtyards in back that were generally used for parking cars. The Chaboseaus' even had a door to access the elevator and staircase, just like the main door.

"I often use the back door. It's really useful, especially if you've been shopping."

"What do you use the courtyard for?" Le Menn kept digging.

It was perhaps three meters by four. A high wall to the left and right, an electric gate onto the street at chest height.

"I used to park my car there."

"And your husband?"

Madame Chaboseau raised her eyebrows. "He's been parking his car in the bigger courtyard across the road for years. He rented a parking space there."

She basically meant—or at least it sounded this way to Dupin—that it was the proper place for her husband's limousine. Both courtyards were on the Rue du Guesclin, a narrow, quiet, one-way street behind the Amiral. Dupin's favorite newsagent was on the corner, run by Alain and Amélia. He bought all his newspapers there and plenty of other things: books, science and cooking magazines for Claire, and his red Clairefontaine notebooks as well as the dozens of pens he was always losing.

"And what do you use your courtyard for now?" Le Menn wouldn't let it go.

Dupin got out his Clairefontaine and made a few notes.

"Just as a private entrance to the house."

"And you two are the only people with a key?"

"And the caretaker, and the maid too. Nobody else."

"And you didn't see your husband's body until the moment the gate opened?"

So far, nobody had come forward who could have witnessed the fall—or who would have noticed the body any earlier than Madame Chaboseau. Which wasn't a surprise, as it wasn't a very busy street. And the gate was at least one meter, forty centimeters high.

Madame Chaboseau nodded.

"What did you talk about over lunch? Did you talk about anything in particular?" Dupin made sure to strike a friendly tone. Madame Chaboseau had mentioned earlier that she and her husband had eaten together between twelve and one thirty, downstairs in the Amiral. In the brasserie, same as every Friday at lunch. According to her statement, she'd gone to the second floor afterward and her husband had gone to his office on the fourth. Apparently he hadn't worked on Friday afternoons for some years now.

"We read the papers. And spoke about various things."

"For example?"

"The harbor."

"The harbor?"

"The harbor expansion."

"I see. And what exactly did you talk about?"

Several articles had come out this week about the new ship-yard that had opened recently. The town had also authorized land to be used for expanding the harbor further.

"How enthusiastic we are about all of this activity."

The harbor expansion had long been one of the main topics of conversation in Concarneau. Because the *ville bleue*, the beautiful "blue town," was essentially one thing: a town on the sea. And the harbor was its center; or rather, the three harbors were. The leisure and sport harbor for amateur sailors and professionals. The legendary fishing harbor—nothing had shaped the history of Concarneau like fishing had. Although the revenue from it had dwindled in recent decades, it was still among the most significant fishing harbors in all of France. And last but not least the industrial harbor with its dockyards, shipbuilding, and ship repairs, which was growing the fastest. When you drove over the remarkably high bridge over the Moros and suddenly had a breathtaking view of Concarneau, the harbor was directly beneath you. You could see enormous ships in the water or in vast dry docks. The tagline for the expansion was "The harbor in the town, the town in the harbor." A line that also referenced the town's excellent geographical location. The town was protected both by spits of land and the river Moros's large, natural pools against the brutal raging of the Atlantic and enemy attacks, of which there had been several in the town's history.

"But surely you must have got into more detail than that when you discussed the harbor."

"No. And how is this meant to be relevant, anyway?"

This was hopeless.

"And what else did you talk about?"

"The weather."

This didn't seem like a barbed comment. And it was probably true. The weather was an extremely popular topic in Brittany even though it—unlike other places in the world—actually didn't influence people's lives very much. Bretons didn't let the weather hold them back from something important.

There was a knock and Iris Nevou came into the room. She launched right into a report: "None of the neighbors saw a stranger at the house between two and four. I've spoken to them all myself." She took her cell out of her pocket and tapped away at it. "Shall I send you the list?" She looked at Dupin. Her deep voice always fascinated him; it was such an incredible contrast to her fragile appearance.

"Please do. And nobody saw anything—or even heard anything? The windowpane cracking? A scream?"

"Nobody, nothing. Paul Girard didn't either." This was the

owner of the Amiral, a friend of Dupin's since his earliest days in Brittany. "And neither did the staff. I've spoken to Ingrid." The wonderful, talented manager of the brasserie. "By the way, Paul Girard is visiting his oyster farmer at the moment, getting new stock."

"And what about the kitchen staff?"

The kitchen was out the back, but it was a good ten or fifteen meters away from the little yard.

"They didn't hear anything either."

This was plausible. It was loud in the kitchen, plus there was the high-performance air-conditioning system and the noise from the Friday market held on the square in front of the Amiral.

"Excellent."

Dupin was pleased that Nevou had thought of everything.

His emphatic "excellent" prompted perplexed looks from everyone present, including Nevou.

The commissaire abruptly turned to go.

He stopped just before the door and turned around. "Thank you so much, Madame Chaboseau. Please get in touch if you need anything."

Madame Chaboseau looked bewildered.

"If anything occurs to you, give me a call. You've got my number. And Le Menn, you wait here—the crime scene investigators are about to come back upstairs."

They would take the computer too. Madame Chaboseau said she didn't know the password, which meant it would be complicated, as it always was. The same was true of the code for Monsieur Chaboseau's cell phone, which they'd found in one of the bureaus. He had barely used the landline for years now. Madame

Chaboseau said she was the only one who still used it for making calls; she didn't have a cell phone.

The team of crime scene investigators had started in the courtyard, and afterward they had spent time in the loft. But then the team moved to the second and third floors so that Dupin could speak to Madame Chaboseau in peace. Dupin had instructed them to take photos of everything, which Madame Chaboseau allowed only under protest.

"And Nevou, you come with me," Dupin said, waving her over to him.

He had a few jobs for her.

"And before I forget, madame, this room will be considered a crime scene until further notice. Along with the courtyard. Nobody will be allowed to access them apart from the police."

He opened the door and hurried toward the stairs. He was not getting in that elevator again.

It wasn't that he didn't have plenty of questions left for Madame Chaboseau, but he needed to get his thoughts in order. And try to get through to Riwal and Nolwenn again as soon as possible. Above all, he couldn't go a moment longer without a coffee. He'd been meaning to have one that afternoon at the Baie des Trépassés. After the cold beer. Which he'd missed out on, just like he'd missed out on the ham crêpes. His relaxing day trip already seemed like days ago.

Dupin was sitting on the terrace at the Amiral. In his usual corner, his back to the whitewashed stone wall. It was seven fifteen and only one other table, right at the other end, was still occupied. Ingrid had just brought him the coffee he'd ordered from her as he crossed the restaurant. He sighed in relief.

Nevou had been standing in front of the Amiral making calls as Dupin walked into it from Avenue Pierre Guéguin. The editors of both *Ouest-France* and *Le Télégramme* had made a bee-line for him. Donal and Drollec. The two newspapers had their offices less than two hundred meters from here on Place Jean Jaurès, the large square to the south of the Amiral.

News of the death of Monsieur Chaboseau would have spread through the town like wildfire, of course. Despite being fond of the two journalists, Dupin had not been in the mood to give explanations. So he had declared, both bluntly and truthfully, that as of yet he had "absolutely nothing" to say.

Dupin leaned back, took a slug of coffee, and let his gaze wander across the square, all traces of the market having already been cleared away.

The massive Ville Close towered up on the left and next to it were the leisure harbor's miles of wooden jetties winding their way in different directions. Dozens of boats gently bobbing, mainly sailing boats. Brightly colored sails hanging slackly, lit up beautifully by the sun, which was still high in the sky. The days had begun to lengthen.

All of a sudden, Dupin couldn't help smiling. There were various reasons for his—inappropriate—emotion. If this was more than a tragic accident or suicide, if a crime had taken place here—and his instinct told him that was the case—then he would be sitting here quite a lot, and he would actually be "on official business." The Amiral would become his office. Besides, there was no way he could go to dinner with Claire's parents today. And in fact, it was very likely he would miss a lot of the family's Pentecost plans.

"Ah, there you are, Commissaire!" Iris Nevou was standing at his table all of a sudden. He hadn't seen her coming. She looked out of sorts.

"Same for you?" He raised his empty cup.

"I don't drink coffee."

Nevou sat down next to him.

"Please talk to Docteur Chaboseau's colleagues at the surgery about their boss's potential enemies. Or disputes."

"All right." Nevou took out a tattered brown notebook. "All right" was one of her favorite phrases and she didn't use it more or less in passing the way most people did, she emphasized it very firmly every time.

"So." Dupin's Clairefontaine was open in front of him and he was scanning the notes he'd made. "So, these projects, what are these projects that Docteur Chaboseau was so admirably involved in"—he quoted Madame Chaboseau's words—"as a 'philanthropic donor and patron of the arts'? Le Menn will help you look into it."

Especially at the beginning, it was mostly a case of hoping for the best. Doing some investigating here, some investigating there. You had to cast as many nets as possible in as many places as possible, and see what you caught.

"Shouldn't we wait until we really know what we're dealing with here? What if it wasn't murder at all? I'm not too sure."

Another phrase Nevou liked to use. And it expressed more than a specific doubt about the thing at hand. Her "I'm not too sure" was more like a policy of questioning everything on principle. And not trusting appearances. A sensible policy, Dupin thought, as a matter of fact.

"I . . ." What could he say? Strictly speaking, she was right. "But if it really was murder, which is currently by far the most plausible theory, we would be losing valuable time."

She shrugged her shoulders. "Okay, then. In that case, if I were in your position I would be taking an interest in Chaboseau's business ventures."

"What do you mean exactly?"

"He and his wife were well known for being entrepreneurs and investors."

This was news. To Dupin, at least.

A dog had settled down next to their table. A large dog with long, dirty fur; it was hard to tell what color it was, but somehow yellowish. He was lying with his snout on his paws, raising his head now and again to look at the commissaire. Dupin looked around for its owner but couldn't see anyone.

"What kind of investments are we talking about?"

"They have interests in various companies and projects. Real estate, a brewery, and also the leisure harbor here in Concarneau. Those are the three I know of. But there might be others."

Brittany produced many successful entrepreneurs. Businesspeople who also recognized their responsibility to be philanthropic, another fine Breton tradition. There were countless examples, including Yves Rocher, who made his first fig buttercup-based cream in the attic of his parents' house. Or François Pinault, the billionaire patron of the arts who founded one of the largest fashion empires in the world. Gucci, Yves Saint Laurent, and Puma were now all Breton-owned.

"Do we know how much of a financial stake the Chaboseaus have in these projects?" Dupin was curious now.

Nevou shrugged. "I'll look into it." She still seemed a little grumpy. Dupin would have been only too glad to order her a coffee. He was convinced that caffeine improved your mood.

"Did he have business partners? Long-standing business partners?"

"I'll look into it."

"Go over the details with Madame Chaboseau too."

"All right."

Dupin jotted down a few key notes in silence, and signaled to Ingrid for another coffee. She was just settling up with the table at the other end of the terrace.

Nevou's brow furrowed. "There must be several million hanging on the walls of the apartment. That's more than your average hobby, I'd say. Another interesting point."

Dupin had dealt with a valuable painting in a case once before, a Gauguin. And while it was true that no painting had been stolen from the Chaboseaus, a crime could look quite different in the art world. Perhaps, and this was just one of numerous possibilities, Chaboseau had been taken in by a sophisticated forger and this had set off a dramatic series of events.

"In her statement, Madame Chaboseau says she was in the Galerie Gloux at lunchtime today about a piece of art."

Dupin wasn't quite sure what Nevou meant by this. But he would still call in to the gallery because it was a good idea anyway. Françoise and Jean-Michel knew the town, the people, all things Concarneau.

"We . . ."

"Commissaire!"

In an instant, Rosa Le Menn was standing in front of them. "The medical examiner called. He wanted to tell you pers—"

"And?"

"A distinct antemortem hematoma on his right shoulder. And one on his upper arm. Fresh, they were caused shortly before death. And I'm quoting here," her eyes widened, "'morphologically everything suggests a powerful push.' Docteur Lafond would, and this is how I was told to put it, gladly swear to it after just one exam."

She broke off, scrutinizing Dupin as if she wanted to give him time to process this news.

"That would mean," Nevou pointed out, "he really was murdered." But she followed this up with an "I'm not too sure" all the same.

Dupin stood up abruptly. He went to the end of the terrace and then walked slowly back. There was actually nothing surprising in this report. And yet—now it was real. And his strong sense of indignation had returned too. In all the time that Dupin had lived in Brittany there had never been a murder on his own turf, in Concarneau. At home, so to speak.

"Did Lafond say anything else?" Dupin was back at the table. Le Menn had sat down next to Nevou while the commissaire stayed on his feet facing them.

"Apart from the hematomas, he couldn't find anything unusual. Lafond has ruled out a heart attack or stroke."

"Has he said anything about time of death?"

"Officially, it was between three and four o'clock. Also, everything suggests Chaboseau died immediately. If you'd like to know why in more detail, he says he will gladly explain."

"What does 'officially' mean?"

"Lafond's personal suspicion is that it likely happened closer to four o'clock."

This was incredible: Dupin had never once known Lafond to be so forthcoming before. The fact he was expressing a "personal suspicion," especially at such an early stage, could prove very helpful to their inquiries.

"But," Le Menn added, "that is, and I quote, a 'question of interpretation.' In the report it will just say 'between three and four o'clock.'"

So it would have happened just a short time before Madame Chaboseau came home.

"Was that it?"

"Yes."

"We really need to speak to the Chaboseaus' maid," said Nevou. She didn't sound at all out of sorts anymore. "She lives just a few doors down."

Dupin should have thought of this himself.

"Definitely. Do that first."

"And maybe Monsieur Chaboseau really did have plans to meet someone," she continued. "Let's see what the phone records tell us."

"That'll take a while." This was always a nuisance, but Dupin was under no illusions.

One thing was clear anyway: he needed Nolwenn. And Riwal. As soon as possible. If the two of them only knew—a murder in their town! Plus Nolwenn knew practically everyone in Concarneau. And not just the people, she knew their stories too. Then it occurred to Dupin that he should really call Docteur Garreg, his grumpy, elderly GP. He would definitely be able to tell him a little about Docteur Chaboseau.

Dupin turned to his two colleagues: "Divide the tasks we've got so far between you."

He felt a sudden unease. He reached for the little coffee cup that Ingrid had placed on the table while he had been walking up and down, and emptied it in one go. Then he turned around without another word, crossing the road to Place Jean Jaurès. His cell already to his ear.

He just got Nolwenn's voicemail again.

A sigh came from deep down inside him. Dupin had no clue what part of her journey through inland Brittany Nolwenn could be on at that moment. Riwal would probably know, or at least what area she was traveling through. Nolwenn had discussed the trip with him in detail. With Riwal's knowledge, Dupin could probably try to contact her via the pubs. He recalled the pubs were mainly named after women—their owners. Or if necessary, he could have contacted her through the local gendarmerie, but that was no good to him so long as he still couldn't get hold of Riwal either. The commissaire remembered them speaking about a local hog roast festival, a traditional Fête du Cochon. This festival's cheerful motto was *"De la tête à la queue je suis délicieux."* "I am delicious from head to tail." Dupin opened the browser on his cell. Maybe he could find one of these festivals happening around now.

There were more than a dozen hits. He went through some of the places mentioned. None of them rang any bells. This was pointless. Although he'd briefly considered it, he wouldn't be able to rustle up enough gendarmes to look for Nolwenn and her husband in all the pubs in inland Brittany.

He'd try Riwal one more time.

Just his voicemail again. Dupin hung up. He'd left enough messages and was desperately hoping that his inspector would turn on the radio or television in that isolated house on Belle-Île and at least find out what happened that way.

"Bloody hell."

By this point Dupin was standing at the bottom of the steps to the magnificent nineteenth-century covered market, the town's great palace of culinary delights.

The next phone call was not exactly a success either: "This is Docteur Claire Lannoy. Please leave a message."

Claire should actually have left the hospital by now, so she must have been on her way home.

The beeps swiftly followed.

"Salut, Claire, it's me, I . . ." Dupin paused. It would be a mistake to leave a message. There was too much to say, and every single part of the message was in itself not easy to explain, but it was no good. "Claire, we've got a murder. Here—in Concarneau." He tried to make it sound dramatic: "Docteur Chaboseau. A fall from the fourth floor. They live above the Amiral. We're just starting the investigation." That was the first thing, now here was the other. She didn't know anything about this yet either. "Your parents are actually coming tonight. They didn't stop off like they were planning. They'll be here by around nine." It occurred to him that he still had the smoked fish in his car. "Please tell them I'm sorry. And we'll probably be busy here for the next few days, you know what it's like. Please tell them I'm really sorry." There was a little pause. "I've got to get going, Claire. I'll talk to you later."

Dupin decided to head straight to the gallery. But before that he would quickly call his own GP, Docteur Garreg.

He pressed his phone to his ear. The voicemail kicked in immediately.

"Damn it." It was practically jinxed. His fourth unsuccessful call. Dupin hung up when he suddenly remembered the practice was closed. Garreg himself had told him a few weeks before when Dupin had been to see him for a checkup. Garreg was visiting his daughter in Canada. She lived with her husband and children somewhere between Québec and Montréal. They were going to go hiking together on the Saint Lawrence River. For two weeks.

Out of the corner of his eye, Dupin saw a white Citroën van coming around the corner. It was Paul Girard, returning from his trip to the oyster farmer. Paul had a parking space in the same courtyard as Chaboseau.

Dupin was walking toward him as he got out. His sparse gray hair shone more brightly than usual today.

"Salut."

Paul was standing behind his van. Docteur Chaboseau had landed diagonally opposite, on the other side of the street. The gateway to the courtyard was cordoned off with two or three lines of police tape.

Usually, Dupin was very glad Paul was a quiet person, but right now he was really counting on a good chat.

"What do you make of Chaboseau?"

Paul shrugged. "Tragic story. And strange."

"Did you know him well?"

"We used to say hello to each other. That was it. I'm not important enough."

Paul's expression spoke volumes.

"You never chatted for long?"

"Not really, no."

"Were the Chaboseaus already living here when you took over the restaurant?"

"Yes."

Paul had bought the Amiral almost two decades before.

Like all restaurateurs, he had the phenomenal gift of being able to get on with almost anyone. But this didn't mean he became friends with everyone.

"They're not my kind of people, those two."

"Do you know of any disagreements or arguments he may have had?"

"He's friends with Brecan Priziac, the pharmacist, and Jodoc Luzel, the wine merchant. They come into the restaurant fairly regularly, usually in the evenings. Sometimes the brasserie at lunchtime too. As do Chaboseau and his wife."

That wasn't the answer to his question, but Dupin made a note of the names. He remembered seeing the men now and again. Like Chaboseau, they were well respected in the town but he didn't know them well. He just knew that Priziac was a widower, an aristocrat. He also belonged to one of the powerful, wealthy families in the area. Over generations, his family had built up a real empire of pharmacies. So he was old money.

Totally different from Luzel, a confirmed bachelor in his early fifties who had started to build up an ambitious wine business ten years before, initially in Brittany but then throughout western France. It was clearly extremely successful. Just last year he had opened a large shop on one of the roundabouts outside the town. With its shameless sales, it gave Dupin's favorite wine merchants, Cave Moros and La Petite Cave, a run for their money.

"Are they business partners too?"

Paul nodded. "I think so. But I don't know any more than that. Or anything about any disputes."

"Got it."

Paul opened the back door of the Citroën. There were about

a dozen blue boxes filled to the brim, a feast for the eyes: inside the boxes were oysters, crabs, and clams, including *praires,* Dupin's favorite clams. His stomach rumbled loudly at the sight. Only some of the shellfish was destined for the restaurant, the rest was for Paul's new fish shop, La Roche, on Place du Général de Gaulle. Very close by, it sold all manner of delicious seafood, it was a real maritime paradise. Paul had taken over the shop from Gisèle, who had run it for decades. And not only that, he had inherited her legendary recipes too, like the one for scallops *à la Concarnoise,* prepared with shallots, parsley, fennel seeds, and sea salt, braised in plenty of butter and Muscadet. The people of Concarneau had been relieved to learn that Gisèle's recipes would still be used.

Paul was grappling with the boxes.

"I think," he added in a strangely sinister tone of voice, "Chaboseau kept his business to himself. Just like his friends. How shall I put it? The mafia—but not the good kind."

Dupin knew what Paul was referring to. The topic had been all over the news for days. There had been a spectacular scene during a visit by the French president and foreign minister to the pope: the foreign minister, a Breton, ran into an old friend in the Vatican. He was a priest, also a Breton, and they had been at school together in Pontivy. So here were two old friends, delighted to see each other. And this led the president to make the harmless remark, *"Bretons partout!"* which was, in fact, a Breton dream come true, of course: "Bretons are everywhere." However, the president then turned to the pope and added, *"Les Bretons, c'est la mafia française."* "The Bretons are the French mafia." This had unleashed a storm of outrage, although there was some Breton pride in the mix too. In the end, the smart foreign minister had come up with a wonderfully Solomon-like solution that was music to Breton ears: *"La mafia bretonne, c'est la mafia du bien!"* "The Breton mafia is the good mafia." Or more accurately: "the goodies' mafia." But that was not the mafia Paul had meant just now.

"Are you talking about any particular incidents?"

"No."

"You just mean in a general sense?"

"Right."

"But you're referring to these three friends?"

"Yes."

That was enough for Dupin for now.

"I've got to go. Salut, Paul."

"See you soon." The owner of the Amiral picked up the first crate of oysters and carried it into the restaurant.

Dupin reached the *tabac-presse* on the corner in no time. He ought to speak to the owners at some point too. As well as Valérie, the ceramic artist Dupin liked so much. Once he started to think about it, he kept thinking of more people he could question. The good thing was: he could trust every single one of them unconditionally; he wouldn't be wondering whether they were holding something back, manipulating or deceiving him, putting him off the scent. Any one of his friends, and he had made quite a few of them during his nine years in Concarneau, could be helpful in solving this case. A very unfamiliar situation but extremely convenient for an investigation. This was a home game. After the conversation with Paul, Chaboseau's friends and possible business partners now ranked very high on the priority list; ordinarily Dupin would now have phoned Nolwenn and she would have put together a perfect file on them both very quickly.

Dupin crossed the street and found himself on Place Jean Jaurès again. He was walking parallel to the quay in the leisure harbor, past the pretty old fishermen's houses.

He stopped halfway to the gallery. Something had struck him.

He walked back a few paces and stopped outside a narrow, picturesque building. An ornate wooden bay window, the wood-paneled ground floor painted a deep blue, the logo of the newspaper in bright red above the door: *Ouest-France*.

Maybe this was a crazy idea, but Dupin was going to give it a go anyway.

He flung the door open. He knew that Drollec's office was on the first floor. The two surprised employees on the ground floor nodded at the commissaire as he ran up the stairs without saying a word.

A remarkably rotund man, Drollec was sitting at his desk, looking at him in bewilderment.

"I'd like to make an official statement. On the Chaboseau case."

Drollec leaped to his feet.

"Call Madame Donal from *Le Télégramme* afterward, I want everyone to know."

"And what statement do you want to make exactly?"

Drollec reached for his cell and turned on the recording function.

"It was murder. The medical examiner's office found an antemortem hematoma on the victim's right shoulder. Everything indicates a deliberate push. Therefore we're dealing with a capital offense, committed between three and four in the afternoon. In the attic of Monsieur and Madame Chaboseau's private home,

Avenue Pierre Guéguin 1. The police are requesting the public's active cooperation. Any tip relating to any incident that is even potentially suspicious, or relating to any person who is even potentially suspicious, any detail, as insignificant as it may seem, that anybody noticed during the time in question could help to solve this case."

Dupin was aware that this statement was, in a way, utter madness. They would get dozens of tips, including some very odd ones, no doubt. In the worst-case scenario, he would be spreading fear and anxiety through the town.

"Is that everything?"

Dupin nodded.

Drollec stopped recording.

"Publish it on your website as soon as possible," Dupin instructed him.

Riwal and Nolwenn had enabled news alerts from *Ouest-France* and *Le Télégramme*, so they should finally find out about the case. That was the commissaire's priority. Admittedly Riwal didn't have either internet or cell phone reception, but perhaps he would find out about it if he went into a restaurant or pub.

"At once, Monsieur le Commissaire! And on the front page tomorrow morning! Even Six Cent Soixante-Deux will have to make way for this."

This was meant as a joke. For weeks now, no other Breton news reports had been the focus of such fervent emotional attention as the ones about Six Cent Soixante-Deux. An injured seal had been found on the beach in Plouarzel. An arctic seal. It had been treated, nursed back to health, and released again, fitted with a transmitter. Then it had set off on an epic mission—its journey far north into the Arctic. Five thousand kilometers. And all this on its own, separated from all of its kind. It had covered a thousand kilometers so far in just ten days. All of Brittany had joined in the excitement. Would it make it, would it dodge all the killer whales and sharks? Usually, animals that came to the attention of the Breton public—a fearless dolphin, a lost whale shark, or an escaped kangaroo—were given a pretty name, but with the seal it was the registration number, always uttered with deep affection, that had become the animal's name: Six Hundred and Sixty-Two.

"That's it, thank you so much." Dupin turned on his heel. Drollec looked just as bewildered as he had at the outset.

"Have you got a hunch then yet, Monsieur le Commissaire?" the editor called after him, but Dupin was already at the stairs.

"Haven't the foggiest."

This had sounded practically cheerful. Even Dupin didn't know why.

Soon he had left the building and was back in the mild evening air. He stood still for a moment.

The retreating tide had exposed the seabed around the Ville Close and along the quay. The tide was at its lowest point. Six or seven meters of the Atlantic were missing from the harbor. Instead you could see muddy, slimy, and in some places sandy seafloor and patches of bright green seaweed. There were some multicolored plastic dinghies lying on dry land and a ramp down from the quay. The waterline was some distance away from the Ville Close.

"Commissaire!"

Dupin had set off in the direction of Galerie Gloux again. Rosa Le Menn was walking toward him, incredibly athletic and quick for her size.

"I saw you"—Le Menn stopped right in front of him—"from the Amiral."

"Yes?"

"Nevou has already spoken to the Chaboseaus' housekeeper."

That had been very quick. Excellent; Dupin loved a brisk pace.

"She was terrified, just absolutely distraught. Nevou wasn't able to get anything of interest out of her."

"Nothing at all?"

Dupin had been hoping for something, at least. She was coming and going regularly at their house, after all.

"No. Nevou would like to keep looking into her a little bit, she wanted me to tell you. She doesn't think she's totally above suspicion."

"What does that mean?"

"Just a kind of feeling she had."

At the moment, anything was possible. Any potential scenario.

"I see."

"I'm going to start by speaking to the staff at the practice."

"Great. By the way, we now know that the pharmacist Priziac and the wine merchant Luzel were friends with Chaboseau. Perhaps even business partners. Please find out as much as you can about them both. I'd like to pay them a visit as early as this evening if possible."

"We'll find out where they are."

It was going to be a long night, that much was for sure.

"Great. That's it for now."

"Brilliant."

Le Menn headed off again immediately.

Two minutes later, Dupin was standing in front of the Galerie Gloux, the second-last building on the square. Set right above the sea, there was nothing beyond it but the quaint Café de l'Atlantic and the Atlantic itself.

There was nobody visible through the window of the ornately carved wooden door.

Dupin knocked.

The gallery was already closed, but it wasn't unusual for Françoise and Jean-Michel to work in one of the exhibition spaces or workshops until late into the night. What's more, they lived on the two upper floors of the building. Their life and work, or rather their life and passion, were closely intertwined here. The building itself was a work of art. It had been built by Françoise's ancestors in 1883 with Norwegian-inspired half-timbering. The decorative elements were well balanced by the austerity of a modern art aesthetic. The building was painted dark green while the supporting beams and the frames around the doors and windows were painted a rust red. Françoise's famous great-grandfather, Théophile Deyrolle, and his brother-in-law had been painters, but entrepreneurs too. Among other things, they had traded ice from the Norwegian port of Bergen. It had been shipped to Concarneau in enormous quantities on large ships and then used to keep the fish fresh in the harbor.

Françoise and Jean-Michel had opened the gallery together nearly fifty years before. Dupin had sat upstairs in the extremely cozy loft with them many times, and on mild summer nights they sat on the balcony too with its incredible view of the Ville Close and the sea. It wasn't unusual for them to be there till dawn. The two of them recounted the history of the building during these evenings. By the end of the nineteenth century and beginning of the twentieth century, Concarneau had become a center for art, with its own artists' colony—not quite as well known as Gauguin's in Pont-Aven, but still significant. Before long, artists had taken up residence in the building. Conveniently, there was a bistro on the ground floor, and therefore plenty to drink. In 1905, one of the artists designed the poster for the first Festival des Filets Bleus, the town's most important festival today. It had been born out of necessity at the time. The usual shoals of sardines failed to appear and the fishermen were suffering from poverty and hunger. The money the festival brought in was helpful.

Dupin knocked a second and third time, and then the door opened. Françoise greeted him with her familiar smile and without a trace of surprise.

Her dark eyes sparkled; she was an extremely beautiful woman. She was one of those people who would never look old, no matter how old they were. She was wearing a thin white sweater with jeans, simple, casual, but with a great sense of style, and round horn-rimmed glasses that really suited her. In her left hand, she was holding an enormous hammer.

"It was murder, right?"

"It was murder," Dupin confirmed, and stepped inside.

Even the walls of the gallery's entrance hall were covered in paintings right up to the ceiling; every square centimeter of space was used. They were by artists with a connection to Brittany, especially those who had stayed in Concarneau, so there were quite a few. On the right was a glass cabinet of precious objects. Among other things, there were two ships in bottles. There were two low tables with books, art catalogs, old pottery, and—Dupin got excited every time—a penguin sculpture. More specifically: a pair of penguins, black with silvery-white tummies, a good forty or fifty centimeters tall.

Françoise walked over to her wooden desk at the back of the room and gave the commissaire a thoughtful look.

"An awful business."

She was an extremely clever woman; wise, people might have once said. Essentially what she was saying was: "This is going to be complicated."

"I'm afraid you're going to have to delve into every social circle in town. Dig deep. Deeper than you'd like."

"What do you mean by that?"

It had sounded ominous. Reminiscent of dark realms and secrets. As if the town were a sinister being. Dupin knew a different side to Concarneau: bright, light, wide, open, free, or rather: Atlantic. He had the impression Françoise looked a little pale all of a sudden. But maybe that was just because of the low lighting.

"If it involves the wealthy, old families, then money, business, connections, and power are almost always involved too. A lot of it dates back years."

"Are you talking about something specific?"

"No. Not at all. But the town is stuffed full of secrets. Including some dark secrets nobody will speak about willingly." She gave a laugh and winked at him.

"You just need to read *Contes de la Ville Close* sometime, Georges. Or this"—she reached over to a stack of old books lying on the desk—"*V'là la Revue*—fantastic! An overview of the town and its community from 1925. Fourteen stories from the heart of the town's collective memory. Even Vauban himself makes an appearance." Vauban was Louis XIV's master builder who had built parts of the old town's fortifications. In a husky voice she added, "There's an important warning at the end too: against greed and craving status. People can never get enough. But"—she smiled and put the book back down on the desk—"back to the present. I started hanging paintings earlier. By Jean-Pierre Guilleron, you know him, of course. You can give me a bit of a hand. Jean-Michel is in Quimper."

Without waiting for an answer, she went into the exhibition space next door. Dupin followed. In the middle of the room was a massive fireplace made of pale granite. A dark brown chest of drawers and a few small tables were scattered around the room. On top of one of them was a dark-colored bear by the same artist who had made the penguins.

On the left-hand side was a blank white wall—the only one not made of stone—and Françoise was standing in front of it. There were lots of paintings leaning against it. Pieces by Guilleron. A set of quite small paintings had clearly already been sorted. They were of animals native to the Atlantic—bass, red mullet, halibut, sea bream, crabs, langoustines, lobsters, and mussels. In a very special, unique way, they were both totally realistic and highly artistic. Which was down to Guilleron's unusual process—he painted real fish and pressed them onto the paper. He then essentially painted on this print. The result was extraordinary: some fantastical creatures. Mythical beings. It had the incredible effect of making the familiar look unfamiliar all of a sudden.

"Madame Chaboseau says she was with you this afternoon."

"Yes, she was."

"Around what time?"

Françoise thought about it. "About half past three, maybe."

"Why did she come and see you?"

"To talk about two paintings. Docteur Chaboseau was a great collector, they both are, in fact. His father and grandfather were collectors before him and there are even some paintings dedicated to them. The couple make purchases at the really big auctions, at Sotheby's, Christie's, Phillips. And in France too. From us too, now and again. Expensive ones. And we do all of their framing."

She had taken a few steps backward and was surveying the wall.

"Madame Chaboseau only mentioned one painting to me, not two. Why?"

"I don't know, I'm afraid."

Dupin had taken out his notebook.

"When . . ."

His cell rang. It had been quiet for a surprisingly long time.

It was Kadeg's number. Dupin couldn't believe his eyes.

"Excuse me, Françoise, just one moment."

"No problem. Go into the annex, the reception is better there."

Dupin nodded.

"Kadeg?"

"Is that you, Commiss—"

There was no time for that.

"What is it, Kadeg?"

"I heard about the murder."

"And?"

"And I heard your public statement. And . . ."

"Kadeg! I'm in the middle of an interview. You're on parental leave! What do you want?"

Dupin had walked into the annex.

"I've heard Nolwenn and Riwal aren't there."

"And?"

"I would definitely have come and helped, I just wanted to let you know. But my wife is away for work this weekend."

"I'm managing, the two new people are doing an excellent job, thanks, Kadeg." Much as Dupin tried, he couldn't deny feeling somewhat touched.

"Does anything occur to you about the whole thing?" he added. Since he already had his inspector on the phone . . .

"Chaboseau was friends with that pharmacist. He's a piece of work, be careful."

"Anything else, Kadeg?"

"No, that's it. I'll be in touch again."

"But only . . ." Dupin broke off. "Stay in touch. Speak to you then."

The commissaire went back over to Françoise, who was waiting for him with a smile on her face.

"So," he picked up right where they'd left off, "I'd like to know what the situation is with the two paintings that Madame Chaboseau was here about."

Françoise bent down to pick up a painting that had six pink sea bream all swimming in one direction in an orderly fashion and a shoal of small blue sardines coming toward them.

"Hold this, Georges. At this height." With a slight movement of her head, she pointed at the spot she wanted on the wall. Dupin took the piece and held it to the wall quickly. Françoise took a nail out of the back pocket of her trousers, placed it in position without making any kind of mark first, and hammered it into the wall with two decisive blows.

"One painting comes from the Rockefeller Collection that was just sold in New York. A smallish Renoir. A landscape scene. The other is a Matthieu Dorval. Madame Chaboseau picked out a frame for each of them."

Claire had bought a painting by the Breton painter Dorval a while ago. They had even gone to his studio together on the Presqu'Île de Crozon. A picture of the sea—blue in all its nuances, bright white here and there, rough brushstrokes. Dupin was very fond of it. It hung in their bedroom.

"Where is the Renoir? Here?"

It must have been very valuable.

Françoise took the sea bream painting from Dupin, hung it up, tilted her head to one side—and looked pleased.

"It's still at their house. They want a new frame for it. Docteur Chaboseau was petrified of woodworm, they get even the most beautiful old frames replaced. But what can you do?" There was regret in her voice.

"How much is the painting worth?"

"It's not one of the really expensive ones. They paid one point three million. You can take a look at it on the Christie's website, they put up the prices they're sold for."

Apparently "expensive" meant something very different in the art world.

"Is it possible there was something a bit suspicious about the painting?"

Françoise looked at Dupin in amazement.

"You mean it might be a forgery? If you buy a painting at Christie's, that is practically out of the question. They employ the most respected experts, the painting has a verified provenance."

"What would you say the total value of the couple's collection was?"

"Now this one." This time Françoise reached for a dark blue lobster that was apparently going to go next to the sea bream and sardines. A very similar lobster by Guilleron was hanging in the Amiral, and it also appeared on the restaurant's new logo that Paul had chosen last year.

Dupin followed Françoise's brief instructions and held the painting on the wall.

"Thirty or forty million. For sure."

"Not bad," Dupin blurted out.

Françoise nodded vaguely, Dupin standing to one side as she hammered the nail into the wall.

"With a focus on impressionism and post-impressionism. But also certain contemporary artists. Occasionally artists who are still unknown. You've got to hand it to them: they are passionate collectors."

"And this painting by Matthieu Dorval, could there be"— even Dupin himself didn't know what he meant—"something unusual about it?"

Françoise had hung up the lobster piece. It looked perfect.

"Not at all. Matthieu has a big exhibition in Paris soon. This could be his big break."

She reached for three small paintings, apparently intended for the spot next to the lobster. They were all of red mullets. Dupin adored eating them. That delicate, slightly bitter taste.

"Anything else? Does anything occur . . ."

His cell. Again.

"Sorry, Françoise."

Dupin walked into the annex again.

"Yes?"

"We're here, Georges. We're standing in front of your house."

This time he recognized the voice straightaway. Hélène Lannoy. His mother-in-law. This could not be happening. Dupin glanced at his watch.

Twenty past eight.

"We can't get hold of Claire. She must have had another emergency come in. But I'm sure you'll be here any minute now."

It took Dupin a moment.

"I—we've got a case." He needed to make the seriousness of the situation crystal clear to her. "A murder."

"Oh—that must be very recent then. There wasn't one earlier." She made it sound like Dupin had made up the murder.

"Very recent, yes. I . . . sorry, Hélène, I've got to keep going here. I'll call Claire again."

"So you'll be a bit late?"

"Right—I'm afraid I'll be a bit late, yes. It's a real shame, I had bought smoked fish for us especially. But it's in the car." He hoped his efforts would be appreciated.

For a moment there was a suspicious silence on the other end of the line.

"All right then. We'll go for a bit of a walk." Dupin had been expecting worse. "Your house really is in such a wonderful location. When did you say you'll be here?"

"I'm afraid I don't know."

He couldn't say. Not when he'd come home—not where Claire was, not when she would get home or when he would get through to her, and not how the fish would make its way from his car to them.

"But I'll try and get hold of Claire!"

If Claire was dealing with an emergency at the hospital, she probably didn't know about any of this. About her parents arriving early or about the murder.

"Excellent. That's all sorted then. See you soon, Georges."

She hung up.

Dupin let out a sigh of despair.

A moment later he was back with Françoise again and she was handing him one of the paintings of the red mullets. "Above the lobster."

"I wanted to ask," he said, picking up where they'd left off, "whether anything occurs to you about the Chaboseaus in general? Do you know of any enemies or disputes they had?"

Dupin held the painting higher and higher until Françoise nodded.

"Both of them have always behaved very discreetly. I know almost nothing about them, to be honest. Just that they had a lot of money at their disposal. As well as a very powerful network of contacts that extended throughout Brittany and as far as Paris."

"What do you know about their business dealings?"

"Real estate. He and his family have owned the hill directly to the west of the Sables Blancs"—the most beautiful and famous beach in town, one of Concarneau's upmarket residential areas—"for generations now, and they used to own the land directly behind the beach too. But the family sold that a hundred years ago. When summer homes came about, it was worth its weight in gold."

"He owns the entire hill?"

"Yes."

The land was in a fantastic location. Dupin estimated a good twenty houses had been built on it a few years before. Spacious houses with equally spacious yards.

The first of the three small red mullet paintings was up. Françoise put the second nail in place without making any more measurements.

"He also invested in the thalassotherapy spa there. But I don't know if he still has a stake in that." The next piece was up in an instant. "Then a few years ago he invested in the huge brewery up by the Leclerc Roundabout. Although he is always very careful to keep a low profile there, as he does everywhere else. Oh yes, and very recently, he invested in a fish cannery he has big plans for, Délices de la Mer."

Dupin made notes while Françoise went over to the next painting.

"A cannery?"

"Yes. Fish-canning factories are really making a comeback, a great tradition is being revived." Françoise seemed very much in favor of this development. The canneries had been an important contributor to the economy of Brittany since the middle of the nineteenth century, particularly in Concarneau. They had been in decline more and more in recent decades. But they were booming again now. There were the handful that had survived to this day and lots of new, young businesses. With a wonderful mix of the old savoir faire, the best ingredients, and plenty of fresh culinary imagination, they conjured up pretty jars of fish and seafood.

"Could this be about rivalry?"

"No idea. But I could ask a client of mine. Sieren Cléac. She has opened a little cannery herself. An artisanal workshop. She only uses fish from inshore fishing."

"Please do."

There really were advantages to investigating on your own doorstep.

"The poor woman, her mother died three weeks ago."

Françoise's expression turned sad.

"I'm sorry." Dupin cleared his throat. "And this brewery?"

"You mean Roi Gradlon."

The third red mullet was up. Perfectly placed.

Roi Gradlon was a well-known brewery. It did a huge amount of marketing and had made a big show of advertising that it wanted to compete with the oldest and biggest brewery in Brittany. This big brewery was called Britt and it was on the very edge of Concarneau. Besides Britt, also known as the *bière de la Bretagne*, dozens of small breweries had sprung up in the area. Beer was a hot topic in Brittany, including the patriotic implications of it: flourishing beer production in Brittany could at least go some way to making up for the stigma of not producing their own wine. They had Breton beer, and of course, Breton cider!

"I don't know anything about . . ." Françoise seemed to be searching for the right words. ". . . specific incidents to do with that either, though."

Her expression was suddenly very grave. But her dismay seemed to have more to do with the placement of the remaining painting. She picked up a portrait of a very red crab. Then one of three elegant, silvery bass.

Dupin glanced at his notebook.

"Do you know anything about the Chaboseaus' stake in the leisure harbor?"

The window at the end of the room gave a direct view of the harbor.

"As far as I know, they haven't even invested in it at all yet. The plans to expand the harbor are under consideration. As is the possibility of setting up a company to do that. Chaboseau wanted a share in that. But it really hasn't got very far. Right now the harbor belongs solely to the town."

Françoise seemed better informed on this point than Nevou.

"Is it a controversial project?"

She had put the bass next to the crab and carefully scrutinized the painting. Now she reached for the crab.

"No. It's not, actually." She handed the piece to Dupin and the familiar process happened again. "Just a long, drawn-out one. Your best bet is to speak to the mayor about it."

That would be a good idea anyway. For several different reasons. Kler Kireg, a young, dynamic guy in his early forties, had been elected at the end of the previous year. Part of the reason the citizens of Concarneau trusted him was the fact that he came from the highly respected Gouillen family—although he was adopted, as the whole town knew. The family owned one of the biggest and oldest canneries in town, but Kireg himself had nothing to do with the business.

"What about Chaboseau's work as a doctor?" It was an absolute shot in the dark, but this was what it was like at the beginning of any investigation. "Have you heard about anything . . . out of the ordinary in relation to his work?"

"A little bit higher . . ." Françoise gestured upward with her head and Dupin held the crab even higher. "No. Chaboseau was a very good doctor. He was incredibly successful at everything he did. He's had a second doctor at the practice since the middle of last year. Presumably she was meant to take over the practice once he retired."

This second doctor was news to Dupin. And not uninteresting.

"What's her name?"

"This is ridiculous," Françoise said sharply, "it's got to be the bass!"

She took the picture of the crab firmly out of Dupin's hand and put it back on the floor.

"Here!" She held the bass out to him.

"Evette Derien," she continued calmly, "mid-thirties, pretty, and very ambitious."

She said this almost in passing.

"Do you know of any tensions between the two of them?"

"I haven't heard anything about that."

"Do you know of any mistakes that Chaboseau ever made as a doctor?"

"No. I've never heard anyone talk about that."

She uttered this emphatic "No" at the same time as hammering the nail into the wall.

"And all of his volunteering work, and the patronage of the arts?"

"He keeps a low profile on that too, but in such a way that you still know it's him who's the patron. The one making things possible."

"Do any of these projects spring to mind in particular?"

"He was involved in the restoration of the sand dune at the Plage de la Belle-Étoile. The project had its grand unveiling last week."

The town had decided to take better care of the—once famous—downtown beaches. A wide-ranging initiative. It involved the ecological side of things too.

"Really good," she commented on the bass hanging on the

wall. "Then there was also that project with the environmental boat. By those three boys from Concarneau. It turns plastic into oil."

Riwal had talked about this project at the station with great pride, almost as if it were his own invention. It really was remarkable: three young researchers had designed a large, elaborate boat, and apparently as it crossed the sea it could collect the wretched plastic that was polluting the whole world, and turn it back into oil using a patented process.

"He bought a stake in that?"

"I don't know if it was just an investment or a case of him having shares."

The list of topics in Dupin's notebook was getting longer all the time. Chaboseau had really been a tireless businessman.

"What is Madame Chaboseau like as a person?"

Françoise looked Dupin in the eye. "Not easy to answer that one."

Dupin waited. Instead of answering, she shook her head and handed him a picture of four spider crabs with long, thin, hairy legs. Magnificent monsters.

"Is she actively involved in her husband's business dealings?"

"Absolutely. But I couldn't tell you exactly how they split it up between them." She paused for a moment. "So sad, this whole thing."

The picture was big, the biggest one so far, and Dupin had to stretch.

"Higher. There is good."

Dupin groaned softly. Françoise was holding the next nail.

"Does she have girlfriends?"

"Within *her* circles, maybe. I don't know. For a few years

now, Madame Chaboseau has been staying in her house in La Trinité more and more. Her husband didn't go there that much."

Dupin hadn't heard of this house before. La Trinité-sur-mer was one of the most outstanding seaside resorts in Brittany. Located on the gorgeous Golfe du Morbihan, it was very ritzy.

"Monsieur Chaboseau," Dupin just wanted to have this confirmed again, "was friends with Brecan Priziac, the pharmacist, and also with the wine merchant."

"Priziac and Jodoc Luzel, yes. They were good friends, as far as I know."

"Do you know anything about their business relationships?"

"They don't speak about that with outsiders. None of the three do."

She had walked to the opposite wall and was leaning against it, checking the hanging of the pictures so far, from that angle. She seemed pleased.

"Did Madame Chaboseau seem different to you when she was here today? Not her usual self?"

"There was no difference at all. Although that doesn't mean anything. She's an extremely self-possessed person. Determined, class-conscious—and above all: unreadable."

"She hasn't even shown much emotion at the death of her husband yet."

"That doesn't surprise me."

"Do you know anything about her marriage?"

"You must be joking. No, absolutely noth—"

Dupin's phone rang again.

A local number.

"Yes?"

"Monsieur Georges Dupin?"

"Whom am I speaking to?"

"Brecan Priziac."

The pharmacist.

A dramatic pause.

"A colleague of yours called me. But I would have got in touch anyway."

He left another long pause. Dupin was about to say something but the pharmacist beat him to it.

"I think we ought to talk at some point, Monsieur le Commissaire."

He sounded aloof and arrogant.

"Indeed we should. Best to do it right now. I'll come to you."

"Brilliant." Priziac wasn't going to let Dupin rattle him.

"Where exactly can I find you?"

"In Beg Meil. Pen ar Roz. The house at the end of the lane. Right on the water."

Beg Meil, a marvelous little seaside resort, was just a few kilometers from Concarneau as the crow flew, in the bay across the way.

"I'm on my way."

Dupin hung up without waiting for a response.

Françoise had walked over to the desk in the entrance hall during this phone conversation.

"I suppose I'm losing my assistant?" She smiled.

"That was Priziac."

"Speak of the devil . . ."

"Thank you, Françoise. You've been so helpful."

Dupin had learned quite a lot. Plenty of new information. Potentially important information. Criminal cases were crazy in so many ways: sometimes, there was that one clue right there at the beginning of an investigation that was the key to everything. From the very first moment, the solution was there in plain sight, perhaps almost grotesquely obvious. Unfortunately, this was usually apparent only in retrospect, but not always. On the other hand, sometimes that crucial clue didn't appear at all for a long time. Unlike in crime fiction, it was totally arbitrary.

Dupin turned to leave.

"You know," Françoise said as he walked away, "that there was an attempted murder at the Amiral before?"

Dupin stopped abruptly and turned around again. It must have been before his time, long before his time, otherwise he would know the story.

"In 1931. A poisoning, though, strychnine to be more specific." The sinister tone she had adopted was already turning into a laugh. "And it was in a novel. In *The Yellow Dog,* one of Maigret's most famous cases, the greatest commissaire of all time. The attack in the Amiral is actually the second attempted murder. Before that, a wine dealer gets a bullet to the stomach, right next to Alain's newsagent's, as it happens."

Dupin couldn't help smiling. The legendary crime novel was part of the town's rich cultural heritage. Its author, Georges Simenon, had stayed in Concarneau several times and had made the Amiral, as well as the town, the setting of the book. And it was not the only case that brought Commissaire Maigret to Concarneau. The town honored him in all sorts of ways, including with the famous annual literary festival, Le Chien Jaune.

"All right, take care, Georges!" Now it was Françoise turning away. "And like I say, read the stories from the Ville Close! Maybe it's all connected to the mysterious dark sorcerer . . ."

Dupin wasn't going to ask; he had heard of the legend before. A tragic love story.

"Thanks again, Françoise."

Within moments, Dupin had left the gallery.

The finest bright white sand and crystal-clear water so transparent that you had to look carefully to make out where it even began. The colors of the sea intensified only gradually. A pale, elegant emerald blue that turned greenish a few meters farther out, then turquoise, finally transforming into an azure blue farther out into the bay. Below the horizon it was a dark ultramarine. If this view were a photo, you would bet there had been plenty of photo editing, too much color correction.

The beach was perhaps fifty or sixty meters wide, flanked by rough granite cliffs in elegant gray tones. There were quite a few of these beaches, called *criques*, along this woodland-bordered stretch of coastline, each one more idyllic than the next. The water was dotted with rocks, most of them washed smooth, others overgrown with bright green seaweed, some with those dark green threads that unfurled like in an underwater botanical garden. This seaweed was edible; Dupin had been served it recently, in the same way rosemary is used elsewhere, as a garnish in a gin. A *gin marin*, from Brittany, of course. Dupin had been impressed by the fresh, subtly iodine-esque flavor.

The Mediterranean atmosphere here had nothing in common with the rugged Pointe du Raz where the commissaire had been just that lunchtime. A handful of tall pines towered up in front of him, and everything seemed gentle and mild, even the air. It was still a good twenty degrees. A man and woman were dozing on a rock, enjoying the ambience of the early-summer evening. An older woman with bright white hair was swimming parallel to the beach, two boys were having a kickabout with a heavy leather ball, you could see the effort they were putting into every single kick. Dupin's prehistoric sat nav had directed him to the wrong cul-de-sac, Kerengrimen instead of Pen Ar Roz, even though he had put it in correctly. So he had decided to walk to the pharmacist's house across the beach.

He looked eastward, out across the bay toward Concarneau. There were the Sables Blancs, then the kilometers-long Corniche, the coastal path to the Marinarium. With a pair of binoculars, Dupin could have seen his house on the stretch of land in front of it. Then there was the wide, sheltered entrance to the harbor and, on the other side, the famous Le Cabellou peninsula, one of the wealthiest areas in town.

It was almost nine, the light was golden, the sun was still above the horizon. It didn't go down yesterday till just before ten—Dupin had been sitting on the patio on his own. They were heading toward the longest day of the year, still a good month to go, and this was the season of spectacular light. Dupin had been even more pleased about the light returning in recent weeks than he was about the heat. March to November had been extremely unsettled months this year, with lots of storms. Sometimes it had rained all day long, and once for weeks. This was really unusual, because Breton weather generally changed every day, not just once but several times. The possible reasons for this had been eagerly discussed. Dupin had personally noticed deep worry lines on the foreheads of longtime residents of Concarneau when they talked about it. What if climate change was on its way to the End of the World now?

Dupin had tried Nolwenn and Riwal again on his way to

Beg Meil. No answer, just like there was no answer when he then tried Claire. He had left her another message. Where on earth was she? Still at the hospital?

Nevou answered straightaway. She had spoken to two receptionists at the practice. They hadn't noticed anything out of the ordinary that day or over the last few days. They had nothing to report about any unusual "incidents" either. Dupin had not been particularly surprised to learn that Madame Chaboseau had not agreed to another interview with the two policewomen for now. She had informed Le Menn on the doorstep that she was "indisposed" and would be putting off everything till the next day. She would also give them a list of her husband's business commitments then, although she considered this "ridiculous" and "an unreasonable demand" anyway, according to Le Menn. Apparently Madame Chaboseau had actually seemed more upset during this—short—conversation than she had earlier. But she refused all offers of help again. She still didn't want to see a doctor who could prescribe her a sedative. Dupin would pay another visit to Madame Chaboseau the next day himself.

Dupin had got through to Alain, the owner of the newsagent's. But unfortunately he had nothing to report that Dupin hadn't known before. The same was true of Valérie, Dupin's ceramic artist friend.

Dupin had rejected two calls. Both from Claire's parents. Who were presumably still waiting for their daughter.

On the journey, he had checked whether the regional radio stations were also reporting on his appeal for the public's help by this point. They were.

Priziac's house turned out to be a magnificent villa. Dupin guessed it was probably from the twenties. The front garden was enclosed by an enormous stone wall and it was dominated by a statuesque spruce. There were purple rhododendrons in the borders. Beyond the garden sprawled the villa, just a stone's throw from the sea. It was dusky pink, with pointed gables, a dark slate roof, and a turret. The windows were framed by pale gray granite. The highlight was that the entire ground floor had a gigantic glass window with a breathtaking view of the bay.

The front door was around the side. A massive wooden door.

Dupin pressed the doorbell and an old-fashioned bell sound rang out.

"Here."

It was hard to tell where the voice was coming from.

"Down the gravel path."

A narrow path ran past the house toward the sea—at the other end was a car park with a silver SUV. Dupin went down the path to the back of the garden.

"Over here, young man."

Dupin could see a teak table and six majestic chairs. Nearby were three lounge chairs, the same design, with dark blue upholstery. Priziac was lying stretched out on one of the lounge chairs. He hadn't deemed it necessary to stand up.

"Come over here."

He gestured to the lounge chair next to him with his head. Priziac had a high forehead, thick silver-gray hair carefully combed back, coarse but not cruel features, piercing eyes, a fleshy nose. He was probably a little older than Docteur Chaboseau.

The commissaire leaned on the stone wall opposite and took a long, hard look at the pharmacist. With maddening calmness and without wasting time on a greeting, he said:

"Three lounge chairs. For you and your two friends. Friends and business partners."

A smile appeared on Priziac's face. He was a stout man and wore an expertly cut gray suit, no doubt custom-made. With shiny black shoes.

"When did you last sit here together?" Dupin asked after a brief pause. "You, the wine merchant Monsieur Luzel, and the murder victim Docteur Chaboseau?"

Priziac instantly became serious.

"I suggest you urgently speak to the mayor, Monsieur Dupin. Our surfer boy."

Priziac was referring to the fact that the mayor liked to pose for the press with a surfboard.

"Tell me what businesses you and Monsieur Chaboseau invested in together. Or all three of you including Luzel."

Priziac had turned away from Dupin and was pointedly gazing out across the bay to the open sea.

"Pierre and our mayor"—he was acting as though he had not even heard Dupin—"had a huge argument recently. They had had arguments several times before. But this wasn't even about ludicrous town politics or that ambitious technocrat's ridiculous initiatives." Priziac spoke in an openly condescending way. "Although those alone would be reason enough for a bitter argument. It was about granting extra brewery licenses. Pierre invested generously in Concarneau over the decades—in the infrastructure and the economy, he created hundreds of jobs directly and indirectly—and now the town merrily grants licenses to anyone who just happens to feel like brewing beer."

"Did you personally invest in Roi Gradlon too? Did Monsieur Luzel?"

"As I say—pay attention to the mayor." His voice was dark and dramatic. He paused for a moment, and a few seconds later he declared in a different, almost soft voice:

"It's a tragedy. For Claudette, for Pierre's friends, his son. And the entire town."

"Chaboseau has a son?"

Nobody had told Dupin this yet. His police colleagues had not—they seemed not to know—Paul hadn't, Françoise hadn't. Apparently this was one of the potential disadvantages of an "investigation at home": quite a few people—including and especially Dupin's closest friends—would just take a lot of knowledge for granted, thinking something was so obvious that it wouldn't even occur to them to share it. But the strangest thing was this: even Madame Chaboseau hadn't mentioned anything about a son.

"They weren't in touch a great deal. Almost never."

"Had they fallen out?"

"No."

"But they didn't have a very close personal relationship?"

"No, none at all."

Dupin thought he could detect a scornful undertone.

"Is he the son of both Claudette and Pierre Chaboseau?"

"Félix, yes. Forty years old, trying his luck with flour at the moment."

There was open contempt in his voice now.

"Does he know yet? That his father is dead, I mean. That he was murdered."

"Yes."

"When did Madame Chaboseau call you, Monsieur Priziac? To inform you of the death, I mean."

He was just assuming that she had done it.

"Around quarter past five, maybe."

"On your cell?"

"Yes."

"Does Chaboseau's son live in Concarneau?"

"On the Cap Sizun, not far from Douarnenez. Right next to the Pointe du Millier."

The rocky cape was one of Dupin's favorite places. There would hardly be a single place in this case that he didn't know. And know well.

"He owns the mill there."

This was the answer to the question Dupin had just been asking himself. There was nothing right next to the Pointe du Millier apart from a little white cottage near a lighthouse. A few hundred meters away stood the ancient, completely original water mill, which was still in operation. A stream with a strong current drove the enormous wooden paddlewheel. The mill produced famous organic flour, mainly dark buckwheat flour, *sarrasin*, used to make delicious *crêpes au blé noir*.

Dupin would put the two policewomen on Chaboseau's son. And of course, he would meet him himself. But now he needed to focus.

"So, Monsieur Priziac, what investments did you make together? The two of you, or the three of you?"

Dupin was still leaning on the stone wall, his eyes locked on the pharmacist.

"The brewery—what is the story there? Are you involved in that too? The real estate?" Dupin had opened his notebook to the relevant page. "The new fish cannery? And here's another thing

I'd really like to know, do you know of any other business deals your murdered friend was involved in?"

Priziac gave him a searching look.

"Good deals rely mainly on one thing: trade secrets."

There was a hard edge to his voice now.

"Besides, you're wasting your time. I've already told you all I've got to say. You're better off paying attention to the mayor. If you're smart—and people say you are—take me up on my tip."

This was frustrating. Dupin didn't have any police powers to grill him any further. Of course it was simple to find out who officially owned a company, but not whose money was tied up in it in one way or another. They would need to be able to prove a specific, serious suspicion against Priziac. But for the moment, he was nothing more than a friend of the victim. And he wasn't the only one. If Madame Chaboseau wasn't willing to volunteer all the information on her business and financial activities, this was going to be difficult. They would have to wait and see.

"I . . ."

His phone. It was Iris Nevou.

"Excuse me." Dupin walked a few paces away. A steep set of stone steps led down to the beach. He didn't answer the call until the last step.

"Yes?"

"Your appeal for the public's cooperation." There was a clear note of disapproval in her voice. "The phones haven't stopped ringing. Everyone's got tips."

For Dupin, it had mainly been about getting the urgent "message" to Nolwenn and Riwal—but in fact, it couldn't hurt to take the tips into consideration. Even though such a public investigation was not usually his style.

"I'm all ears."

He was walking across the sand. He was completely alone. The shadows of the trees behind the beach were getting longer and longer, the sun had sunk quite some way and it had taken on a slightly orange tinge that it was now imparting to everything around it.

"Docteur Chaboseau and Evette Derien, this doctor who works in his practice, they met twice in a pub in Saint-Guénolé, in the evenings. The first time was three weeks ago and then again two weeks ago. At Chez Cathy. They had an 'intense discussion' over drinks there, according to the tip-off."

Saint-Guénolé was right by the Pointe de la Torche and the famous sandy beaches that were kilometers long. Not far from Beg Meil, where Dupin currently was.

"What does that mean? Intense?"

"I don't know."

"Where did you get this information?"

"From the owner of the pub. He heard your appeal . . ."

"Does he suspect an affair?"

It sounded a little like that.

"He didn't put it like that."

"But maybe that's what he meant."

"Maybe."

Nevou was silent.

"Why would they meet there?"

"She must be there quite a lot. She's a surfer."

La Torche was Brittany's legendary surfers' paradise. Surfing, wind-surfing, kite-surfing, body-boarding. Everything you could wish for. Even land-sailing.

"Le Menn tried to get hold of her."

"And?"

"She's surfing right now."

"At La Torche?"

"Yes. She has only just arrived. She asked Le Menn to call her back later."

Dupin knew that surfers were very fond of taking to the water at dusk.

"I see." He thought this over. "She's clearly not exactly grieving."

Her colleague had been murdered a few hours before. No doubt she would have heard about it by now.

"Maybe this is her way of processing it. There's something meditative about surfing."

Before Dupin could respond, Nevou carried on with her report. "And there's something else."

"Yes?"

"One of the Chaboseaus' neighbors, an older man, got in touch. It has occurred to him that this afternoon, contrary to his first statement, he, and I quote, 'did in fact see something on the staircase.' And this was around four o'clock or a little after. He says he saw someone there who was, and I quote, 'apparently a total stranger.' Just for a fraction of a second because then the stranger went out the door. Unfortunately he couldn't describe him in any more detail. And before you ask: the statement fits with a dozen other statements from people who also noticed 'strangers' supposedly acting suspiciously in some way, following your appeal . . . In all sorts of places. Some people suspect it's connected to that big submarine docking."

There had been stories in all the papers, a large naval submarine had docked in the harbor for three days. But of course, it was preposterous to suppose there was any connection.

"We've got access to the phone records now. The phone calls and texts from Chaboseau's cell."

This seemed incredibly quick to Dupin. So Nevou's optimism had been well founded.

"There are quite a few calls, I have the lists. Le Menn and I are combing through them. I can send them to you."

"Please do."

"All right. We still can't access the data saved on the phone, though, and the same goes for the computer."

Dupin had not expected any different.

"In terms of the phone records, we've started by concentrating on today."

Sometimes Nevou's rather long-winded manner reminded Dupin of Kadeg. But maybe in his impatience he was just imagining that.

"He spoke to Priziac this morning at nine thirty and to Luzel at nine fifty-four. For around four minutes each. He must have been at the surgery by then. He called his wife for two minutes at two twenty P.M."

Madame Chaboseau had not mentioned this either. Why not? Dupin put this on his list of questions for when he next spoke to her.

"At eleven oh three there was a phone call from one Sieren Cléac. We have not been able to get hold of her yet. And that was it."

"Sieren Cléac." Dupin repeated the name automatically. He had heard it before.

"She owns a new little canning factory in Concarneau."

Bingo. Dupin remembered now. Françoise had spoken about her. A client.

"What could that have been about?"

"No idea. I'm sure we'll get hold of her soon. That's all I have for now," Nevou finished. "Oh wait, actually, the chief called. He was a little . . ." She seemed to be searching for the right words. ". . . taken aback to have found out about this 'appalling case' from the media. He would like you to get in touch, but of course only, and I quote, 'if that suits you.'"

Dupin couldn't suppress a grin. Locmariaquer. His unbearable, bad-tempered boss; he had actually expected the call much earlier. And usually in a situation like this there would have been a massive outburst of rage from the prefect. But since the events surrounding Dupin's last big case, the prefect had been keeping himself in check. During the complex case in Brittany's Artus Forest, Dupin had worked—against his will, but "extremely successfully" in the media's opinion—as a special investigator with the Parisian police, and in the end he had received a very attractive job offer from the capital. The offer was for him to be a *directeur central*. Dupin had wanted to turn it down on the spot but in fact hadn't. He realized to his astonishment that he kept putting off turning it down for the flimsiest of reasons. He would never really have genuinely considered it, but the idea of going back to Paris did appeal to him in a way, in a very small way. When Dupin did finally turn it down some time later, they had been undeterred, telling him that the retirement of the current incumbent "was unexpectedly delayed for a while" so he still had time to keep thinking. That he shouldn't rush into anything, to take his time instead. Dupin had not told the prefect anything about turning down the job, only about the extension to the offer. And Dupin's calculations had worked out perfectly: it was hard to believe how friendly, even deferentially, the prefect had been acting ever since. The commissaire was downright enjoying it, he had to admit. Not that Dupin staying would really have meant anything to the prefect, of course, but the public would possibly interpret the commissaire leaving as a defeat for the prefect—and this was where Locmariaquer's boundless vanity always came into play.

"Good. I have a few more jobs for you."

Dupin went over the new issues with Nevou. Among other things, they would urgently need information on Chaboseau's son. The two policewomen had not been aware of him either, which was extremely odd. Evette Derien, the doctor, had ended up high on their list too after the tip-off from the pub landlord. Dupin needed a bigger squad. There were so many potential connections and very loose connections in this case at the moment—but he had never had such a small team.

The commissaire had walked to the end of the beach and back three times during this conversation. Once he had hung up, he walked unhurriedly back up the stone steps into the garden.

Priziac was on the phone. He looked like he had stretched out even more comfortably on his lounge chair than before.

"Right. I'll call you back later."

He put the phone on a stool next to the lounge chair and sat up a little straighter at least.

"A friend?" Dupin asked, his brow furrowed.

"That's right."

"Where . . ."

Dupin's phone rang again. He was still holding it in his hand.

Claire. She was finally getting in touch.

"One moment." The scene from earlier repeated itself, with Dupin disappearing down the steps.

"I'm so glad you've called."

"I'm just coming out of the hospital, Georges, a complicated case . . ."

Clearly the world was full of complicated cases.

". . . an emergency," she specified. "I've just listened to your message. Or should I say your *messages*." This meant she already knew everything. "So yeah, what can I say?" Dupin couldn't interpret her tone. "There's nothing we can do. This is just the way it is. A murder. And you're investigating." She didn't sound angry or even disappointed. "Where are my parents now?"

Dupin had walked to the middle of the beach and now he stopped.

"They've gone for a walk. Or to have something to eat."

"Okay. Maybe we'll see you every so often. You'll need to have something to eat now and again. So we could do that together."

An absurd idea.

"Maybe the case will be solved quickly. Remember the last one. That was less than twenty-four hours."

That was true. But in his whole time as a commissaire it had happened that way precisely once.

"Quite unlikely. But we'll see." This was not the right time for a discussion.

"Great. Then let's do it that way. I'll call my parents now."

"I . . . let's talk later, Claire."

"Speak to you then." She hung up.

Dupin walked up the steps again. He was a little out of breath when he reached the top. The pharmacist had now sat up fully.

"Where were we, Monsieur Priziac?" Dupin really had to think for a moment. "Oh yes. Was that Monsieur Luzel you were speaking to on the phone just now?"

"That's right. And now I need," the pharmacist made to stand up, "a drink. I think we're done here, young man."

Even as a young man, Dupin had hated the old-fashioned phrase "young man." He pretended not to have heard it.

"We are, of course, looking into all of Docteur Chaboseau's business activities very carefully. That means we will know about everything very soon. And all about his business partners too," bluffed Dupin. "So you can just tell me right now what exactly you were up to together."

Priziac was impressively agile given how old—and overweight—he was, leaping to his feet in one deft movement.

"As I say: business and trade secrets are carefully guarded in this country."

He made a point of speaking in a polite way.

"Did Chaboseau have a stake in his son's mill?"

"No, he didn't want that. Félix didn't want that."

The pharmacist was standing next to the lounge chair.

"Pierre suggested it to him. Several times. He didn't want to interfere in the day-to-day operation in any way, he just wanted to allow his son a—bigger start."

"What do you mean by that?"

Having started to leave, Priziac now stopped and turned around.

"Pierre saw real potential in his son. But Félix lacks ambition. With the mill, with everything." He made no attempt to tone down the note of coldness that crept into his voice as he said this. "It really upset Pierre."

There they were: a handful of sentences containing a tragedy, a tragedy with the potential to dominate an entire life. An overbearing father and a son who "failed."

Dupin didn't want to let Priziac go just yet.

"Tell me more about the dispute between the mayor and Chaboseau. About the breweries."

"I've said what I have to say. The rest is your job." Priziac turned around and kept walking.

Dupin followed him, feeling a little ridiculous, but he still had questions.

"Did they have a serious argument?" he said, catching up.

"Yes, they did."

"In public?"

"Yes. At the meeting on Tuesday evening."

"What kind of meeting was this?"

"The city council meeting. Pierre never really went to them. But they were due to discuss the granting of licenses for new breweries."

They had reached the gravel path.

"Were you there too?"

"No. Pierre just told me about it."

"When?"

"Yesterday."

"You saw each other yesterday? Here? In the evening?"

"Yes, and before you ask, Jodoc Luzel was here too."

Why was Priziac only telling him this now?

"And what else did Monsieur Chaboseau say about what happened? Did he mention anything that could be linked to his murder?"

They had now drawn level with the house.

Dupin had begrudgingly started to speak very quickly, although he didn't want to let it seem like he could be rushed.

"I've said what I have to say," the pharmacist repeated.

He reached into his jacket pocket and took out a key. They reached the door.

"You don't have any children?"

"No."

Priziac turned the key in the lock, and the door opened. Without casting another glance at Dupin, he stepped into the hallway.

"Where were you this afternoon between two and four o'clock, Monsieur Priziac?"

"I was in Concarneau until noon. Then from one o'clock I was here," the pharmacist answered over his shoulder.

"Are there witnesses?"

Priziac turned around again.

"No."

"Where exactly are your pharmacies?"

"Aren't you funny, young man." Priziac smiled condescendingly. "That's another thing people say about you. And apparently it's true. There are twenty-three pharmacies. All over Brittany. My great-grandfather set up the first one at the end of the nineteenth century, here in Concarneau." Now he abruptly turned on his heel. *"Au revoir."*

Priziac let the door slam shut behind him.

The La Torche beaches were thirty kilometers away, not a long journey this late in the evening—it was almost nine thirty.

One of the many offers the prefect had made in recent months was to provide Dupin with a new official car "of his choice" that came "with all the extras." This offer actually went far beyond the police service car guidelines. Dupin had gratefully declined, to everyone's frustration, especially Nolwenn's. The stylish new Citroën DS 5 had already been completely "configured"—they would only have had to place the order. Of course Dupin had again clung on to his old, or as he preferred to call it, "character-ful" Citroën—XM V6 24 V Exclusive. Its value was, at a favor-able estimate, three thousand euro. The repair costs alone for the accidental damage during the last case had come to double that, which was "objectively" a questionable investment, but Dupin still had not hesitated for a moment. Nolwenn and even Claire had put forward every conceivable argument for a new car—the environment, safety, reliability, even the prospect of being able to drive more recklessly in a four-wheel drive, which was a real advantage in Brittany. To no avail.

Dupin saw the sign for the Cinémarine on the right-hand side and drove straight to the car park.

"Die Hard—the late showing, one adult?" asked the young man at the cinema kiosk as Dupin walked in. "Popcorn and a beer?"

Dupin was in a hurry, the sun would be setting very soon, but without caffeine he wouldn't be able to take another step.

"Just two coffees, please, that's it, thanks."

The Cinémarine, the popular cinema in Bénodet that always showed classic action movies on Friday nights, was one of Dupin's ports of call when he urgently needed caffeine. It didn't matter where the commissaire was in the general vicinity of Concarneau, he could have listed in his sleep where to get a reasonable coffee at any given time of day or night. Along with the restaurants and cafés, he also knew the petrol stations, supermarkets, bakeries, hotels, clubs, cinemas, and train stations.

"Got it," the young man responded smoothly, "four euro, please."

He busied himself with the chic coffee machine and its enormous screen while it hissed and steamed.

"Here you go."

The two little paper cups were in front of Dupin in an instant. He drank the first all in one go, grabbed the second, and was back at his car in no time.

It was just like it always was during an investigation: he would have liked to speak to every person of interest on his list at the same time. His decision to speak to Evette Derien next was an impulsive one. He would try to keep the conversation as short as possible. And then he would try Madame Chaboseau again, despite everything that had happened earlier. There were some important issues that needed to be clarified.

Before stopping off at the cinema, Dupin had called Rosa Le Menn. She had got through to Félix Chaboseau. His mother called him that afternoon to share the terrible news with him, around five o'clock—quite late in Dupin's opinion. The son had wanted to come over straightaway, but her son said Claudette Chaboseau was "not at all pleased" with that idea. He would not be coming to Concarneau until the morning now. Félix Chabo-seau had spoken about a "huge distance" between himself and his parents and emphasized that he knew "almost nothing" about his father's current life or latest business deals. The young po-licewoman thought he sounded "very credible" and had seemed miserable. She had, of course, asked Félix Chaboseau about his whereabouts that lunchtime and afternoon. By his own account he had spent the whole day at the mill where his four colleagues could see him the entire time. It was not until shortly before five that he had driven home to Beuzec-Cap-Sizun, a small village not far from the Pointe du Millier. If this account was accurate, the son was beyond suspicion, he had a solid alibi.

His phone call with Françoise—she had only just hung the very last painting—had been short. She couldn't imagine why Sieren Cléac, the owner of the small fish-canning factory, might have called Pierre Chaboseau that day. Françoise had not even been aware that they knew each other personally.

Dupin sank down into the comfortable upholstered driver's seat and put down the little paper cup. What other car still had this kind of thing in this day and age: two decent-sized drinks holders built-in between the armrest and the gear stick. The best thing of all was this: although they were intended for regular-sized cans and bottles, they were fitted with an extra dip in the middle—exactly the size of a small coffee cup. This was reason enough never to give up this car, ever. Especially when this was coupled with the ultrasmooth "air suspension" that made every bump in the road disappear as if by magic. Under normal cir-cumstances at least, it prevented any drink spillage.

Dupin started the engine and the radio came on.

"Bernadette, elle est très chouette," Nino Ferrer sang, a song

for eternity—and for right now. Dupin had not heard the song for a long time. A smile was spreading across his face. Then he stopped.

Bernadette! Of course—that was it! He had forgotten the name and the whole story connected to it, but Nino Ferrer had reminded him. Nolwenn had mentioned the Chez Bernadette café in passing. She was very keen to stop off there on her bike tour.

Dupin searched on his phone, he was sure to find it. There! Bernadette was eighty-three and an institution. She had grown up amidst the counters, tables, and customers in her parents' legendary café that had opened in 1903. Bernadette, who was simply called the *"grande petite dame,"* ran the café, now in its third generation, and had done so for fifty years now. She would be retiring soon and devoting her time entirely to her chickens and her garden, according to what he read on the internet.

The café was in Callac, far inland, between Concarneau and the Pink Granite Coast.

Dupin immediately called the number.

It took a moment.

"Bernadette's, *bonsoir*!"

He needed to make this sound as urgent and official as possible, it was going to seem odd enough as it was. "This is Commissaire Georges Dupin, Police de Concarneau. I'm looking for one of your customers. Madame Nolwenn. She might be there today, or maybe she was there in the last few days or hasn't come yet, she is . . ."

"I'll get Bernadette," the woman interrupted him. A few seconds later Dupin heard her loudly calling:

"Bernadette—some nutcase wants to talk to you."

Bretons' respect for official authorities was notoriously lacking.

"Yes?" Dupin suspected this one tiny word had never been more loaded with skepticism.

There was nothing for it, he would have to start all over again.

"Commissaire Georges Dupin. Police de Concarneau. We are looking for a customer. Madame Nolwenn."

"Nolwenn? You're looking for Nolwenn?" Suddenly there was warmth and enthusiasm in Bernadette's voice.

"Right."

"Are you Nolwenn's colleague?" A bit more skeptical again now.

"That's right."

"Nolwenn's commissaire?"

"Correct."

She was silent for a moment. Cleared her throat.

"She was here, your Nolwenn! She is absolutely wonderful." Bernadette sounded like a little girl now, speaking about her best friend. "She left the day before yesterday. With her husband."

This was not quite what Dupin had been hoping for, but still, he was on her trail now.

"And do you know where she was headed next?"

"No."

"She didn't say anything to you about it?"

There was some more silence.

"She wasn't sure yet."

"I . . . thank you so much, madame . . ."

"Please, just call me Bernadette. A friend of Nolwenn's is a friend of mine."

Dupin couldn't help smiling. There it was: Nolwenn's effect on people.

"Take care, Bernadette," he said warmly.

"Say hello to Nolwenn from me when you speak to her."

She hung up.

Dupin leaned back.

He thought things over. He may not have found Nolwenn, but he could narrow down the search radius a bit better now.

He drank his second coffee.

He dialed Nevou's number on the car phone, then drove off at top speed.

Two euphoric minutes later, Dupin reached the bridge over the Odet. Ten minutes after that he stopped at the big car park right before the Pointe de la Torche.

Despite the high speed, he had given Nevou precise instructions: all gendarmeries were to search for Nolwenn immediately in every bistro and café within a forty-kilometer radius of Chez Bernadette. They just had to give it a try.

After some initial confusion, Nevou had promised to take care of it all.

Dupin got out and walked in the direction of the Plage de Pors Carn, one of the top surfing spots in the world. Paul Girard had taken Dupin along once when the official World Cup had been held here in front of tens of thousands of spectators. It was also Robby Naish's favorite spot, ahead of Hawaii or California, and he was the greatest surfing legend of all time.

By now the sun had shrunk to a pale yellow, almost inconspicuous ball. There were evenings when it turned into a spectacular blazing ball of fire as it went down—and evenings like this when it got strangely small, with no dramatic colors or shades. No red, no pink, no orange. It had just tinged the sky immediately around it pink, a subtle effect. The rest of the sky glowed a pale bluish color. It seemed like the sun was primly holding back today. To make some space for other twilight ambiences. For the waning of the light, the fading of color, the lengthening of the shadows and approaching darkness. You could watch it minute by minute.

While there had been just a gentle breeze at the rugged Pointe du Raz that day—and in the small bays of Beg Meil there was not even that—there was a stiff wind blowing here. Powerful and remarkably steady. It was coming straight in off the sea and it carried the sea with it: salt, iodine, and seaweed, every breath was saturated with it.

But the real stars of the evening were the waves. Towering four or five meters up into the air, visible even far out where they broke for the first time, before re-forming and finally coming toward the beach in one long, drawn-out motion, where they broke a second time.

Dupin had walked from the car park to the beach along a narrow sandy path through the majestic dunes. Now he came to an abrupt stop.

This had been an idiotic idea. Two or three dozen surfers were splashing about in the water. Many of them far out, lying in wait for the best wave. Of course this stretch of beach was reasonably small enough to scan compared to the never-ending beaches to the north—but still: How was he meant to find Evette Derien? He didn't even know what she looked like. Let alone in a wet suit.

Dupin walked straight down to the water. Two young surfers

were coming toward him, their boards clamped sideways under their arms.

"Bonsoir, messieurs!"

Dupin had to shout, the waves were making a horrendous racket.

It took a moment for the young men to realize that Dupin meant them.

"Can we help?"

One of them, tanned, with designer stubble and a lovely, open smile, spoke to Dupin as if he needed to help a confused old man. The other man stood next to him in silence.

"I'm looking for . . ."

Dupin had been caught by a wave, right up to his knees. He tried to act as if nothing had happened. The Atlantic was still less than fifteen or sixteen degrees.

"I'm looking for Docteur Derien. It's urgent."

They both stared at him as if he had asked for an alien.

"Oh, right, you mean Evette," said the surfer with the designer stubble after a brief pause. The other man nodded.

"Evette Derien, yes," Dupin confirmed.

"Careful, another wave is about to hit you, monsieur. The big ones always come close together." The young man looked pointedly at the legs of Dupin's jeans.

"Evette is the one in the purple Rip Curl wet suit with the green floral pattern on the arms." He turned and pointed to a spot in the sea where some surfers were lying quite close together on their boards.

"Thanks."

Dupin set off straightaway and was immediately hit by a second wave. He walked stoically on.

The sun had sunk halfway below the horizon by now. Far out to sea, two particularly impressive waves towered up into the air, and Dupin could tell that an excited, nervous energy was spreading among the surfers.

The first of the two waves was about to reach them, they were starting to paddle with their arms, picking up speed. The surfers stood up, practically in synchrony, all but one of them catching the wave. It was an impressive spectacle. Several sections of the wave did collapse but—with the surf constantly churning—they kept going, while other sections remained intact. Both daring and incredibly elegant, the surfers glided through the wild chaos of the unruly forces around them.

Now Dupin could also see the purple wet suit with green on the arms. That must be her. Docteur Evette Derien. She was at the edge of the little group. She was surfing toward the beach, pulling off some daring moves.

Dupin waved harder and harder.

The wave she was on was running out, you could tell the doctor was using the usual maneuvers to prolong the ride. For one last moment she stood on the board with maddening nonchalance, only to leap gracefully into the water a second later.

Dupin strode toward her. He was immediately up to his knees in water.

Evette Derien was standing up to her hips in the water, around twenty meters ahead of him, and she still hadn't noticed him yet. She ran both her hands through her long, dark hair and pulled the board—which was attached to her ankle with a cord—toward her. All of this was done with practiced ease—then she turned around and headed back into the raging surf.

Standing up to his thighs in water, Dupin called after

her, but to no avail. Now he saw one of the surfers signaling to Evette Derien and pointing in his direction. She turned around, not in any hurry. And spotted Dupin waiting for her with wildly disheveled hair, wearing jeans and a polo shirt in the ocean.

They had left the beach and were walking past the dunes, the noise of the breaking waves receding.

"Yes, it's dreadful."

Despite her words, she was smiling, an endearing smile. Strangely, it didn't seem inappropriate.

"I saw him just this morning."

Dupin could feel the water sloshing around in his shoes. His jeans, soaked to the thighs, seemed to be clinging tighter and tighter to his legs.

Evette Derien had left her surfboard on the beach. Dupin looked at her from the side as she walked. She was not particularly tall; she was very athletic, extremely fit, but willowy. Long jet-black hair, thin, dark eyebrows, elegant, wide cheekbones. But the most striking thing about her were her green eyes that positively sparkled.

"And did he seem the same as always this morning?"

"Just like always, yes."

"What time did you meet?"

"We met for the first time today just before eight o'clock at the practice, then of course we met now and again over the course of the morning."

Her voice was soft but also wonderfully clear.

"You didn't notice anything unusual about him?"

"Nothing at all."

Dupin had got his notebook out of his trouser pocket; luckily it had stayed dry. "What did you talk about?"

"We really just said hello to each other." She hesitated briefly. "I presume you know that Docteur Chaboseau wanted to take a bit of a step back? He brought me into the practice in the middle of last year. With a view to me taking over fully one day."

"Was that the explicit arrangement?"

They had reached the sandy plateau behind the dunes. The sun had gone down but there was still a glow in the sky. The wind was blowing much more gently here than down by the sea.

"Of course." That smile again. "For me, it was a precondition of moving to Brittany. I come from Paris, from the Sixth. Same as you." An assertive undertone, just briefly. "I worked in a thriving practice on the Place de l'Odéon. There came a point where Paris was getting to be too much for me, although it took me a while to realize it." She paused for a moment. "My mother is Breton. Her family comes from here. That leaves a lasting impression."

Dupin liked Derien's frank way of talking. People were usually more reticent in the initial interviews after a murder.

"In any case." She gave the commissaire a very serious look. "To return to your question: yes, that's what the arrangement was. It's all working out brilliantly, my patient base is growing. I just made the mistake of not fixing a specific deadline with him for the handover, contractually, I mean. He always talked about one or two years. I've been trying to have a word with him since March to get it clarified."

Suddenly a strange noise came from off to one side. They turned around at the same time.

And they saw a flock of sheep running directly toward them.

Shaggy white fleeces. Fat balls of wool on four legs. One particularly large sheep was out in front, bleating excitedly.

Thrown for just a moment, Dupin swiftly turned his attention back to Evette Derien. They had just been talking about the issue he was most interested in:

"This conversation to clear things up, did you have it in Saint-Guénolé, by any chance, at Chez Cathy?"

"That's exactly where it was." She didn't seem at all surprised by Dupin's question. "We met there twice to speak about that exact thing: when he would be retiring for good."

She was completely open about it.

"I'm often here at the Torche, I love the space and the wildness here. I have a little second home in Saint-Guénolé, just one bedroom, right near the beaches. We met in Concarneau once too, in the Sables Blancs hotel. My real home is in the new neighborhood on the hill to the west of the beach. We—"

"The neighborhood that was built on Monsieur Chaboseau's land?"

An odd coincidence. Perhaps.

"Yes, he told me that too. That the land once belonged to his family. I didn't know that when I rented the apartment."

Dupin made a note, although he really didn't know whether anything would come of it. The Chaboseaus would have sold the land to a real estate firm, and the whole thing was long ago.

Derien returned to their original topic: "This issue meant there was some real tension between us over the last few months. He was dead set against setting a specific date."

She was very firm in the way she put this, but she was neither arrogant nor aggressive.

"I wanted a binding agreement, a contractual one."

For some reason the sheep seemed to take an interest in them all of a sudden. Or at least, the ringleader sheep had decided to stop the flock in front of them. In the middle of the path. Which did not seem to faze Evette Derien in the slightest, who was squeezing her way through the flock unperturbed. The animals stared at her in silence. Dupin copied her.

"Clearly you're right to try and speak to me immediately. The simplest thing"—she glanced over her shoulder to see if he was following—"would have been for me to get rid of him."

Dupin ignored this.

"Did you come to a conclusion in your conversations?"

"He promised to set a final deadline by the beginning of July. This deadline would in turn be at the end of next year at the latest."

"Is there a written agreement on this yet?"

"It was meant to be ready by the end of the month."

They had made it through the flock of sheep without incident.

"I see. How was your relationship otherwise?"

"We had a good working relationship and business relationship. It was important for me to keep a certain distance personally, as it was for him. I'm sure you're asking because you've found me surfing, not grieving."

Out of nowhere—the sheep had been quiet the whole time apart from the leader of the flock—a loud bleating started up behind them. Dupin looked around. The flock was following them. Derien didn't seem bothered by this.

"Do you surf, Monsieur Dupin?"

"No."

His sport was running, which, as he was aware, had a reputation for being one of the most boring kinds of sport in existence.

"It's an opportunity to find yourself fully, by getting away from everyone else. Including yourself. There's nothing left but the waves, the wind, the sea."

This sounded a little too esoteric for Dupin's tastes, but he could more or less imagine what she meant.

"From a financial point of view, did you run the practice together—or is it actually two practices under one roof?"

"We bought certain pieces of equipment together, and of course, we consulted each other on complex cases. He is—he was a good doctor, but we each operated independently. We just shared the two receptionists. All scrupulously fair. There were never any disagreements on that front."

Dupin couldn't help casting a look behind him every now and then. The sheep were hardly bleating anymore now, but they were still trotting along behind them. The scenery behind the dunes was a different world, the ground still sandy but covered in short, scrubby grass. Like a large green carpet, but yellow and rust-red in places.

"And are you aware of any disagreements Docteur Chaboseau had with other people?"

"No. But to be honest I didn't pay much attention to him anymore, even privately." It didn't sound cold, just honest. "I wanted that practice. Nothing more. We don't have any acquaintances or friends in common either."

"You're not aware of any unusual incidents occurring in the practice recently?"

"No, none at all."

"Do you have any knowledge of Chaboseau's other business activities?"

"I hear about them sometimes. But only in passing. From other people. He has a share in a cannery, for example. Frankly, I couldn't care less."

"Do you think that—"

Dupin was abruptly interrupted. Not by the sheep this time, but by a man's voice.

"Hello! Hello! Monsieur le Commissaire!"

A gendarme was running toward them.

Dupin gave Evette Derien an apologetic look and was met by an understanding nod.

"Thank you so much." Dupin had already turned away, leaving the doctor and the sheep behind as he ran toward the policeman.

"You've got no reception here, Commissaire. That's why we've come."

Dupin could now make out a second gendarme farther away, coming up the path from the beach.

"One of the surfers . . ." The gendarme had stopped in front of Dupin, panting hard. "Told us you came up here, he—"

"What's this about?"

"Something terrible has happened. Four injured, two of them seriously. They're at the hospital. They were taken in an—"

The man drew breath.

"What on earth has happened?"

"An explosion in a shipyard. At Héros Naval, the shipbuilding company in Concarneau. Probably not an accident, at least according to—"

"A deliberate attack?"

"Apparently there is some indication of that, but I am specifically supposed to tell you that for now, that is just—"

"What company is this?"

"A company that Jodoc Luzel has a stake in, Nevou told me to tell you."

"The wine merchant?" Dupin spoke as if his mind was elsewhere.

"And Docteur Chaboseau too?"

"That's as much as I know from our colleague."

"And Monsieur Priziac, the pharmacist?"

"I don't know that either." The policeman was gradually getting his breath back.

"When?"

"Half an hour ago."

"Let's go, then."

Dupin charged toward the car park, the gendarme struggling to follow him. It would take him a few minutes to get to his car.

"Do we know any more details about what happened yet?" Dupin called over his shoulder as he ran.

"There was an explosion, that's all I know. I was just meant to find you."

Dupin sped up again.

What was going on here? Shipbuilding had not been part of his investigation before now. But the fact that Jodoc Luzel was a co-owner of the shipyard and that an explosion had happened there on the very day his friend died could not be a co-incidence.

Whatever was really going on here—apparently it was not over yet.

Night had fallen. Which made the entire scene unfolding before Dupin's eyes even more spectacular. The enormous dock, the ship under construction, the smoke, the fire engines and police cars with their flashing blue lights and the high-performance flood-lights that had been set up especially. All of this in the middle of the large harbor and shipyard complex full of technical equip-ment, cabins and piles of materials, an old world of industrial production, but very real. A world made of steel. Steel and rust.

It was the biggest of the docks in the industrial harbor. For a stretch of a hundred and thirty meters, water could flow into the deep dock, along with boats for repair and maintenance. Then the enormous lock gates could be closed and the seawater could be pumped out of the harbor again. Or conversely, as was the case with the *Ampez,* the ship that was now damaged: you could drain the pool to begin with, build the ship, and then let the water in until the ship floated.

A terrible scene of devastation lay before them. They were standing at a safe distance at the edge of the complex. An acrid stench hung in the air.

"I'll say it again—yes!" Dupin had already asked this ques-tion once. "We're completely certain, in fact." The head of the fire brigade, also responsible for the harbor, seemed extremely competent. She had immediately brought Dupin right up to the—strictly cordoned-off—scene of the accident and explained what they knew at that point. "Somebody deliberately detonated one of the gas tanks for welding. One of the smaller ones."

There were no more than a handful of strangely warped steel remnants from the original gas tank visible on the ground. The manager of Héros Naval was standing next to the head of the fire brigade, yet to utter a word; an inconspicuous, pale figure in a dark jacket. He was looking around anxiously.

"We also know how it happened, we have the piece of evidence. The gas pipe on the tank was turned on, cut at a safe distance, and used like a detonating fuse. All you would need is a simple lighter. We've found the end piece that was cut off, along with the welding head. Your crime scene investigation team have already seized it, and it's on its way to the lab. It's very clear the pipe was cut through cleanly. There's no way that was an accident."

Dupin nodded. Her account was undramatic, a professional report.

"During the explosion of the smaller tank," she continued, "one of the larger tanks was apparently hit by the pieces of steel that were flying around. We have not been able to find anything unusual on this larger tank, or rather on what is left of it." From where they were standing, they could also see the wreckage of the larger gas tank, much closer to the edge of the dry dock. "You've got to picture them as projectiles. They instantly caused the second tank to explode, and this was unfortunately right next to the ship, where the shift changeover was taking place at the time. Work takes place night and day here. Four men were injured as a result."

It was horrendous. Dupin had asked for a report on the men's condition on his way over; Nevou was handling it.

"The explosion of the smaller tank alone would definitely have caused damage to the ship, and in the worst-case scenario it would have caused some minor injuries to the workers—but absolutely not on the scale that it has now."

This reconstruction sounded plausible.

"So there were," Dupin summarized out loud, "two explosions in quick succession."

The head of the fire brigade did not go into any more detail. "We have the situation under control now. In the vicinity of the smaller tank, some wooden pallets and beams that caught on fire have already been put out. There is no further danger as far as possible secondary explosions are concerned. We—"

She was interrupted by a loud, strident voice.

"I don't care . . . Just arrest me then, it's up to you."

Spotlit by one of the enormous lights like something out of a film, a man came striding toward the little group, a police officer on either side of him. They must have been part of the team guarding the site. Dupin recognized the man straightaway: Jodoc Luzel, the wine merchant. The third one in the trio. And most importantly, of course: the owner or co-owner of the company building the ship targeted in the attack.

"What exactly happened?" Luzel snapped at the head of the fire brigade. Only then did he cast a fleeting glance at Dupin and his manager, clearly intended as something akin to a greeting. His clean-shaven head, which highlighted his remarkably angular skull with its massive forehead, glinted in the floodlights. Neither particularly tall nor short, he was wiry and thin, a fit fifty-year-old. A totally different kind of person from his much older friends, Priziac and Chaboseau. Jeans, a pale pink polo shirt. Stylish glasses with dark frames.

The head of the fire brigade was about to explain again but Dupin beat her to it.

"A targeted attack on your company, Monsieur Luzel. Who's got it in for you?"

Luzel's eyebrows rose, his expression darkened.

"Sabotage?"

He stared at Dupin.

"Looks like it," the head of the fire brigade confirmed, then explained the facts of the case to Luzel in the same way she had done for Dupin.

Her final word was barely out when the commissaire took over again: "Monsieur Luzel, who's got it in for your company, and why?"

Luzel ignored the question a second time, turning to the manager instead: "How are the staff?"

"No news yet." It was difficult to understand him; his voice kept breaking and he seemed distraught. "Leroy and Moreau are fighting for their lives." He faltered.

Now Luzel turned his attention to Dupin.

"There's no reason anyone would have it in for me or Héros Naval," he said calmly.

"Do your friends Chaboseau and Priziac have a stake in the business?"

"They have a stake in the business that owns Héros Naval. Just like me. Yes."

"What kind of business is it?"

"I'm off," the head of the fire brigade interjected firmly. "If you need me, you'll find me back there." She gestured vaguely in the direction of the fire engine and turned away.

"If you would—excuse me too." The manager saw his chance

and took it. "I'd like to go and see the other workers to reassure them. Of course only if you"—he looked at Dupin and Luzel in turn—"agree."

"No objections," Dupin declared. The manager would find Nevou there, speaking to the shipyard workers to find out whether they had noticed anything unusual.

"I'll be right there." Luzel nodded to him. "Feel free to go."

Every now and again, cheerful, completely inappropriate music drifted over to them on the mild night air. Very likely from the Ville Close. There were numerous concerts at the back of the Ville Close in the summer—in the most beautiful part of it.

"It's a holding company"—Luzel came back to Dupin's question of his own accord—"and it owns quite a large shipyard, as well as this one and two smaller shipbuilding companies in Saint-Nazaire."

Saint-Nazaire was the most significant shipbuilding port in Brittany. And not only that—it was the most significant ship-building port in France. An outstanding shipyard, 150 years old. The *Symphony of the Seas* had been built there, the largest cruise ship of all time.

"What does the exact division of ownership between the three of you look like?"

Dupin needed to keep reminding himself: even though the friends' day jobs were wine merchant, pharmacist, and doctor, they were also investors, perhaps primarily so.

"I hold the most shares, fifty percent, the others each have twenty-five."

Luzel was behaving very differently from the pharmacist; he was giving information readily, and plenty of it.

"Your co-owner and friend, Docteur Chaboseau, was murdered this afternoon. And this incident was clearly an attack! Four people have been injured, some severely!" Dupin was suddenly furious. "So I'm asking you again: Who's got it in for you, for the company you jointly own—and why?"

It took Luzel a while to answer this time. He looked devastated all of a sudden, his face drained of much of its color. It was not as though up until this point he had seemed unmoved by what had happened, but for some reason he was only revealing his raw emotions now.

"You see a connection between the events?" This wasn't really a question. Luzel had said this to himself, as if he needed to do this in order to be able to think properly about it.

"Surely you're not that naïve, monsieur."

Luzel shrugged forlornly. He stared uncertainly at the ground, and was silent again for some time. Then he seemed to recover. His next words were clear and firm:

"I assure you, Monsieur le Commissaire, I can't even begin to think why someone would carry out an attack on Héros Naval."

"I think you—"

Dupin's cell phone. He glanced at the screen.

Claire.

He would phone her back in a minute. If he got the chance.

Dupin forced himself to be matter-of-fact. "What other businesses do you have a stake in, Monsieur Luzel? Just you or with your two friends?"

"My portfolio is very straightforward. I come from the wine trade, as you know. My only other investment, apart from shipbuilding, I mean, is in a brewery."

"Roi Gradlon, I take it."

"That's right, with Pierre and Brecan. Those two joint investments are the only ones the three of us made together. I run the wine business by myself."

All the same. For the first time, a clearer picture of the joint business ventures of the three friends was emerging.

"You're not involved in the art trade or real estate business? Or the fish-canning factory sector?"

These were the other sectors Dupin had come across so far.

"No."

"And your friend Priziac?"

"He'll have to answer that himself." Luzel did not say this in a harsh way.

"How did you hit upon shipbuilding, Monsieur Luzel?"

"A tip from my friends. Shipbuilding is booming. As is this shipyard."

"And why did you put up the biggest stake?"

"I had the money available."

It sounded arbitrary—but there were people who were fairly indifferent to what they were investing in, who were mainly interested in the profits themselves.

"Were there tensions between you and the other two?"

Luzel's expression changed. "What makes you say that? Not at all."

"What kind of ship is this? The *Ampez*?"

Dupin ducked under the cordon. The boat must have been about a hundred meters long. A gigantic green hull, something resembling an enormous round weight at the bow, the railing and the deck painted a matte red. The upper deck with the captain's bridge in dazzling white was way down at the back, practically at the ship's stern, which was positively glowing in the light from the floodlights.

"A multipurpose vessel." Luzel had followed the commissaire. "Sand, gravel, stone. Eighty-nine meters long, three thousand, seven hundred tons of deadweight-loading capacity."

Dupin had stopped dangerously close to the edge of the dock. There was a steep drop and no railings anywhere. He felt a sense of unease. He couldn't help thinking about Docteur Chaboseau.

"Who might benefit from this boat not being finished on time?"

"Nobody, really. The demand for this kind of boat is high, the production lines at the relevant companies are at capacity long in advance. So nobody else can just deliver one if there is a delay in building a ship. And for the last time: I can't for the life of me imagine a rival sabotaging us in this way."

"Do commissions go to public tender?"

"Sometimes. We're building the *Ampez* for a company we work very closely with."

"And had disagreements with?"

Dupin was walking toward the bow, Luzel following behind.

"Maybe somebody just wanted to damage you in general? The three of you—or one of you, who knows? Or just wanted to send you a warning, a message."

These were all possibilities. But if so, they would be back to square one on whatever was really going on in the murder case.

Luzel responded calmly. "And what kind of message would that be, and about what? I just cannot get my head around—"

"Commissaire!"

They both spun around.

This time it was Kler Kireg, the mayor, who suddenly appeared in the light from the floodlights. Le Menn was following him.

The mayor was dressed in a noticeably casual way, dark blue cargo shorts with a pale blue slim-fit shirt that showed off his athletic physique. He was tanned, with short hair and dazzlingly white teeth. But the most striking thing about him was the determined expression he deliberately put on whenever he was in public. He was always keen to make sure people could see his relentless enthusiasm. Even tonight.

"We need to talk, Commissaire!" His manner was friendly but very firm.

He had stopped right in front of Dupin.

"I've already had myself brought up to speed by the head of the fire brigade and the site manager. One thing is crucial now: we cannot allow panic to spread through the town. The probability of it being sabotage may seem 'high' at first glance, but it's definitely not confirmed yet. And that's exactly what we should be saying publicly too, please." As with most politicians, everything about this speech came off as polished. It was not clear what was for show and what was real—Dupin suspected there was no difference anymore. "I was at Didier Squiban's concert in the Ville Close when it happened. News of the 'alleged attack' spread like wildfire, some of the audience left. The loud noise alone caused some commotion."

It sounded like a criticism.

Squiban was one of Brittany's greatest musicians, a jazz pianist, composer, and improviser. He had long been a legend, the Breton Keith Jarrett in a sense.

"And you yourself were totally calm and kept on enjoying the concert?" Dupin asked.

It was unbelievable—just a few hundred meters away there had been an attack in which, intentionally or not, four men had been injured, two of them critically. And the mayor refused to lose his cool, and more than that: he was complaining about other people who did.

"I deliberately stayed a little longer. Tonight is the start of Concarneau's l'Été en Fête, the most important series of events of the year! So it's basically my duty to keep calm and composed, Monsieur le Commissaire. Of course I left the concert some time later to see to this matter."

Besides the great annual institutions like the Festival des Filets Bleus, the literary festival Livre & Mer, the crime fiction festival, and the famous sailing regattas, dozens of other events took place under the umbrella of the Été en Fête: markets, exhibitions, medieval performances, readings, concerts, boat tours, and barbecues. The clue was in the name: *en fête*! Dupin had completely forgotten it was starting that evening. The festivities obviously appealed to the crowds of summer visitors, but they mainly appealed to the Concarnese themselves. Celebrations were one of the fundamentals of Breton life. The Fest-Noz, the classic Breton festival, a cheerful, sociable gathering with traditional music and dance, had in fact been declared part of world heritage by UNESCO recently. Just like the mystical music of Bengali minstrels, shrimp-fishing on horseback in Oostduinkerke, or Mongolian Khoomei throat-singing, as Riwal had proudly explained.

"Do you know," Dupin tried to focus, "of any arguments involving this shipyard, Monsieur Kireg? Do you have any suspicion as to why someone might have carried out an attack on Héros Naval?"

"Of course not. And as I say: it's important to me that we don't talk unnecessarily about an attack, Commissaire. Oh yes and"—it was a clear reprimand this time—"we should also hold off on spontaneous appearances in the press from now on. After all, we don't want to frighten people."

Dupin turned to Le Menn. But he spoke loudly enough for both Luzel and the mayor to catch every word loud and clear. "We must find out everything about Héros Naval. Everything there is to find." Typically these were actually tasks for Nolwenn. "Get some backup at the station and externally. Speak to experts from the trade, to rival firms. You and Nevou need to speak to the manager and all of the workers. Probe the entire company, the accounts, the tax documents . . ."

Le Menn made a note of everything on her phone. A habit that irritated Dupin every time he saw it.

"But surely you can—" Luzel tried to intervene.

Dupin interrupted him curtly: "Where were you at ten P.M., when the sabotage was taking place, monsieur?"

"Me?"

"You."

"At home. Having a wine tasting with friends. I—I live in Le Cabellou."

"Will your friends be able to confirm that?"

"Of course."

Dupin turned back to Le Menn. "We need to speak to these friends at some point then. Monsieur Luzel will draw up a list for us right away."

Le Menn nodded. "First thing tomorrow morning. It's almost midnight."

She was right. Dupin lost all sense of time passing and what time of day it was during a case. Or rather, during his investigations, his manic impulse to make progress in solving the case overrode everything else.

"If you would excuse me now, Monsieur le Commissaire." The mayor made to leave.

Dupin looked back and forth between him and Luzel. "Do you two actually know each other? What is your relationship to each other?"

It took a moment for either of them to respond. Dupin could have been wrong, but he got the impression the occasional glances the two had been exchanging were a touch frosty.

"It's a wonderful thing!" The mayor put his right hand casually in his trouser pocket. "I'm so glad that a citizen of the town as distinguished as Jodoc Luzel is considering becoming politically active. If that is what you mean, Monsieur le Commissaire."

"What are you talking about?" Dupin had no idea what he was referring to.

"I'm weighing up a run for town council," Luzel explained. "As an independent candidate."

"Interesting." Dupin ran a hand through his hair. Everyone was linked to everyone else here in some way.

"And I suppose you have different views and hold opposing positions. Can you give me some examples of what you disagree on?"

The mayor was the first to answer again:

"For example, Messrs. Chaboseau and Luzel, or rather, the

Roi Gradlon company, is of the opinion that the town should be much more conservative in granting licenses to microbreweries."

It was impressive, how much of a dyed-in-the-wool politician the young mayor was—in his gestures, speaking style, behavior.

"And because of this dispute, Monsieur Luzel, you want to go to the trouble of joining the town council?"

"A policy offering security for people's investments would be in the interests of the town in general. Across all sectors." Luzel was pleasant and matter-of-fact in his answer.

"Well, that is just—"

The mayor was interrupted by Dupin's phone.

It was Claire yet again. Damn. He needed to call her back very soon.

"Be that as it may," Dupin shook himself, "let's draw a line under this topic: this attack might not necessarily be to do with the shipyard and shipbuilding."

The men's faces didn't give much away, despite the rather enigmatic conclusion Dupin had drawn.

"Let's talk about something else. A different business sector. One which both you, Monsieur le Maire, and Docteur Chaboseau are involved in. Or were. The canneries. How competitive is it as a sector?"

"It's common knowledge I'm not involved in my family's cannery business in any way. So in that respect, there was no competition between us."

"But what about between Chaboseau's business and your family's business?"

"I don't mind repeating that I have nothing to do with the business whatsoever. And unlike with beer production, there is no and can be no comparable issue of restrictions on competitors—anyone can open a cannery if they feel like it—so there is no possible point of contention there either. The more of these kinds of entrepreneurial initiatives there are, the better. We must encourage entrepreneurial spirit in whatever way we can."

The official position, of course. Dupin would not be hearing anything else on this issue.

He glanced at his notebook. There were still some topics he needed to cover, given that he had both men—who were very high up on his list—here already: "Sieren Cléac opened a little cannery in Concarneau last year, how is her business doing?"

"It's called Fête de la Mer. I understand it's doing really well. Very promising." There was a note of genuine respect in the mayor's voice.

"She called Docteur Chaboseau toward late morning—do either of you have any idea what that might have been about? Whether the two of them knew each other well?"

Both men shook their heads.

Dupin turned to Jodoc Luzel: "Did your friend ever mention Madame Cléac to you?"

"No. I don't recall him ever talking about her or her company."

"You live in Sables Blancs, Monsieur Kireg?" Dupin turned back to the mayor abruptly.

You could tell Kireg was wondering about the possible hidden meaning behind this sudden change of subject.

"That's right. In the old Ker-Jean villa. That Georges Simenon used to rent when he stayed here in the thirties," he said with undisguised pride.

"Your wife didn't go to the concert in the Ville Close with you this evening?"

"No, she's at her mother's in Saint-Malo. For the whole Pentecost weekend."

The town's "first lady." A neat, slightly tomboyish woman in her mid-thirties, a lawyer with a very good reputation.

"Where exactly do you usually surf?"

The mayor was looking more and more baffled.

"La Torche, I presume." Dupin answered the question himself with a guess, a shot in the dark.

"That's right. Like all serious surfers in Finistère."

"And you know Docteur Evette Derien."

"Of course."

"And do you also see her there occasionally when you're surfing?"

"Yes."

"You're friends?"

"I wouldn't say that. But we chat sometimes. We chatted last week in the lighthouse."

"In the lighthouse?"

"After the famous 'vertical race'—in the Phare d'Eckmühl."

These "vertical races" were a mystery to Dupin. They had been taking place all over the world for some years now, in the most spectacular multi-story buildings. Sometimes they were half a kilometer high, thousands of steps. And of course, this sensational sport had been invented in Brittany, in the Phare d'Eckmühl, in fact. This meant that both the mayor and the doctor must be extraordinarily fit.

Dupin made a point of addressing his next question to both

men: "Do you know anything about the dispute between Evette Derien and Pierre Chaboseau? About the final handover of the practice?"

The mayor shrugged, at a loss.

"I just know she was really pushing for the handover," replied Luzel. "Pierre mentioned it a few times, but he was sure they would come to an agreement they were both happy with."

Dupin decided to leave it at that for now; he needed to go. And call Claire.

"I'll just sum up the most important points again." The two men looked at him, all ears. "Monsieur Kireg, you were at Squiban's concert in the Ville Close at ten P.M.—and you, Monsieur Luzel, were at home. At a wine tasting with friends."

Neither of them—it crossed Dupin's mind—had been far from the scene of the attack when it occurred. You didn't need to have graduated from police training school to know that an alibi that looked airtight at first glance did not mean a thing if there were any doubts about it.

"Why do you think . . ." the mayor began.

"All right then, good night, gentlemen."

Dupin gave the suggestion of a farewell with one subtle gesture, turned on his heel, and swiftly left the light of the floodlights.

"Where are you, Georges? Is everything all right?" Claire sounded really worried, which was rare. She usually stayed completely calm even in difficult situations. In fact, she became more and more calm the trickier the situation became. "We were at the concert in the Ville Close and suddenly there was this explosion. And then there were sirens and squad cars."

"You were in the Ville Close? At Squiban's concert?"

"Yes. Is everything okay with you?"

"All fine, I'm in the shipyard where the explosion was."

"What happened?"

"Sabotage. Somebody detonated a gas tank."

"Is it true about people being injured?"

"Four injured, two of them badly. But we don't know any more yet."

"Awful. Is it related to this afternoon?"

"Presumably. In all likelihood."

"Do you have a hunch yet?"

"No."

This was the unfortunate truth. Dupin had reached the last cordon in the harbor complex and it wasn't much farther to his car.

"At first, Didier Squiban kept playing, as beautifully as ever. But once it got around that there had been injuries, the concert was called off."

"Where are you now?"

"We're sitting in Café de l'Atlantic drinking Lambig." The delicious Breton apple brandy.

"Great. I'll be in touch again later, Claire."

"What do you mean *later*? It's after midnight. Don't you want to call it a day for today? Come and see us. Have you eaten anything?"

"I can't."

"Well, be careful then."

Unusual words for Claire.

"Speak soon, Claire."

"Speak soon."

"Wait." Dupin had almost hung up. "Are you still there?"

Claire normally ended phone calls even faster than he did.

"Yes."

"One last thing: When did you get to the concert?"

"Around quarter to ten."

About a quarter of an hour before the explosion.

"Did you see the mayor, by any chance? He claims he was there."

"Yes, I saw him, but only as he was leaving."

"Approximately what time was that?"

She thought about it.

"Twenty past ten, maybe. Twenty-five past ten."

"You didn't see him before that?"

"No."

"Was he alone?"

"I think so."

"Okay. Thanks."

"Salut, Georges."

They hung up at the same time.

Dupin breathed deeply in and out, then ran a hand through his hair.

He still couldn't get his head around the fact that Concarneau of all places had become the focal point of his investigation.

By this point he was at his car. He hadn't actually eaten anything since that morning. And he could really feel it now. He got in, started up the engine, and dialed Nevou's number on the car phone.

"Yes?" She sounded like she was in a bad mood.

"Where are you?"

"At the office."

"At the office?"

Unbelievable.

"Let's meet in the Amiral in five minutes. And let Le Menn know. Team briefing."

"I've spoken to *all* of the shipyard workers," Nevou said again, her deep voice cracking, her dark bob disheveled. "To everyone on the night shift. They were absolutely shattered. Some of them are friends with the injured men."

It was clear how shaken Nevou was. She seemed exhausted, drained of energy. Even more petite and slight than usual. The strain of the last few hours was plain to see. No doubt he was not the only one who had pictured the Pentecost weekend very differently.

All the same, there was some good news: Le Menn had called the hospital again on her way to the Amiral. Neither of the seriously injured people were in critical condition anymore. That was something—the most important thing right now.

They were sitting in the brasserie of the Amiral, at Dupin's favorite table, one of the small wooden tables that lined the walls. The commissaire was sitting on the bench covered in Atlantic blue fabric, the two policewomen on the comfortable chairs opposite him. Officially speaking, the brasserie was closed, so they wouldn't be disturbed here; in the restaurant next door, two tables were still occupied by couples. The two tall lamps on the bar bathed the room in light, giving it some atmosphere. It was a magnificent spot: through the windows opposite, you could see the fishing harbor, and beyond it the start of the industrial harbor where they had just been. And through the front window to the right, you could see the illuminated ramparts of the Ville

Close and the tower at the entrance with the famous clock. It gave the town the time, the rhythm to its days. The door onto Place Jean Jaurès was open, the fresh, wonderfully mild night air streaming into the room.

"None of the workers have a clue why someone might have had it in for the shipyard and the ship. Nobody knows of any kinds of problems or disputes," Nevou finished up her report. "Not within the company and not outside it. There has never been an unusual incident of any kind. According to them. And," she broke off briefly, "nobody noticed anything unusual this evening. Mind you, they're extremely focused on their work. Especially the welders."

She propped her elbows on the table.

It was Le Menn's turn: "I haven't been able to find out much about Héros Naval or shipbuilding yet." She pushed back some hair that had come loose from her braid. She seemed to be in surprisingly good spirits. "Or, to put it another way, we won't make real progress on that until tomorrow morning. But I have already looked online to see if I could find any interesting articles about the company. Nothing of note so far. There was an article in *Le Télégramme* from last December reporting on the business year just ended. And how well the company is doing."

"When exactly was it founded?"

Le Menn glanced at the notes on her phone.

"Eight years ago."

"Who founded it? All three of them?"

"It didn't say anywhere."

"Jodoc Luzel owns fifty percent of Héros Naval, the other two own twenty-five percent each." Right at the outset of the briefing, Dupin had relayed to the policewomen the most important points from his conversation with the head of the fire brigade, the wine merchant, and the mayor, but he had forgotten this point.

Nevou sat up straight. "So the wine trade must bring in a decent amount. I'm not too sure."

"Have you been able to find out anything about the manager of Héros Naval?"

Dupin's red Clairefontaine lay on the table in front of him.

"The workers don't have a bad word to say about him. Without exception. They like him. By the way, none of them know Luzel, Chaboseau, or Priziac personally."

Interesting. The manager hadn't exactly seemed like a friend of the workers to Dupin, but perhaps he had been mistaken.

"I spoke to him too, just briefly, though. He was at home at the time of the explosion. Wife and three kids. He had just as little to say about what happened as the workers." Nevou seemed to be speaking more and more concisely.

"I've got something else on Héros Naval, although it's got nothing to do with shipbuilding." Le Menn took over. "I don't know whether you've heard of this, Commissaire. '*La capsule*' from a team of researchers called 'Under the Pole.' It's a compact underwater capsule with a three-hundred-sixty-degree plexiglass dome and you can live in it underwater for up to three days, on the seafloor."

It had been in the papers in Brittany. There had been an impressive photo of it, in fact.

"A very special project, the first of its kind in the world." Le Menn seemed really excited. "It allows marine researchers to do long-term observations that are impossible on dives. You can sleep, eat, but above all, you can observe. You can even go into the sea and come back again via an airlock. Nothing short of a revolution for science."

"And Héros Naval designed this?"

"They're contracted to build it. It was designed by a team of scientists in 2011."

Dupin had just remembered: Le Menn was really into diving. No wonder she was so interested in this project.

"Did the company invest money in it too?"

"No. That comes from three other partners. Two hundred thousand euro in total, from Région Bretagne among others."

"Has the project been affected by the explosion?"

"No. But the hangar where it is being built is very close by. I think it was pure coincidence that it was spared."

"Do some asking around. See whether there are any interesting stories relating to this project. Next point." Dupin had been meaning to bring this up earlier. "The mayor was at the opening concert in the Ville Close this evening. I'd like a few witness statements. The most important question is what time he arrived at the concert. And whether he was alone. At the moment we only know that he left the concert at approximately twenty past ten."

"You think the mayor is suspicious?" Nevou seemed—and this was rare—impressed.

"Yes, and a few others too. And I want to know where Priziac was. Actually, have you heard from Madame Chaboseau again?"

"No." Le Menn took over again. "She's probably already in bed."

"We . . ."

"Do you want anything to eat?" Paul Girard had appeared at their table. "Or drink?"

"A large bottle of water, please. Plancöet." Le Menn was the first to respond.

"A Coke for me," said Nevou.

"I . . ." There was nothing else for it. "I'll have a glass of white Gascogne." This was exactly what Dupin needed now. A light, refreshing table wine that would definitely perk him up. The commissaire had briefly considered a Pernod but then decided against it.

Dupin gave his colleagues an encouraging look.

"Count me in," said Le Menn cheerfully.

"I'll stick with the Coke."

No coffee, no wine; Dupin was starting to worry about Nevou.

"There was grilled turbot this evening. I've got two wonderful ones left."

Paul's turbot was legendary. Grilled over a charcoal fire. The crispy skin with the chargrilled stripes, the firm white flesh. Some *fleur de sel*, some *piment*, some pepper, and if you wanted, you could also have some of the wonderful ginger sauce. Hands down, one of the best fish. If turbot was on Paul's specials menu, Dupin even skipped his entrecôte.

"All right—absolutely," Nevou agreed, to Dupin's relief.

Le Menn nodded too.

"*Pommes sautés* on the side." Dupin put the finishing touch to this perfect moment. Paul used particularly tasty Breton La Ratte potatoes. Pan-fried in a mixture of salted butter and olive oil, with a touch of *piment d'Espelette*. The skin turned firm while the insides were really soft.

There was no protest from either Le Menn or Nevou.

Satisfied, Paul withdrew.

"I've got some"—Nevou's voice had become a little stronger almost instantaneously—"information about this boat. That turns plastic back into oil. Chaboseau has not invested in it. I spoke to one of the owners on the phone myself."

Back to taking turns, it was Le Menn who took over now:

"Docteur Chaboseau had a stake in So Breizh. And he sits on the advisory board for Produit en Bretagne."

Produit en Bretagne was a consortium of several hundred Breton manufacturers of everything from clothes to food and cosmetics. Alongside their effective advertising and a shared sales department, they had created a label that guaranteed special quality, a mark of the highest prestige for a product. It was a fixed point for Bretons in an endless sea of consumer choice.

"So Breizh?" Dupin had never heard of this one before.

"It's an organization that gives grants to Breton businesses that are particularly dedicated to sustainable and ecologically sound initiatives and projects. Like hemp growing in Concarneau."

Dupin raised his eyebrows quizzically.

"Legal hemp growing. For food production. Oil and flour."

Whatever next. "Do you see any possible link between the case and these two commitments of Chaboseau's?"

"Not yet. But there might have been, let's say, conflicts of interest. Or to put it another way, maybe his own companies were also awarded grants? Who knows? I'll look into it."

The Breton mafia, thought Dupin. Le Menn was absolutely right. "Do it."

"What about the Chaboseaus' maid? Have you interviewed her again?"

"I have. But she seems really quite unsuspicious. Airtight alibi."

"And Chaboseau's real estate? Have we found out anything of interest about that?"

Dupin looked at a double page in his notebook that he had headed—almost illegibly—with the words "The Topics."

Le Menn explained: "He only invested in the construction phase of the thalassotherapy spa, which was then sold to a management company six months later at considerable profit. So he wasn't involved after that. The permission to turn the hill west of the Sables Blancs into building land seems to have been aboveboard, by the way. I phoned two real estate agents I know. And there was nothing online that would indicate anything irregular. The expansion was in the interests of the town, that was the decisive factor in allowing building on Chaboseau's land." Le Menn spoke like an old hand sometimes. "There was a broad political consensus on it at all levels. It seems Docteur Chaboseau did not exert any obvious influence."

If Dupin correctly understood the phenomenon of the "notables"—the long-established, well-to-do families—"obvious influence" was not actually necessary for the kind of power they wielded. And in any case, it was well known that the town was in favor of new building land.

Nevou and Le Menn had done some good research considering how little time they'd had.

"And still"—this was also noted in Dupin's notebook—"no sign of Sieren Cléac, the owner of the Fête de la Mer canning factory?"

"She's not at home. We got the contact details for a girlfriend of hers from Françoise Gloux. Unfortunately she doesn't know where she is at the moment either. But she was still in touch with Madame Cléac this morning by text. The friend has sent her a message telling her to get in touch. But I was able to get hold of a member of the staff from her cannery who tells me Madame Cléac will be at the factory from seven tomorrow morning. They got a delivery of fresh sardines."

"Voilà!"

Paul Girard came to their table with the water, the wine—he brought a whole bottle straightaway—and the Coke for Nevou.

He also put out three glasses and then was gone.

Dupin wordlessly poured some wine, first for Le Menn, then himself. Took a mouthful of it immediately. And then another.

It really did the trick.

Le Menn and Nevou seemed relieved too. A relaxed silence stretched out.

Dupin emptied his glass. Poured himself a second one.

He had sat here hundreds of times before. He could have shut his eyes and described the room in detail. The picture of the black-and-white lobster on a bright red seabed opposite. More lithographs along the wall between the windows, fish in Atlantic colors and shades. Magnificent posters by Valérie Le Roux, who had her studio very close by. Right next to Dupin hung the reproduction of a historic advertisement from the early thirties that, unbelievably, described the Amiral exactly as it still was today: *"Gourmands, gourmets et bon buveurs! Tables abondantes and variées"*—"For gluttons, foodies, and wine lovers! A wide and varied menu." *"Sans chichi ni flaflas—la bonne vie."* "No airs or graces—just fine living!" That was Paul's maxim to this day: produce something incredible from simple things. *"Venez un jour,"* ran the final, crowning sentence of the poster, *"vous resterez une semaine!"* "Come by one day—you'll stay a week!" That was exactly what had happened to him, Dupin thought, and couldn't help smiling.

He topped up Le Menn's wine.

"This is the exact place where that crime novel with the yellow dog is set." Le Menn looked around the room. The sentence hung in the air, a strange non sequitur. Next to the door to the brasserie, there was a sentence from the beginning of the novel in a small frame: "Maigret stayed at the Hôtel de l'Amiral of course, the best in town. It was five o'clock in the afternoon and night had already fallen when he walked into the café . . ."

Unlike Commissaire Maigret, his inventor Georges Simenon, who traveled to Concarneau in 1930 and 1931, lived in a villa by the Sables Blancs beach. The novel *The Yellow Dog* was published in 1931.

"People even say—" Le Menn took a mouthful of wine with some relish. "—the restaurant owes its name to the novel."

A hotly disputed topic—much like the historic origins of everything in Brittany—because there were several different stories to explain anything and everything.

They needed to focus on the task at hand; Dupin could feel himself becoming uneasy again. "So once more from the beginning, what motives could there have been for an attack on Héros Naval?"

"The thing that seems significant to me"—Le Menn topped up Dupin's glass and her own, knitting her eyebrows together as she did so—"is the fact that clearly only the detonation of the smaller tank was intentional. The second explosion was presumably an unlucky accident. The perpetrator, whoever he or she is,"

Le Menn hesitated briefly, "could not have factored in the second explosion."

They were interrupted by loud police sirens. A moment later—clearly visible through the large windows—two police cars rounded the corner at speed and braked in front of the Amiral's terrace.

Le Menn, Nevou, and Dupin jumped to their feet at the same time.

They were charging out the door when the passenger door of the second car flew open. In a flash, she was standing in front of Dupin, to his absolute amazement.

A movie-worthy entrance. Like in a magic show.

"Nolwenn!" cried Dupin.

"Now really, you take a little trip away and chaos breaks out here. Bloody hell, as you would say, Monsieur le Commissaire!"

Dupin's crazy idea had worked. The gendarmes had found Nolwenn.

"How are the injured shipyard workers?"

"None of them are in critical condition anymore. They'll pull through," said Nevou.

"That's the most important thing! Come on." Nolwenn strode between Dupin and Le Menn. "I need to know everything. Every last detail!" She disappeared into the brasserie, Dupin and the two policewomen hurrying to follow her, still dumbfounded.

"In our town, of all places!" Nolwenn headed automatically for Dupin's regular table. "A murder! An attack! What audacity!"

All four of them sat down.

"And where is Riwal?"

"Can't get hold of him."

"At his sister's house?"

"Right."

"All right, I'll take care of that."

These were the words Dupin had missed.

"*Bonsoir*, Nolwenn." Paul Girard came to the table with a large tray. Three plates on it with grilled fish and potatoes along with—unasked for, but it went without saying—another bottle of Gascogne Blanc.

"This is the way to do it." Nolwenn nodded firmly. "*Da heul al labour emañ ar boued!*"

One of the wisest Breton sayings that Dupin knew: "The food follows the work." There were two meanings to this: once you've done some work you can eat, and this meaning was important enough in itself. But the second meaning was even more important: the food must be worthy of the work. Which essentially meant: if you've worked hard for a long time, you deserve a particularly delicious and particularly large meal.

"Are you hungry too?" Paul had put everything down and turned his attention to Nolwenn.

"No thanks. We ate an entire pig earlier. But I'll join them for a glass of wine."

Paul nodded and fetched another glass.

"So I want to hear everything now, Monsieur le Commissaire." This was a command from Nolwenn. "Don't leave out any details!"

The fish and fried potatoes in front of them smelled heavenly. Dupin took his first large mouthful. "So . . ." He didn't get any farther, instead taking a second, even larger bite. It tasted phenomenal: the essence of the sea with the salty, buttery taste of the fried potatoes.

It took a good half an hour—including questions—to bring

Nolwenn up to speed. The second bottle of wine was swiftly polished off.

"Hmmm" was Nolwenn's summary once the report was finished, equal parts serious and mysterious.

For a while she fell into pensive silence. Then she sighed.

"Evil, truly evil. This will be complicated. We'll need to give it our all. And we'll need more help."

She stood up abruptly.

"But all tomorrow morning. There's nothing more to be achieved tonight." She glanced at her watch. "It's quarter past one."

Dupin wanted to protest. But Nolwenn was right.

He had felt a profound, fundamental sense of relief spreading through him since she had returned. He had missed her, her support, her inimitable manner.

"Back here, seven o'clock?" Nolwenn looked around at everyone.

"Back here, seven o'clock," Dupin confirmed.

Nevou and Le Menn seemed glad of Nolwenn's intervention too. If he was lucky, he would catch Claire still awake. And at least be able to chat with her a little after this crazy day.

The soft grass at the Pointe du Raz, the relaxed lie-down he had had up there, felt like weeks ago, maybe longer.

It was exactly 1:37 when Dupin opened the front door.

There was no noise. No light visible. Maybe there were still some lights on in the back bedroom on the first floor—where Claire's parents were staying—but not in the sitting room and not in their bedroom, both of which were at the front, facing onto the sea; the sitting room was on the ground floor, the bedroom above it.

Apparently Claire was already asleep, after all.

Their house was on a small hill, thirty meters from the sea. There was the wonderful small beach—Coat-Pin, next to the Plage des Dames—then the quay wall with the wide promenade, the Boulevard Katerine Wylie, a thick hedge on an old stone wall, then an overgrown front garden and their house.

Dupin didn't put on any lights. The moon shone brightly through the large windows on the ground floor and it was a starlit night. Dupin could see enough to navigate his way around the house. He stashed the smoked fish quietly in the fridge, although he wasn't sure it was still edible after the day in the car. Then he went over to the little wooden table in the sitting room that had been his great-grandfather's and that they had turned into a "bar." It was the only heirloom that Dupin owned, this and the chair that went with it. He could never decide if the chair was very comfortable or very uncomfortable. He picked up a bottle of whisky, poured himself a glass, and sat down. Armorik, his favorite whisky—Breton, of course.

There was still too much going through his mind—despite his crushing fatigue. Hopefully the whisky would soothe him and stop his thoughts endlessly churning until he went to sleep. It was as pointless as it was grueling when his thoughts became shapeless, out of all proportion, when some of them took on absurd dimensions, his mind focusing on random details and creating agonizing loops.

Dupin grasped the bottle and the glass and they clinked together softly. Suddenly he gave a start.

He had heard something.

A voice. A whisper.

"Georges . . . Over here."

Claire—a little louder this time, but still very quiet.

Her voice was coming from outside. Only now did Dupin notice the open door onto the patio.

Claire was lying on one of the two loungers facing the sea.

"I was waiting for you, but I must have fallen asleep for a little while. Sit with me."

Dupin could see that she was smiling. He was smiling now too.

"Look at this crazy sky!"

They would simply sit there. Looking at the sky and marveling at the moon that hung low over the Atlantic, conjuring a faintly shimmering beam on the perfectly smooth sea. Not only were some bright stars visible, but immense nebulae too. You could see the Milky Way, so vivid and vast that you could suddenly envision the extent to which our little Earth is a part of it, one component of that colossal phenomenon. There were so many stars, it was like there was no void, no blackness.

The Second Day

It was 6:32.

Dupin had been sitting in the Amiral for a few minutes. He had left the house at sunrise and driven toward the center of town. He liked being out and about this early in the morning, watching the town slowly wake up, the world slowly waking up.

He wasn't in bed for long. And his dreams had been strange. He had been wide awake at half past five. He drank his first *petit café* at quarter to six. On the patio where he had sat with Claire till quarter to three. On their way to bed they had briefly discussed the rest of the "schedule" for Claire's parents that weekend. Dupin found it easy to agree enthusiastically with Claire's suggestions; he would not be there anyway.

His dreams, or the fragments of them he could remember, had been about the strange, dark sorcerer Françoise had mentioned in the gallery yesterday. The case and the ancient legends from the Ville Close had mingled together in an absurd way. The sorcerer had set the entire town on fire and set off explosions, and in the end Concarneau had gone down in fiery flames.

It was a crazy story, the story of Siprian and the supernaturally beautiful Emilia, two young lovers who find themselves faced with a terrible dilemma one day. The town is under threat from a ship of savage pirates and the only way out is to accept a shady offer from a mysterious stranger who suddenly turns up promising to save the town if Emilia will be his for one night. The young woman accepts. The stranger reveals he is a powerful sorcerer, and when the pirates attack, he makes massive stone walls shoot up from the ground all the way along the island. Emilia tricks the sinister sorcerer with a sleeping draught so that she can spend a night with him without coming to any harm, but then he puts a terrible curse on them the next morning: Siprian and Emilia will be immortal and their love will never die. But Emilia will never leave the Ville Close and its town walls again and Siprian will never be able to enter them. That's as tragic as it gets, Dupin thought. Siprian and Emilia had appeared in his weird dreams too.

The commissaire had taken a seat outside, at the end of the terrace. The same place he had been sitting yesterday with Le Menn and Nevou.

It was still cool, but you could tell that this Saturday would turn out to be another glorious early summer's day. The pretty cobblestones shone in the sunshine. The square in front of him would only come to life bit by bit; but in the fishing and ship-building harbors, there was already hustle and bustle.

Dupin was updating the list of people he needed to speak

to. He was also trying to reorganize things; to work out what the most pressing questions and issues were at the moment. Nolwenn and the two policewomen would arrive soon and they would have a quick discussion. Despite the lack of sleep, Dupin was full of energy.

"Morning, boss!"

Dupin couldn't believe his eyes.

"Here I am."

He leaped to his feet.

"Where—" He broke off.

Inspector Riwal was standing right in front of him!

"How—I mean . . . Where have you come from all of a sudden?"

"A police car pulled up outside my sister's house at four minutes past five. With sirens and blue lights. They drove me to the harbor at Le Palais, where the boat was waiting."

Incredible. Nolwenn must have arranged everything last night.

"Nolwenn and I have already spoken on the phone—I'm more or less up to speed, boss."

"Great. I am—" How should he put this without sounding too sentimental? "—glad you're here, Riwal!"

Riwal would never know *how* glad he was. Dupin had lost all hope. After Nolwenn's sudden return, this was the second wonderful piece of good fortune.

The inspector sat down without further ado. He looked wide awake. Ready for action.

"Good morning, Riwal! A coffee for you too?" Ingrid walked out onto the terrace.

"Absolutely!"

Everything was starting to feel normal again—or as normal as possible under the circumstances. And with the two police-women and more reinforcements at the station, a powerful team was now in place.

"Don't you find it a little creepy, boss? A murder in the Amiral? And involving a pharmacist and a doctor, of all people? Just like in *The Yellow Dog*, Simenon's famous case. There's a pharmacist and a doctor in that too. Although the doctor is not a practicing doctor at all. And strictly speaking, the pharmacist is not one of the main characters."

"No." Dupin's answer was very clear. "I don't find it creepy. And the murder didn't take place in the Amiral itself, anyway."

The inspector scratched his head. "There's a wine merchant in the book too, by the way. Mind you, he's shot right at the beginning and he doesn't figure very much after that." Françoise had also mentioned this detail earlier. "But there is a journalist, which we don't have in our case."

"I see."

Dupin's head was spinning.

"It wasn't just *The Yellow Dog* that Georges Simenon set in Concarneau, by the way. Commissaire Maigret visits us in several books! And comes on holiday too. And some of Simenon's other novels are also set here, including *The Evil Sisters of Concarneau*, a . . ."

"We need more details on Héros Naval, Riwal. There must be something shady there. And we need," Dupin hesitated, "more information about the three friends' other joint financial commitments."

"Maybe this is to do with the company's crooked dealings? But it's possible the three fell out among themselves too?" Riwal's voice had immediately turned serious. "There's clearly a lot of money, power, and respect at stake. Maybe one of them tried to cheat the others? And now they're attacking each other?"

A solid analysis, one that Dupin had not yet formulated in his own mind so explicitly or logically.

"Possibly."

A scenario like this would, in theory, explain everything. If it were true, either Priziac or Luzel had killed the doctor. And, for some reason or other, detonated the gas tank.

"There's one problem with that." An extremely logical weighing up of the possibilities was another of Riwal's specialties, or "discussing it with himself," as it were. "The three of them have been in business together for a long time and know each other well. That creates a bond. Therefore they would presumably, if at all possible, be more likely to try and get the upper hand by forming an alliance against other people than they would be to turn their skills on each other."

Still, Dupin had seen it all. The most important investigative principle was not to rule anything out.

"Do you know Docteur Evette Derien personally, Riwal?"

"Only by sight. And one of my wife's friends is her patient. This friend is, shall we say, very demanding—and very pleased with Derien. She must be extremely nice and good at her job. Really into surfing."

"And Docteur Chaboseau, did you know him?"

"I went to see him with extreme back pain once, when Docteur Garreg was on holiday. Around four years ago or so. He gave me an injection. An aloof person. And an extremely discreet businessman, I hear. Aristocratic in his discretion. He was of the opinion that you shouldn't talk about money. Especially if you have a lot of it. He had an impeccable reputation as a doctor." Riwal shrugged his shoulders. "We just moved in different circles."

"And this Sieren Cléac, the owner of the cannery?"

"My wife knows her, she really loves her food. I do too, as it happens. We both visited her factory once, she invited my wife to see it. You've absolutely got to try the *rillettes de sardines aux trois algues*! Sardines caught inshore, dulse, nori, and wakame seaweed, with salt from the Guérande peninsula and Breton crème fraîche—exquisite . . ."

He stopped short and steered himself back to the subject: "Cléac seems very friendly. She has only been in Concarneau for a few years, I think."

They were silent for a moment. Then Riwal went on.

"And I wasn't even aware Chaboseau had a son. But still, it's an interesting point: perhaps there might even be a dramatic family story behind all this. A complicated marital crisis? Or was it to do with the inheritance?"

"What do you make of Madame Chaboseau?"

"She is not to be underestimated. I know her from a few previews at the Glouxes'. Her husband almost never came with her. She is formidable and she has a will of iron. Tough and tenacious. The pharmacist, Priziac"—Riwal seemed to want to go through everyone one by one, and that was fine by Dupin—"is an ice-cold tactician. Unscrupulous. I think he's capable of anything."

Dupin agreed.

"The wine merchant is your classic rogue. Very sociable. And business-minded, too. He can turn aggressive when it comes to business and make life difficult for people. Mind you, most people only know him as a generous playboy."

Riwal's analyses were clear-cut.

"What about the mayor? Did you know about the dispute between him and Luzel?"

"The public were aware of a few run-ins but they seemed harmless enough. Jodoc Luzel loves spreading the rumor he's going into politics."

"He's done that before?"

"Yes, quite a few times, but he has never followed through on it. The dispute between Chaboseau and the mayor was much more serious, though. My second cousin has a microbrewery himself. They're putting the wind up the big breweries at the moment. Roi Gradlon and a few others are having a hard time of it. Only Britt is growing. Plus the carbon dioxide shortages are coming this summer."

Dupin was not going to probe any further. Their case would probably not revolve around carbon dioxide shortages. Whenever he heard the name Britt, he was reminded of the company's amusing origin story: at the beginning of the twentieth century, Célestin Heurtaud had come up with a recipe for a "drink" with "healthy, bordering on miraculous properties," especially for sailors who spent a long time at sea. The alcohol was the miracle, Dupin presumed. It was actually "medically prescribed" on a mass scale and happily knocked back. The beer of today still had its origins in that original recipe.

"Is Roi Gradlon in serious trouble?"

"My second cousin says it is."

This was interesting.

"Look into that. What about this underwater capsule that Héros Naval is building? Is there an unusual backstory there?"

Riwal's eyes lit up.

"That capsule is just the beginning! What the researchers are actually planning is to build an entire underwater station. A whole team could live in it for months. A real Jules Verne project."

Dupin waited for Riwal to follow this up with the fact that Jules Verne had also been Breton, but he didn't.

"I'm sure the debris from the explosions last night could just as easily have hit the hangar where the underwater capsule is being built. Do you know of any disputes around this project?"

"No."

"All right. Le Menn and Nevou will handle that."

Dupin could tell Riwal would definitely have been keen to do it himself, but he needed him for other things.

"What exactly will the capsule be used for?"

"There's a mission starting in the Pacific about the influence of the lunar cycle on the marine environment. Another mission will probably be taking place in the bay in Concarneau." There was a dangerous level of enthusiasm in Riwal's voice now. "While we're on the subject"—this was how his digressions usually began—"of the marine environment and research, have you heard the latest news about Six Cent Soixante-Deux? It's already swum around the south coast of Ireland and it'll probably be at Limerick soon. All in just ten days!"

This was certainly impressive—and Dupin was glad to hear the little seal was doing well—but unfortunately it was beside the point.

"And what does the mission want to research in our bay?"

A careless question, but he was actually interested.

"Scientists from Ifremer in Brest have discovered a geological miracle in the bay, a phenomenon on our seabed that is unique in the world. The underwater landscape is riddled with many, many deep craters that must have been formed over a span of ten thousand years by the release of huge volumes of gas. There are craters in seabeds all over the world, but not in such great density. That is what people want to research using the capsule."

Claire had explained the craters on the seabed to him in detail recently. She was fascinated by scientific phenomena like this. The Bay of Concarneau had not been around long—geologically speaking; about ten thousand years, created by a swift rise in sea level as a result of significant global warming. In the dim and distant past, there had been a twenty-five-kilometer-long valley off the coast of Concarneau. Today's Glénan Islands had been a chain of hills at the edge of it. It was a densely wooded, fertile valley with several rivers running through it, carrying vast amounts of organic material with them. And it was this material, buried by many layers of sediment, that later produced gases in the seabed that forced their way up to the surface due to seismic activity, forming craters. Some scientists, and this was Jules Verne territory again, speculated there was a gas bubble over a hundred kilometers squared underneath the bay, which prompted the most outlandish theories. Inevitably this included the theory that the bubble was on the brink of exploding and that this kind of explosion would blast Concarneau into outer space.

"You know, don't you"—it was as though Riwal had read his thoughts—"that the gas bubble might explain the numerous mysterious maritime disasters that have happened over the last few centuries. The sudden disappearance of ships shortly after they had set sail from our harbor. It's all just like in the Bermuda Triangle . . ."

"Good morning!"

Nolwenn was standing in front of them, radiating good humor.

"As you know: *Abred ne goll gwech ebet*. Early never loses."

She was the epitome of energy, readiness for action, fierce determination—there was no trace of a lack of sleep about her.

"Welcome back, Inspector Riwal! And, straightaway, we've got another piece of good news: I've just heard the workers are all on the road to recovery. The two with minor injuries will probably be discharged as soon as tomorrow. Unfortunately they didn't see or hear anything unusual, nothing that could be helpful. Despite significant blood loss, the condition of the other two has definitively stabilized."

That really was good news.

Dupin glanced at his watch. It was five past seven. The two policewomen still hadn't arrived.

"Nevou and Le Menn"—Nolwenn had seen the commissaire's glance, and made no move to sit down—"are already at the station. And I'll be there soon too." Dupin knew Nolwenn needed phones, preferably several, and computers, also preferably several.

"The renovations are being put on pause until further notice." Her expression turned grim. "I've just given the order."

Dupin couldn't help grinning. *That* was what you called power.

"I've also spoken to Sieren Cléac. She's expecting you at her cannery at half past seven."

Dupin looked at Riwal. "Let's do that together."

"All right, boss."

"And Félix Chaboseau is coming to Concarneau this morning. He's due to get to his mother's house around ten."

Dupin was glad to see the pace of everything really picking up since Nolwenn's return.

"Great. And I need to speak to Priziac again."

"That shouldn't be a problem."

This was another of the sentences Dupin loved.

Nolwenn cleared her throat. "The prefect tried to get hold of you just now. Let's just say I painted a vivid picture for him of what's going on right now. He has asked that you get in touch at some point, but only when you can manage it, I'm specifically meant to tell you. The prefect is busy all day."

Dupin didn't reply.

"The new sign at the exit off the Route Nationale is being ceremonially launched in Quimper today. Then more signs will be launched at hourly intervals."

An extremely emotive topic: in the absence of a proper motorway, the incredibly important Routes Nationales, Brittany's four-lane arterial roads, were the responsibility of the central Parisian authorities. And now at last they had decided to carry out the measures recommended in the 2015 convention on the *transmission des langues de Bretagne et le développement de leur usage dans la vie quotidienne*. A convention that was meant to ensure that the Breton language, so long oppressed by the central government, would be brought back into everyday life. And it began—and this was psychologically very significant—with the place names, all the proper names in Brittany. Concarneau, for example, was not called Concarneau but Konk-Kerne, Quimper was Kemper.

There had, of course, long been bilingual place-name signs on all of the local and regional roads that were Breton property, but the signs on the arterial roads had not been bilingual. The signs had finally begun to be replaced much too late, and only after a public outcry. Controversially, the rule was that initially only signs that needed to be changed anyway because of their "age or considerable damage" would be replaced. At which point all of the place-name signs along the Nationale were suddenly showing signs of damage, serious scratches and dents. So the new signs, hard-won victories, obviously deserved to be celebrated in a fitting way.

"Essentially, feel free to call him and leave a message today, there's no risk of him answering," Nolwenn said with a meaningful smile.

The cannery was in an old stone barn with a pretty slate roof. It was on the outskirts of Concarneau, on the way to Trégunc, right on an idyllic inlet called the Anse de Manioc that meandered inland in the east of the town. At low tide, the riverbed turned into an expanse of endless fine white sand, and more and more dark mud the farther inland you went. The atmosphere here was instantly different, you were in the *campagne,* in the countryside, in woodland. There were fields with little stone walls, meadows with tall, wild grass, dense little woods—bedraggled and bewitched—while streams came from this direction and that, winding inlets of the Anse that looked like lakes. A small paradise, peaceful and quiet. There was at most thirty meters between the barn and the water, you could see it shimmering through a thick row of oaks at the end of the property.

A member of the staff wearing dazzling white overalls and a

dazzling white cap had opened the door to Dupin and Riwal and led them inside, right onto the workshop floor. It was a bright room with concrete underfoot. The entire manufacturing process apparently took place here.

"Madame Cléac will be right with you."

The staff member left the commissaire and the inspector standing in the middle of the room and went over to one of the long aluminum tables that were spread out around the room. There were two large boxes on her table, one blue, one yellow, both full to the brim with sardines. There must have been hundreds of them. The shimmering silvery white bellies, the dark backs, beautiful fish. And very tasty. For quite some time they had been considered "simple" and "cheap," they had been cooked in a careless way, like cod, until they had been rediscovered as extraordinary delicacies. The staff member slipped on plastic gloves and went back to her work without a word. A colleague stood next to her. There were two staff members at each station, all women; nobody let themselves be distracted by Dupin and Riwal, all of them going about their work undeterred. Dupin had never been in a cannery before. Apparently it all began with chopping the sardines' heads off on the first table with an impressive-looking knife and then putting them in a large high-grade steel bowl under running water.

"You wanted to speak to me?"

Fascinated, Dupin had approached the table where the final step in the process was clearly being carried out. There were dozens of jars on the table, with five or six sardines inside each one—and a member of the staff was carefully ladling a delicious-smelling sauce into them. A fresh and fragrant aroma filled the room.

"Absolutely, yes." Dupin turned around to face Madame Cléac.

She was also wearing white overalls and a white cap that looked like a little paper boat. An open, eager smile all over her face. A narrow nose, dark eyes—an intense gaze—her shoulder-length dark blond hair poking out from underneath the cap, disheveled. Her posture was self-confident; she seemed very comfortable in her own skin.

"I'd really like to know what you talked to Docteur Chaboseau about during your phone call yesterday morning." Dupin came straight to the point. "You called him a little after eleven o'clock. Just a few hours before he was murdered."

It was an odd place for an investigative interview, but this was how Dupin liked it best. His favorite thing was to meet people where they felt at home, as they went about their lives.

Sieren Cléac had walked to a different corner—Dupin and Riwal following behind. There was a large deep-fat fryer here, fitted with an ultramodern, quiet extractor hood above it that seemed to be doing its job brilliantly, because there was no smell of frying fat.

"Excellent," Cléac said, watching one of her staff members lowering two special square sieves with fish arranged on them into the oil. Dupin had seen this process before in historical photographs: each sieve had at least a hundred sardines laid out on it in tightly packed rows, the fish tails pointing up into the air.

Riwal couldn't hold back any longer. As it was, it was remarkable he had been silent for so long. "The manufacturing is carried out just like it was a hundred or a hundred and fifty years ago. Everything is done by hand. The fish are fried quickly and then placed in the jars. Then comes the crucial part: every cook adds their own, often secret, spice and oil blend, sometimes vegetables or fruit too. The base is always the same: pure oil and pure sea salt. It's groundnut oil here. That's how sardines tasted in my childhood." There was nostalgia etched across Riwal's face. "People often just use olive oil for everything these days, it's so ridiculous. And usually cheap oil too, but so much depends on the oil."

Sieren Cléac gave Riwal an appreciative look and then returned to Dupin's question:

"I still can't believe it." She seemed really exhausted now. "I spoke to someone and a few hours later they were dead." She stood there motionless for a moment, then turned the temperature button on the deep-fat fryer up to the maximum. "Monsieur Chaboseau had offered to buy the cannery from me. I said I needed to think about it. I thought about it. And then I called him yesterday. That's what happened."

"He wanted to buy Fête de la Mer from you?" Riwal sounded outraged.

"Yes."

Dupin got out his notebook. "When did he make you the offer?"

Sieren Cléac looked like she was thinking. "Four weeks ago."

"Was it a concrete offer? Did he name a price?"

"No, he didn't name a price. He didn't even know any of our financial figures. But"—Sieren Cléac went over to one of the smaller workbenches—"he said he would pay an extremely good price. He said he wanted to keep expanding into the cannery sector."

There were round high-grade steel containers on the workbench, most of which, as far as Dupin could tell, were full of seaweed. In the others were dried tomatoes, thin slices of lemon, and shallots. Next to them were little bowls of coarse sea salt. In the middle were three dishes of oil. Clearly this was where they made up the spice and oil blends.

"Fête de la Mer"—she added salt to one of the dishes of oil—"is relatively small; we specialize in very high-quality preserved food, only carefully selected fish and seafood, all strictly from sustainable inshore fishing. We're stocked by delicatessens and *traiteurs* nationwide at this stage, not just in Brittany. Apparently Monsieur Chaboseau thought we would make a good complement to his cannery."

"How did he contact you? Did you know each other?"

"By sight, yes. But we had never spoken before. He approached me at lunch one day, in the brasserie of the Amiral. Initially, he just asked whether we could meet sometime to speak about something business-related"—she reached for a large pepper mill—"and that's what we did. In the Sables Blancs restaurant last week. We had an aperitif there."

The restaurant's terrace was one of the most beautiful places to have an aperitif. Set right above the beach, and part of the gorgeous hotel. A few meters above the ground, the terrace was made of ship-like wooden planks and it gave you a terrific view over the Bay of Concarneau.

"Was anyone else there when he asked you for the meeting?" Riwal was standing close to Sieren Cléac and watching her, but he was totally focused on the conversation at the same time.

"No. He waylaid me just as I was leaving the restaurant. He walked with me for a while. I was on my way home."

"Where do you live, Madame Cléac?"

"Place du Général de Gaulle. Right above Hops. The white building."

Claire and Dupin had become fond of Hops as a meeting place, often meeting up there after work. Katell, the owner, had put a few bistro tables out front, the perfect place for the perfect aperitif. She sold excellent local beers. They were the handiwork of the small breweries that were a thorn in the side of Roi Gradlon. Like the Storlok by Katell's brother Erwann that Claire and Dupin had drunk there just recently. They had become obsessed with a Corsican goat's cheese too.

The commissaire remembered where he was.

"Do you know whether Pierre Chaboseau is the sole owner of the cannery? Or whether one of his friends and business partners has a stake in it too?" Dupin had been leafing through his notebook.

"As far as I know, it's just him."

"How did he treat you when you met? How did he act?"

"He was unfailingly pleasant and"—Sieren Cléac was by this point crushing lemons with a kind of large pestle in the dish with the oil, salt, and pepper—"friendly. He wanted something from me, of course—and not the other way around."

"So did you consider selling?" Riwal asked gravely.

"No." A clear-cut answer. It was laced with modest pride and there was a flicker in her eye. You believed her. Riwal acknowledged her definitive response with a satisfied smile.

"I told him so at our very first meeting, and then he very politely asked me to take some time to think it over. I told him that definitely wouldn't change anything, but that I would get in touch again."

"So that," Dupin reasoned, "is what you did yesterday?"

"Exactly."

"How did he take it?"

"Very well. He said the offer was always there, in case I ended up changing my mind one day. I just had to give him the nod."

Dupin examined the wall behind Cléac's aluminum table where a few dozen preserving jars hung.

She seemed to have noticed his gaze. "Those are our creations. Our archive, so to speak." That pride in her voice again, but it was discreet, proportionate.

The jars were decorated with drawings of the sea creatures they contained, each one in a different Atlantic primary color, the edge of the jar trimmed in a second color, a simple and memorable design. *Mackerel marinated in Sancerre*, Dupin read. *Mackerel with two kinds of mustard. Mussels with pear and wakame seaweed. Tuna with plums and raisins.* The promise of delicious things. And typical of the cannery's recent creativity.

"How did Docteur Chaboseau seem during the phone call?" Riwal took over again.

"What do you mean?"

"I mean, did he come across as nervous? Tense?"

"Well, I barely knew him. But no. He seemed totally normal. It wasn't a long phone call, though."

"I see—did you speak about anything else during your meeting at the Sables Blancs?"

"No."

"Do you know Monsieur Priziac, the pharmacist? And Monsieur Luzel, the wine merchant?"

"By name, of course. And by sight. But not personally."

"And the mayor?"

"He really advocates for small businesses. Especially for canneries," she said approvingly.

"In what way, exactly?"

For a brief moment she seemed off balance. But she recovered again straightaway.

"We should really have been in one of the industrial estates. But I didn't want that. Since we offer guided tours, among other things, there was some wiggle room in the regulations. He was the one who made me aware of that. And that's how we found this barn."

Dupin made a note.

"Are you friends?" Riwal asked.

"No, we're not. We never meet outside of work."

"Are you the sole owner of the cannery, Madame Cléac, or do you have a partner?"

"It mostly still belongs to the bank. But the rest is mine, yes."

She had put the pestle down to straighten her cap.

"You know Françoise Gloux." Dupin didn't know quite where this comment had come from.

"I like her very much"—an especially warm smile appeared on Cléac's face—"and I love the gallery."

"Do you know Docteur Evette Derien?" Riwal interjected again.

"She's my GP."

"Really?" Dupin blurted out.

This was interesting. New connections were constantly emerging. On the other hand—it was a small town. Cléac's home was close to Chaboseau's surgery, maybe five minutes away from it.

"Did you come across Docteur Chaboseau at the surgery too? Were you ever seen by him?" Riwal followed up.

"No. I haven't been Docteur Derien's patient very long. A friend of mine recommended her to me."

"And do you know Madame Chaboseau? Personally, I mean," Dupin asked.

"No. I saw her from time to time, in the gallery, for instance. She never really noticed me."

That was it—Dupin had nothing else on his list for the time being.

"Thank you for your time, Madame Cléac." He turned to go, but stopped and spun around again. "Just one more thing. Where exactly were you yesterday afternoon between three and four o'clock?"

She didn't seem thrown in the slightest. "I was in my office, like I am every Friday afternoon. Dealing with invoices, deliveries, orders."

She added a spice to the bowl and Dupin recognized it by the smell that spread: Kari Gosse, the Breton curry powder.

"And where exactly is your office?"

"Here, in the annex to the barn."

"Were you alone?"

"Yes. My office assistant left in March. I'm looking for a new one at the moment."

"And where were you that evening?"

After all, they had tried to get hold of her but not been able to.

"At my best friend's house. Michelle Vigourt. She lives near Trévignon."

Trévignon was fifteen minutes away. A tiny, unpretentious harbor and a long quay wall with a few boats belonging to inshore fishermen who sold their superb catch on the spot at around five o'clock. One of Dupin's favorite pubs was there too, Le Noroît. Dupin had been welcomed with open arms by Christine and Pascal as soon as he set foot inside, at the very beginning of his time in Brittany. Your origins didn't matter to either of them. Not even questionable Parisian origins.

"Do you surf, Madame Cléac?" This question had just crossed Dupin's mind.

"No."

"We will leave you to work in peace now. *Au revoir, mesdames.*" Dupin directed this farewell to the room at large—Cléac's colleagues had carried right on working this entire time. There were soft echoes of "*Au revoir, messieurs*" here and there.

Sieren Cléac smiled.

"I hope you make progress with your investigation."

"Thanks. And my sincere condolences on the death of your mother." He should have thought of this at the beginning.

"That's very kind, Monsieur le Commissaire. Thank you so much."

Her eyes glistened; she quickly fixed her cap again and busied herself with the bowls in front of her once more.

A moment later the commissaire and the inspector were standing outside in the early-summer sun. Riwal was getting his bearings on the gravel path that led to the street.

"One moment."

Dupin walked the length of the building and went around the corner. This was where the annex was. It was made of wood and not very big, maybe four meters by three. An enormous window and a narrow, red-painted door on the side. Through the window you could see the door that led to the factory floor where they had just been. A wild meadow surrounded the annex, reaching almost as far as the oaks by the water.

"She could have—" Dupin flinched; Riwal was standing right behind him all of a sudden. "—left her office without being seen."

Dupin nodded. He glanced at his watch.

"Onward. We—"

His cell rang.

Nolwenn.

"You were very keen to meet Monsieur Priziac. He's in the harbor right now. In the offices of Héros Naval. If you're done there, you could drop in on him quickly before you drive to the Chaboseaus. I've let them know you're coming."

"What's he doing in the harbor?"

"He wanted to survey the damage at the site for himself."

"Is he meeting Jodoc Luzel there?"

"He didn't say."

"Thanks, Nolwenn, talk to you soon."

Dupin put his cell back in his trouser pocket.

Riwal gave him a quizzical look.

"We're driving to Héros Naval."

The headquarters of Héros Naval was on the Rue du Moros, not far from the site of the explosion, in the harbor area.

The inspector and the commissaire had driven past the edge of the shipyard and even this morning, in broad daylight and seen from the car, it was a horrifying sight. Work on the ship had been called off until further notice, the dock was cordoned off, and they had seen lots of police officers.

Héros Naval owned the entire top floor of the square building they had parked in front of. There was a sign with large lettering emblazoned on it outside the building. Priziac would be meeting them in the manager's office, because the manager was out visiting the injured workers at the hospital this morning. Riwal and Dupin had been met by a member of the staff. They were told Monsieur Priziac just had a phone call to make.

They walked into a small, very functionally decorated office. A desk, a swivel chair, a small conference table with four chairs, beige plastic. Standard office furnishings like something out of the advertising catalogs the police station occasionally got sent. And since the beginning of the renovation work they "coincidentally" received them on an almost daily basis. An oversized computer screen was the only eye-catching thing in the room. On the walls were photos of ships in cheap plastic frames. There were four small windows, all of them open. Dupin stopped in front of one of them. It looked out onto the bustling shipyard complex. An odd world, it was a world predominantly made up of dozens of different overlapping sounds: hammering, welding, grinding, the sounds of the pressure washers on metal, occasionally amplified by the enormous resonating chambers of the ships where most of the work took place; a hiss, a squeak, a screech, all of it unbelievably loud especially when large metal parts banged into each other, you couldn't help being reminded of the muffled chimes of a clock. Dupin was watching an impressive cascade of sparks coming from a long metal girder being ground behind the building. A chemical smell hung in the air.

"How can I help you, gentlemen? I'm sure you understand I don't have much time."

Clearly Priziac had finished his phone call. He was wearing

a suit again, this time with a white shirt neatly buttoned up to the top and a red tie. His expression was arrogant, even steelier than the day before.

"Your colleagues are combing through everything here anyway, what do you want—"

"Why would someone carry out an attack on Héros Naval?" Dupin interrupted him sharply. "Whom did you provoke that much?"

To Dupin's surprise, Priziac paused a moment in confusion, his eyes wide, his eyebrows raised, before he replied:

"Ridiculous! *We* are the ones who were the victims of a brutal crime! *We*—"

"What's going on here, Monsieur Priziac?" Dupin was struggling to keep his cool. He found the pharmacist thoroughly unpleasant. "Four people were injured, two workers were fighting for their lives. I'm sick and tired of this. Start talking!"

Dupin had suddenly squared up to the heavyset man, towering over him by a head.

"Monsieur Priziac." Riwal, who seemed to fear a violent altercation, stepped in forcefully. "If there's something you've been keeping from us, now is the time to tell us. Otherwise there are going to be even more victims."

"I don't know. I don't know why any of this has happened." Priziac didn't seem keen on things escalating any further. He bowed his head, walked over to the desk, and stopped in front of it, hesitant.

"We will find out." Dupin made a show of following Priziac, coming very close to him again. "We've brought in experts from Quimper, Rennes, and Paris. They're going to scrutinize all of your business activities, every deal you've ever made, every transaction, every business associate. Everything. We will speak to every one of your customers, we will keep searching until we find something."

It was going to be difficult to intimidate someone like Priziac. Still, dramatic scare tactics couldn't hurt.

"And first and foremost, we are going to keep this site closed until we can be sure there's no risk of another attack. Nobody is going to lift another finger around here until I say so. Which means: it could be a very long time before they do."

Priziac fixed his piercing gaze on Dupin.

"You've got to do what you think is right."

Dupin walked toward the window and leaned his back against the wall.

"What businesses do you run with Docteur Chaboseau that we don't know about yet? And with Jodoc Luzel? We're not leaving here without all of the information, Monsieur Priziac."

Dupin hadn't mentioned this yesterday. They had only spoken to Luzel about it so far.

Priziac sat down in the desk chair.

"There's just the two businesses you already know about."

He looked weary all of a sudden, weak, almost slumped. The change came out of nowhere. He rolled backward on the chair and it groaned under his weight. "I haven't even made any other investments. My main business is the pharmacies."

"But you're aggressively trying to expand the shipbuilding firm and the brewery," Riwal remarked.

"There are plans for that, yes, let's put it that way." This sentence sounded more assertive again.

"And plans to buy up other companies too?"

"Absolutely. A shipbuilding firm near Arcachon. Le Grand

Large, the offer is on the table. And we're interested in two breweries in Normandy."

Finally they were getting a few details.

"And this purchase bid," Riwal followed up, "for the ship-building company—are you competing with anyone on that?"

Suddenly there was an ear-splitting noise, a horrendous rattling sound. Priziac took absolutely no notice of it.

"No. We made the offer very discreetly. And I'm not aware of any other offer."

This could all be investigated. And that's exactly what they would do.

"And Docteur Chaboseau? What else did he invest in?"

"Just fish-canning factories, a market where he saw a lot of potential, especially at the higher price points." Priziac nodded as if he wanted to personally endorse this view. Dupin had taken out his notebook. "And he also put a lot of money into art, he was a passionate collector."

This point had been pushed to one side during the course of the investigation so far, Dupin realized. There would be a chance to take a deeper look at it in the conversation they were about to have with Madame Chaboseau.

"Did Docteur Chaboseau tell you about his plan to buy Sieren Cléac's . . ." Dupin broke off. And felt annoyed. He had gone about this wrong, but he couldn't go back now. "Did Docteur Chaboseau tell you about his intention to buy Fête de la Mer from Sieren Cléac?"

There was a flash of uncertainty on Priziac's face but then he recovered.

"Yes. He had a few candidates on the list."

"Who else?"

This was new information. If it was true.

"The other two midsized canneries here in town. JB Océane and Gonidec."

Their products were also delicious.

"Had he already made them offers too?"

"No."

"You know that for sure?"

"I'm pretty sure."

Dupin wanted to find out these details, but he also wanted to know what the pharmacist really knew about Chaboseau. To get a sense of how close the friends had been and how much they had confided in one another.

"What about the plots of land?"

Priziac leaned back. "Pierre was tremendously lucky with the land behind the Sables Blancs. The other land he owned out toward the Anse de Saint-Jean is a conservation area. That's never going to be building land."

Dupin made a note anyway.

"And the thalasso spa?"

"A quick, targeted, and extremely successful investment, but that was it for real estate deals."

Dupin had been checking everything against the notes in his notebook. The list of Pierre Chaboseau's business activities looked like it was complete now, unless the pharmacist and the wine merchant were deliberately hiding something or hadn't been aware of something. He would discuss it with Madame Chaboseau soon.

"Think carefully, Monsieur Priziac." Riwal took over now. "Does anything else occur to you about the attack last night? What does your friend Jodoc Luzel think about it?"

"He's in a state of shock, just like I am. You," Priziac looked at the commissaire, "saw him yourself, last night."

"And his rival Kireg too, there's no love lost there. He'd like to take over from him as mayor."

Priziac attempted a sarcastic smile.

"That would be nice, actually. Did you take my advice and ask the mayor about the dispute with Pierre, Monsieur le Commissaire? And his partisan use of influence, which is clearly damaging Roi Gradlon's business?"

Dupin didn't react. He had had enough.

"Did Docteur Chaboseau speak to you about Docteur Derien's strong suggestion that they fix a date for the handover of the practice?"

"She's very pushy and she was pressuring him. But that didn't bother Pierre. He found it a bit hard to commit himself. You've got to understand that. I don't think she killed him over it, mind you, but you're the only one who gets to decide that."

"Thank you so much"—there was unconcealed sarcasm in Dupin's voice—"for the useful information, Monsieur Priziac. As I say: we think there's a real risk of another attack against the shipyard, so the site will remain closed until further notice."

This was the closest Dupin came to a good-bye before heading for the door. Riwal had already picked up on the signal to leave at "Thank you so much."

They were almost outside when they heard a low, muffled "Wait!"

They turned around.

Priziac was hunched over the desk, typing on the keyboard.

"I'm going to show you something."

Priziac pointed to the screen.

After a brief hesitation, Dupin and Riwal went and stood behind the pharmacist to look at the screen.

"I got this at half past midnight last night."

An email. Just four lines.

You'd better stay out of the yacht world.

We mean it.

You are going to withdraw quietly. And don't tell anyone about this email, especially not the police.

"What does that mean?"

This was unbelievable.

"And why are you only showing this to us now, Monsieur Priziac?" Riwal was furious.

"Jodoc and I were . . . unsure."

"Unsure?"

Dupin was speechless.

"We put in a bid to build a yacht six weeks ago. In the forty-meter class. For the first time. A luxury yacht. For ten people, a seven-person crew."

"Héros Naval is building a yacht?" Riwal asked in disbelief.

"We set up a subsidiary company: Rêves Maritimes." Priziac hesitated for a moment. "The shipbuilding company near Arcachon that we wanted to buy, Le Grand Large, builds exclusive yachts. In various classes, but all in the luxury sector. Custom-built boats."

There was an entire section of magazines about boats and yachts, including luxury yachts, in Dupin's favorite newsagent's. It was near the Amiral and he bought his newspapers there every morning. Although Dupin's interest in all things maritime was very limited due to his severe seasickness, the photos on the glossy magazine covers did look impressive. They were floating luxury apartments, entire villas. The world of the rich and the beautiful.

"So you want to get into the yacht business," Riwal reasoned, "and other people clearly don't like that."

This might be what was going on. It would explain the attack, and also the fact that the aim had probably not been to hurt people, but to cause a certain amount of damage, as a warning. But how would that fit with Chaboseau's murder?

Riwal was clearly thinking along similar lines. "Did Docteur Chaboseau meet up with someone from another shipbuilding firm yesterday? Tell us, Monsieur Priziac!"

Priziac looked at him in bewilderment.

"Not that Jodoc or I knew of, no." He seemed genuinely stunned. "I—I think he would have told us. Who could it have been, anyway?"

"Has anyone commented on Héros Naval's venture into the yacht business before? Another firm, a rival company?" Riwal was obviously trying to flesh out this scenario.

"We deliberately didn't shout it from the rooftops. We—" Priziac broke off, sweat running down his forehead. "But word could have got around, of course. I mean, clearly it's possible another company got wind of it from the client we had put in the bid with."

"Have you got a specific company in mind?"

"No. But maybe," he was speaking slowly now, "somebody turned up at Pierre's house unannounced yesterday. Someone he didn't know at all."

"To threaten him. And then the situation escalated." Riwal finished his theory. "But why would this person have gone to

Pierre Chaboseau specifically? And not to you or Monsieur Luzel? Luzel owns the most shares in the company."

"Well, nobody knows that," Priziac replied.

"Presumably not many people know that you three are the owners of Héros Naval anyway, right?" said Riwal, making an important point. "And those who do know come from the ship-building trade themselves."

Priziac nodded. "Probably, yes."

Dupin felt a deep sense of unease.

"Why would someone do something like this? Somebody just turns up at Chaboseau's to ask him to make Héros Naval withdraw from the yacht business? And after that, once they've killed him, which was presumably unplanned, they attack the shipyard overnight? And then only get in touch with a threatening message afterward?" None of it made any sense at all.

"Maybe it was not particularly well planned out. That happens."

Riwal was right. But still. For the moment, these kinds of scenarios were nothing more than wild speculation.

"Who is the client"—Dupin felt this was their best starting point—"you're building the yacht for?"

There was another almighty crash right next to the building. As if something heavy had landed on the ground.

"Renan Budig. From Saint-Malo."

Dupin had not heard the name before. Riwal—of course—had: "He moves in the same circles as the Goulfart family."

This name did, in fact, mean something to Dupin. Olivier Goulfart, a Breton to his core and from a big business family, had founded a large logistics empire and it currently operated worldwide.

Riwal responded immediately. "I'll get in touch with Monsieur Budig right away. He'll be able to tell us if he told anyone about the bid. Had you requested that he keep it confidential?"

Priziac shook his head. "Not in so many words."

"How many French companies are in the yacht trade?"

"Maybe ten."

"We should ask Nolwenn to draw us up a list of all the relevant companies," Dupin said to his inspector.

Riwal's forehead furrowed. "It's an international industry. A Spanish, Dutch, or English company could just as easily get angry about a new competitor. It's going to be a long list," he finished wearily.

Dupin turned back to Priziac: "And you really have no idea who could have written the email?"

"The email won't have been sent from an ordinary account." Priziac was staring at the screen. There was something condescending about his tone of voice again, something exasperatingly arrogant. "But won't the police have ways to trace it?"

"Our experts will look into it, but someone who is determined to send an email anonymously will find a way. I'm sure the sender's name will be fake. You . . ."

Something had just occurred to Dupin: "Do you know whether Renan Budig owns a yacht already? Or anyone from his family? Which would mean he had an existing relationship with a shipbuilding firm?"

Maybe somebody had been very much hoping for the commission—and would have been unceremoniously done out of a deal because of Héros Naval.

Priziac looked pensive. "His brother owns a yacht. Built by a company near La Rochelle. It's called Dauphin."

"We'll have a word with that company first, then. I'll pass all of this on, boss." Riwal got out his phone.

"I'm coming with you, Riwal. We're done here."

Priziac straightened up. "And what am I meant to do now? I mean, how should we act? Jodoc and I—all of us?"

"You won't do anything, and you will act perfectly normally." Dupin was clear. "You'll look after your injured workers. And their families." Dupin was already heading to the door. "You're going to make sure they get generous benefits. And—you're going to make sure you're available to speak to us. And don't leave town. We'll see you again soon."

Riwal had his phone to his ear as they stepped out onto the street. Dupin could hear him going through the new tasks with Nolwenn.

The car was right by the quay, just a few yards away from them. Dupin took a look around. There was a naval vessel in one of the berths. It was wedge-shaped, narrow, that distinctive pale gray, a small frigate or patrol boat. There was a large, empty area in front of the quay where he could make out three rusty rail-like contraptions running parallel along the concrete floor. There was a boat on the middle one, twenty meters long, Dupin guessed, a technical superstructure, some kind of utility boat. Beyond that he could see gigantic steel ramps leading into the sea. Apart from white, the brownish red of the rust was the dominant color here, and it was surprisingly bright in the sunlight. Opposite was a large concrete berth that marked the edge of the shipyard harbor. Right next to it, looking almost dainty: narrow wooden jetties for the pleasure boats. The Port de Plaisance in the front harbor had long been too small for all of the boats. So the town had opened more mooring spots for smaller sailing and motor-boats in the large harbor around the Ville Close.

"That's fine, yes. Great. Le Menn is to call me directly, yes . . ."

They had reached the car now and Riwal was still on the phone.

The unease Dupin had been feeling during the conversation they had just had was turning into serious frustration. The two events didn't fit together properly, no matter how furiously his mind tried to make links between them; or at least he couldn't see how they fit. There was Chaboseau's murder and then there was the attack which had at least one—anonymous—confessor to it and now a possible motive too. But what good would that be if the two events just didn't fit together? Had two crimes happened independently of each other? Two ongoing, unre-lated matters? That overlapped through certain people "by total chance"? Extremely unlikely. But it was not out of the question. Anything was possible. One of Claire's favorite sayings was you could have fleas *and* lice at the same time. A good doctor knew this, no matter how unlikely "common sense" might deem it, and this exact knowledge had saved countless lives. Claire could give plenty of specific examples. Were they dealing with one such example? Were fleas and lice both at play here?

Dupin started the engine. Riwal was still on the phone with Nolwenn.

The network of paths in this part of the harbor complex was like a labyrinth. It was particularly confusing because nothing was fenced in, all of the construction sites and complexes were openly accessible. You had to drive slowly, very slowly, and be incredibly careful. They went past another warship, this time in a dry dock. Dupin used his turn signal—only to brake hard a moment later and pull over.

He had thought about it on his way to the car earlier when he had seen the Quai des Seychelles and the little leisure harbor on the other side of the harbor. He had no choice. And it would only take a few minutes. His mind wasn't working properly; the commissaire needed caffeine. He would have a coffee in Le Pas Sage, right by the mooring spot for the little ferry that shuttled between the two parts of Concarneau.

Riwal—he was talking about the mayor just now—turned to Dupin for a moment with a quizzical look but then his expression changed, signaling that he understood. Their many years of working together weren't for nothing—he knew his commissaire.

Three minutes later they were sitting at the table right on the edge of the terrace. The terrace was lined with large flowerpots, magnificent bamboo plants and oleander towering up out of them. Small black tables, fewer than ten of them, and comfortable dark red chairs. The *petits cafés* had been ordered. The restaurant was an old fisherman's cottage—Dupin liked this whole neighborhood, which was called Quartier Lanriec. The cottage was painted a pale pink and the door and the windows were framed in granite. But the prettiest thing about it was the contrasting filigree stucco all over the facade.

The view was terrific. The entire place was, with all of its ambience.

You could see the Ville Close in the large harbor, the tall ramparts that had withstood everything and everyone since medieval times: fierce enemies, the raging Atlantic, apocalyptic floods. Dupin couldn't help being reminded of the dark sorcerer who had made the ramparts shoot up out of the ground, the treacherous curse, and the tragic, desperate love story.

"All discussed, all delegated," Riwal said, pleased. After the conversation with Nolwenn he had phoned Nevou. He leaned back with a sigh that was difficult to interpret.

"We're only just beginning our investigations into the yacht company. But Nolwenn has already rustled up a dozen people to find out more about Héros Naval and the three friends' business dealings. No scandals so far, no dirty business practices, no corruption or tax issues. Nolwenn has made a few discreet calls"—one of the sentences that Dupin loved, because it usually signaled new information—"but she didn't find out anything of interest, unfortunately. The three of them are considered shrewd businessmen—tough, assertive, occasionally aggressive, but apparently they haven't crossed any lines so far."

Dupin nodded wearily.

"Apparently Kler Kireg and Evette Derien were voted joint chairpeople of a society called Les Amis de la Torche three weeks ago," Riwal continued.

"What kind of society is it?"

"It's involved in organizing quite large surfing events, it mainly looks after the PR."

"*Et voilà!*" Marie-Ophélie—the manager of the Pas Sage—set the coffees down in front of them. "Anything else? Breakfast, maybe?"

Dupin shook his head, there was no time for that, unfortunately. Which was a real shame because the food was superb here. Marie-Ophélie and Valentin had opened the restaurant together. Before that they had traveled the world together for six years. Concarneau-born Valentin had worked as a chef in the Caribbean, Brazil, Ireland, and North Africa. Even this was very Breton: going boldly into the big wide world. Or at least it was no less Breton than making the opposite life choice: clinging to one tiny scrap of Breton land until the end of your days—and doing so happily. Traveling to far-flung countries had shaped Valentin's cooking. Dupin had eaten here with Claire just two weeks ago and Claire had enjoyed a tandoori steak tartare.

"Nothing for me either, thanks." Riwal was equally saddened he had to decline. He had been awake even longer than Dupin.

"By the way, Georges Simenon also liked to sit here," he said suddenly.

Like the Amiral, the Pas Sage had a famous past and a treasure trove of stories. It had been called Le Café de la Marine back in the day and was run by two sisters. A meeting point for fishermen. Simenon had had the protagonists from his novel *The Evil Sisters of Concarneau* live here.

"What else do we know about this society?" Dupin asked, hoping to head off a digression by his inspector.

"In the next eight days alone there are two important competitions taking place: the second round of the Coupe de France in shortboard, qualifiers for the national championships, and the E. Leclerc Junior Pro La Torche, one of the most significant European competitions for surfers under the age of eighteen . . ."

It was incredible how well informed Riwal was about local events. "In both competitions, surfers from Brittany are best placed to—"

"Aren't Docteur Derien and the mayor in touch a lot then?" Dupin interrupted Riwal's speech.

Derien, who wanted to take over the practice sooner rather than later, and the mayor, who had clashed with Chaboseau over the brewery licenses. Both of these things—according to what they currently knew—insufficient as a motive for murder, they were not important enough or dramatic enough for that. On the other hand, you never knew whether these kinds of connections ran deeper.

"Not necessarily."

Dupin remembered his conversation with the mayor about Evette Derien; he had explicitly asked whether they knew each other well. His answer had been that they exchanged a few friendly words now and again, and that was it.

"They're really ceremonial positions," Riwal clarified. "As chairpeople of the society, they're very unlikely to be involved in the day-to-day running of it."

"I see."

Dupin drank his first coffee in three mouthfuls. Excellent as always. Then the second.

Riwal used this break to drink his coffee too.

Dupin's gaze fell on the newspaper that the last customer must have left on the table—an interview with a biologist. "Penguins Are Total Egoists," the headline read. The scientist did say he was fascinated by penguins' skills—they could swim twenty-five thousand kilometers without ever going on land, and every penguin had its own distinct personality—but then he went on to raise almost only the issues that penguin-lovers like Dupin didn't want to hear: "A penguin colony smells like a fish market in the evening," was one of the statements. And another, totally unscientific assertion: "As teenagers, emperor penguins may look like cuddly coffeepot cozies but once they are fully fledged, they have temper tantrums, run around aimlessly, and beat up any peers in their way." As if adolescent humans are any different, Dupin thought, outraged. Then, to top it all off, this was followed by the remark about egoism. Penguins lived in an icy hellhole that was minus fifty degrees; of course you had to look out for yourself in such extreme conditions. Besides, didn't they usually stand together in that very social way to warm each other up? Systematic misinterpretations, that was always the problem with people and their views of animals. Dupin slammed his empty coffee cup down on the page with the interview.

Riwal got to his feet.

"I'm going to try and get hold of Renan Budig and his contact at Dauphin. And I'll speak to one of our police colleagues in La Rochelle. Maybe they'll know the company. It's best if one of our colleagues pays them a call."

It all seemed a little over the top, but since the threatening email had come in, quite a lot pointed to the theory that a ruthless competitor could be responsible for the attack on Héros Naval. And maybe there was some kind of connection to the murder, after all. Some kind of connection they just couldn't see yet.

Riwal picked up his phone.

"Feel free to drive on ahead, boss. I have several phone calls to make. I'll follow you."

Riwal already had the phone to his ear, walking toward the water a few paces away.

Dupin fished out some change and placed it on the saucer with the receipt. Then he left the terrace.

The little ferry—the *bac de passage*—was just putting to sea from the Ville Close. There had been ferry crossings between the two parts of the town since medieval times. The Concarnese had a grand term for this trip: *"La plus petite croisière du monde."* The smallest cruise in the world.

Up until a few years ago it had been a little green boat, its diesel engine defying the currents. The entire boat had vibrated hard and, with it, every one of the passengers' bones. *Le Vachic* had now taken over the crossing, an extremely quiet white catamaran with an electric engine and a small French flag on the stern. It was the only boat trip Dupin could stomach. He would go so far as to say he actually liked it.

Félix Chaboseau was not how Dupin had imagined him. Not just as far as his physical appearance went—he didn't look particularly like either his mother or his father—but personality-wise too. He couldn't have said why exactly, but Dupin had expected that when he met him, he would be able to tell that this was a person who had had to fight his whole life. His father's devastating assessment, as reported by Priziac the day before, was still fresh in his mind.

But Félix Chaboseau did not seem like a broken man. Opposite Dupin stood a man at peace with himself and self-assured, who was very clearly grieving, yes, but who was not drowning in grief. Dupin put him at one meter eighty, but he was not as thin as his father, with longer, straight hair—dark blond—that fell into his face slightly. A face with gentle, serene features. He was wearing jeans and a dark blue linen shirt, the top buttons undone.

They were in a spacious drawing room on the second floor.

Madame Chaboseau hadn't wanted to go up to the top floor, although Dupin would have preferred that.

Félix Chaboseau had arrived only a few minutes before Dupin. The commissaire had spoken to Nolwenn again on his way to the Chaboseaus' home. Just because it was possible again now. And because it calmed him.

"It's true, we didn't have much to do with each other. Basically nothing. It's a shame." Félix Chaboseau was sitting in one of the stately armchairs, Dupin on the sofa opposite him, and between them was an elegant low table made of untreated oak. The sofa suite was black leather. Just like the top floor, this room resembled a museum, dozens of paintings hanging on the walls.

"It has always made me feel very sad." Félix Chaboseau didn't come across at all melodramatic; he sounded sincere, serious, shaken. "And I have never really made my peace with it." He spoke softly, but his voice was firm. "But it doesn't stop me living my own life anymore. My father was, as far as I can judge, a happy person. And I am too. I am content with my life."

Dupin had started by asking Félix Chaboseau about his relationship with his father—and had received an answer that was honest and impressive, if profoundly sad. Madame Chaboseau had excused herself for a moment after placing a silver tray with a bottle of mineral water and three glasses on the coffee table. Félix Chaboseau had a strong alibi, several people had seen him at the mill the afternoon before, they had checked it. By the looks of things, he could not be the murderer.

"It's awful his life had to end like this." Félix Chaboseau looked Dupin in the eye, his gaze gentle but piercing. "Who could have done this, Monsieur le Commissaire? And why? Do you have a lead yet? A provisional theory about what's behind this?"

It was remarkable that Chaboseau's son was the first person in this murder enquiry to ask this question—a very natural question, in fact. Dupin was usually tormented by this question throughout a case.

"Nothing concrete, I'm afraid. It's possible that the murder of your father is linked to the attack on the shipbuilding firm Héros Naval. If that's the case, there must be one narrative that unites both crimes."

Félix Chaboseau allowed what had been said to sink in. He drank a mouthful of water.

"When did you last see your father?"

"January. He was in Douarnenez. He had an errand to do there. We ate lunch together. In Ty Mad."

Dupin had got his notebook out and was writing in it.

"He was able to spare me more or less forty minutes. He offered to get my flour distributed in huge quantities by one of his friends. He thought I desperately needed to increase my production. The usual."

"What was your parents' relationship like?" Dupin decided to go for the direct approach. "Your mother is one of the suspects, of course."

Félix Chaboseau fell silent for a while.

"If I'm honest, I couldn't say. And there is no point in my life when I could have. For a while I thought I understood their relationship, and I hated it. But then it became clear to me I don't understand anything about it at all."

"And when you thought you understood the relationship—how did it seem?"

"Like their marriage was a prison, a binding marriage of convenience. And they'd be better off splitting up."

"And then what did you think later?"

"Then I realized that the marriage was exactly how they wanted it. Both of them. Because they were both getting something out of it."

"Did your father have other women? Affairs?"

"Oh yes, or he did during my childhood, at least. Not many, but all quite long-term."

"And your mother knew about them?"

"She has a very odd way of knowing something and not knowing it at the same time. She doesn't repress things completely, but she represses their significance. That is much more effective."

These were smart observations. Dupin knew exactly what he meant.

"Did she hate him?"

"That would be to put it too simply."

Dupin understood this too.

"The important thing is this: my mother was never just the passive one."

"Did your father have an affair recently?"

This would be an important lead, of course.

"I don't know. I went to boarding school at fourteen. I haven't seen my parents much since."

"Do you know anything about your parents' business dealings, or your father's? About the investments they made?"

"Only very little. My mother used to be involved in all of the decisions. I remember the thalasso spa project, for example."

"What do you know about Héros Naval?"

"That was more my father's thing, but like I say, I don't know exactly. My maternal grandfather owned shares in one of the big shipbuilding firms in Saint-Nazaire."

"Does your mother still own them?"

"No. My mother did inherit them but she disposed of them. A good twenty-five years ago, I'd say."

"Are you familiar with any of your father's business plans in the shipbuilding sector, did he mention anything specific in January? Maybe just in passing? That he wanted to expand, for example?"

"No. If I understand correctly, his two friends are also involved in most of his deals. I'm sure you'll have spoken to them."

Dupin nodded.

He was writing in his notebook again. They had to bear in mind that if Félix Chaboseau was telling the truth—and they had no reason to doubt it—then he was one of their worst informants, because he knew the least.

"So do you actually inherit," Dupin changed the subject abruptly, "directly now? A direct share from your father, I mean? Or does your mother inherit everything?"

An important point. Dupin had thought of this a couple of times but not followed up on it yet.

"I'm so sorry, I have absolutely no idea."

"Do your parents have a prenuptial agreement, I mean, what about the assets, the paintings, the companies, does that all belong—"

"I don't see what that has to do with the police, Monsieur le Commissaire!" Madame Chaboseau had come into the drawing room through the double doors. "Those are entirely private matters."

"I can tell you exactly what it has to do with us." Dupin stood up. He was going to make her talk today. "It has everything to do with us. Absolutely everything." He walked toward her, struggling to control himself. "We are trying to solve your husband's murder and you are one of the suspects. And you are going to tell us and show us right here, right now, everything that we need for this investigation. If you do not, we'll have a search warrant within five minutes and we'll take everything away. It's up to you."

Madame Chaboseau fixed Dupin with a deeply contemptuous look. Then she went over to a waist-high drinks cabinet. She reached swiftly for a crystal carafe—cognac, Dupin suspected—poured herself a rather full potbellied glass of it, and drank a large mouthful.

"All right then," she said, an icy note in her voice, and went over to the armchair next to her son's. Félix Chaboseau shot her an inscrutable look. She sat down as if in slow motion. She smoothed out her black silk dress—a flower pattern that was so dark you almost couldn't make it out on the black fabric—and took another mouthful. Her hairdo was not quite as perfect as it was the day before, but Madame Chaboseau seemed to be wearing more makeup today instead.

"What do you want to know?"

Dupin sat down again too. He took his time in answering.

"For one thing, exactly what I just asked your son: how your prenuptial agreement—if you've got one—settles the estate. And more generally: how the ownership of assets between you and your husband is settled. Who owns what share of the estate, the assets? The companies and company shares?"

"We don't have a prenuptial agreement, that's new-fangled

nonsense. Everything of value that we brought with us to the marriage, as well as everything that has been generated by us jointly or by one of us since then, belongs equally to us both. The same goes for the companies and shares too. And that's all there is to say on that."

"And what are the inheritance arrangements? Is there a will? I take it you're familiar with it?"

Dupin was watching both mother and son very carefully.

Indignant, Madame Chaboseau's eyebrows shot up.

"Of course there's one, and of course I'm familiar with it." That sharp tone of voice again. "Félix inherits a quarter from my husband's share of our joint assets, on certain conditions, mind you. The remainder comes to me."

Three-quarters, in that case.

"What kind of conditions?"

"He can access it to make investments." She didn't dare glance over at her son.

Dupin had turned to Félix Chaboseau, expecting him to say something. But he did not.

After a while the hint of a smile appeared on his face. Not a cynical or sarcastic smile. More like a smile to break the tension. He closed his eyes briefly, opened them again. Dupin wouldn't ask any more about this. Mother and son needed to figure it out between them.

"So, Héros Naval"—Dupin needed to move on—"who dealt with the company, Madame Chaboseau? You, your husband, or both of you?"

"My husband. All I did was back the investment at the outset."

Félix Chaboseau had stood up. "I don't think you need me anymore." Without waiting for an answer, he strode toward the door to the library, which was right next to the drawing room.

Madame Chaboseau nodded, although her son could not see her anymore.

Dupin was silent for a moment, then returned to his questions. "Why did you back Héros Naval?"

"Shipbuilding is a lucrative business."

"Did you make the suggestion to your husband?"

"No. Brecan Priziac did."

"What about the plans for further investments? Getting into the yacht business? Setting up Rêves Maritimes?"

"I think they were both the right decisions to make. The demand for luxury goods is growing."

An astonishingly forthcoming answer by her standards.

"Did you discuss these issues with your husband?"

"Yes."

"And the business discussions"—this was another thing that interested Dupin—"between your husband and his two friends? Were you there for them too?"

"No."

The relationship setup the Chaboseaus had found for their lives was strange and unusual. Assuming Madame Chaboseau was telling them the truth.

"Does anything specific occur to you that might explain the attack on Héros Naval?"

"No."

Madame Chaboseau had finished her drink by now, but was still clutching the glass.

"I'm sure you'll be in a position to tell us if we are now aware of all of your and your husband's business activities—or if there are any more?" He read aloud: "The cannery, the shipbuilding, the brewery, the pieces of land, the investment in the thalasso spa, the art collection—and of course, the medical practice."

Madame Chaboseau nodded almost imperceptibly.

"That's everything."

"What about the underwater capsule and the three researchers' boat that makes oil out of plastic?"

"None of our money is tied up in either of those projects. Héros Naval is just building the underwater capsule, we have nothing to do with the financing."

"Another thing." Dupin glanced at his little notebook. "Your husband called you yesterday afternoon at two twenty P.M.—a call you never mentioned to us. Was that your last conversation with him?"

"Yes. He just wanted to remind me about something."

"What was it?"

"I needed to sort something out at the Galerie Gloux. His call was totally unnecessary, I had it on my list anyway."

Dupin could feel his impatience growing.

"Your visit was about *two* paintings—you only mentioned one yesterday."

"Oh well!" A scornful shrug.

"But there were two."

She looked at him, pulling an exaggerated, baffled face. It was no good. Dupin couldn't make anything more of this point.

He stood up and walked over to the window onto the harbor. He couldn't stand being on the sofa any longer. He stopped in front of a painting right next to the window, his back to Madame Chaboseau.

"The painting won't mean anything to you." Her voice was disdainful.

Paul Signac. *Concarneau, 1931.* It struck Dupin that this was the same year the Maigret crime novel that took place in the Amiral came out. In the foreground of the painting was a boat with two majestic masts. From the time when Concarneau had been the most significant tuna-fishing port in the world. Behind the boat were the enormous ramparts of the Ville Close. It was a painting full of over-the-top color. The boat a dark blue, the sails orange. The sea green with several islands of color that were simply intoxicating: a pale whitish blue that glowed almost phosphorescent. That's exactly how the sea sometimes looked in Brittany. The sky all sorts of pink shades. The roofs of the old houses leaden gray. The trees of the Ville Close an almost supernatural bright green. The world as color. The crazy thing was: the artist saw the world the way it really was.

Dupin turned back to Madame Chaboseau abruptly. "What did you advise your husband about Docteur Derien's request? She clearly put quite a bit of pressure on him."

"Disgraceful! The audacity of that woman!" Her reaction was fierce. "Our position on it was that only we would fix the date and only when *we* thought the time was right."

"How often did your husband meet Docteur Derien to speak about it?"

"That's completely beside the point," she snorted.

"How much did the dispute between them escalate?"

"Where that woman was concerned, my husband was far too . . ." She broke off. "We haven't reached any kind of binding arrangement yet."

"Are you going to sell the whole practice to Docteur Derien now? She's sure to approach you with that suggestion soon."

"We'll see."

"I've got to ask you something, Madame Chaboseau." Dupin didn't know why he was introducing this question in such a roundabout way. "Did your husband have an affair recently?"

He was met with another venomous look.

Dupin didn't let up: "Did he?"

"No. Absolutely not."

"Do you know that for certain?"

"I do, yes."

"Would you tell us if it wasn't the case?"

"Never."

Dupin was not surprised.

"Well, in any case. There was a second enterprising young woman who met up with your husband."

Madame Chaboseau's brow furrowed.

"My husband always had lots of business ideas, not just in the shipbuilding sector." A smart retort.

"In the cannery trade too?"

"What are you trying to get at?"

"Your husband met up with Madame Sieren Cléac."

She gave an exaggerated shrug of her shoulders. "He met all sorts of people."

"You didn't know he wanted to buy the Fête de la Mer company from her?"

It was clear Madame Chaboseau was keen to answer as casually as possible. "As I say, we were always considering expanding. The canneries are really booming, especially the upmarket ones."

"You didn't know anything about it, did you?"

Dupin was certain of it. It seemed Pierre Chaboseau had told his friend Priziac about it but not his wife.

She was silent.

This must have been tough for Madame Chaboseau, having just done her best to try to make it clear that she and her husband had made all of their business decisions together.

"Madame Cléac phoned your husband just a few hours before his violent death. To turn down his offer. A phone call you were also unaware of, I take it."

"You seem to take particular pleasure in trivial matters and insignificant details, Monsieur—"

She was interrupted by Dupin's phone. He took it out of his trouser pocket.

Nolwenn.

"Just one moment, please."

Dupin went into the spacious hallway and closed the door behind him.

"I've got something very interesting, Monsieur le Commissaire, especially as you're talking to Madame Chaboseau right now." She got right into it, just like he knew she always did. "It's about the mayor and Docteur Chaboseau."

"Yes?"

"They were seen together two weeks ago in Café de l'Atlantic, late in the evening, at around eleven o'clock on a Thursday. This is coming from Anne and I've had it confirmed by Aurélie. Anne was only sitting two tables away from them."

The investigative machine was in motion. Dupin may have had no idea who Anne was, but he knew the two owners of Café de l'Atlantic, the sisters Aurélie and Diane Gavoué.

"She heard them having a heated argument. She couldn't understand everything but apparently Chaboseau threatened to stop all of his financial contributions to town and local causes and even pull Roi Gradlon out of the town if Kireg continued granting brewery licenses the way he had been doing."

It was unbelievable. Why hadn't Madame Chaboseau told them this dispute had worsened? Had she not known anything about this either? And why had the mayor kept it from them? And why had Priziac? And Luzel? Surely Chaboseau had told his wife and two closest friends about it.

"How did Kireg respond?"

"She couldn't hear, he was speaking very quietly, she says. Judging by his facial expressions, he was being quite conciliatory."

"Did Anne catch anything else?"

"No."

"Is there anything on Dauphin yet, that yacht company?"

"As soon as we have anything on that, I'll be in touch. Another thing." Nolwenn sounded strangely upbeat. "Since your piece in the press, a steady stream of tips has been coming into the station from the public. Apparently five portable toilets were stolen from the Sables Blancs beach overnight. They had been put out for the concert tonight. And also someone remembers seeing an unusual stranger last night. Unfortunately they couldn't see him clearly."

"That's crazy."

"I know. Especially for the event organizers. If the portable toilets don't turn up again, the festival committee will have to cover the damages, one thousand five hundred euro. Speak soon."

With these words, Nolwenn hung up.

Dupin went back into the drawing room.

"Madame Chaboseau, I hear you concealed a really quite remarkable piece of information from us: your husband met the mayor two weeks ago to deliver a serious threat to him. He let him know he was going to pull Roi Gradlon out of the town, along with all of the jobs. These are more than—as you called them—trivial matters. Why did you keep this from us?"

For a moment she seemed genuinely thrown. "I—we discussed it in principle. Yes! And that's exactly what happened."

"Who discussed it? You and your husband?"

"That's what I meant." She seemed reasonably composed again. "I meant that we jointly decided to take a strong line on this issue. And—"

"Why didn't you tell us anything about this dispute yesterday?"

The mayor hadn't mentioned it either!

"Perhaps you'll recall, Monsieur le Commissaire—I had just found my husband dashed to pieces on the asphalt, it can make you slightly addled now and again." She sat up straight on the edge of the armchair, the fabric of her dress rustling.

"A little birdie tells me"—Dupin was not prepared to back down that quickly—"that the brewery is in financial difficulties."

A well-judged shot in the dark.

Madame Chaboseau's eyes widened.

"That is outrageous. And damaging to our company's good name. Who is spreading such barefaced lies? I'd be all too pleased to—"

The doorbell rang.

Madame Chaboseau got to her feet. Without another word, she rushed out of the drawing room, emotions etched across her face now—it was just difficult to tell what emotions they were.

Dupin followed her into the hall.

Madame Chaboseau wrenched the door open.

Rosa Le Menn was standing outside, pale and struggling to catch her breath.

"Jodoc Luzel," she gasped out, "he—he's dead. Murdered." For a moment they froze; Madame Chaboseau still had the door handle in her hand.

"The wine merchant?" Dupin broke the spell. "Murdered?"

"Yes. He . . ."

"Damn it."

He ran a hand through his hair.

"What happened?"

"Probably killed with a bottle. In the Roi Gradlon brewery. He—"

"In the brewery? In *his* brewery?"

"That's right."

"Who found him?"

"Monsieur Priziac. Just a few minutes ago."

"Priziac?" This was getting crazier and crazier. "But we've only just seen him. In the Héros Naval offices. Why did he go to the brewery?"

"I don't have any information on th—"

"So is the brewery open today, then?"

"No."

Dupin turned to Madame Chaboseau. Her expression was difficult to read. There was horror there, but not just that; there was something else there too. Dupin couldn't tell what it was.

"This is your husband's friend, madame. The second one in the trio. What's going through your mind?"

"Nothing."

She sounded weary by her standards.

"*Can* you not," Dupin said in a strained voice, "or do you still not *want* to tell us what is going on here? Clearly it's definitely something to do with the three of them. And your husband's business dealings are your business dealings too. I think you could potentially be in danger too. Your life could be in danger."

This was the truth.

Madame Chaboseau jutted her chin out. "I have told you everything I know." She had recovered her haughty manner.

"Whatever you say," Dupin was moving off, "whatever you say, Madame Chaboseau. We need to go."

Without turning around again, he hurried down the steps.

"Come on, Le Menn."

This order was unnecessary; the young policewoman was right behind him anyway.

"Does Inspector Riwal know?"

"His phone was busy the whole time."

"Where exactly is the brewery?"

Nine minutes later the commissaire's Citroën was stopping in an empty car park right outside a modern building.

They hadn't spoken on the journey there. Dupin had been lost in frantic thought, but it had not brought him the slightest bit closer to solving the case.

But one thing seemed undeniable now: this was about the three friends—the trio—of whom two were now dead. The whole brutal business had something to do with them, that was the only thing Dupin was sure of.

Nevou was waiting for them at the entrance to the brewery, having had a few minutes' head start.

"You've—"

"How long has he been dead? When did it happen?"

"Only the medical examiner will be able to tell you that. He should be here any moment now."

"Where is Priziac?" Dupin asked impatiently.

"Inside, with two of his colleagues."

Dupin strode inside, Nevou and Le Menn hot on his heels.

"First on the left," Nevou instructed. "He's in the Espace Création."

"In the what now?"

It sounded mystifying.

"It's a separate brewery plant. Where the new beers are developed," Nevou explained clearly as they hurried along the corridor. "I've spoken to the head of the brewery on the phone. There's no production on Saturdays and Sundays at Roi Gradlon. So none of the staff were in today. But of course, Luzel has a master key."

"Does Priziac have one too?"

"He says not. He says the brewery is mainly Luzel's thing. I mean," Nevou added drily, "it was. It was his thing."

"So either Jodoc Luzel had something to do in the brewery and the murderer knew that he would come here—maybe even followed him—or Luzel and the murderer arranged to meet here," Le Menn reasoned.

That was the situation they were dealing with.

"Someone who definitely did know he was here anyway was Monsieur Priziac," Nevou added drily.

One of the oldest, simplest tricks in criminal history: you "found" the dead person that you yourself had killed. Brazen, callous and, time after time, extremely effective. If you hadn't left any traces behind and there were no witnesses or hard evidence, nothing could be proved against you, even if the crime verged on the obvious. Or at least there wouldn't be enough to convict you. The pharmacist would have the chutzpah for that kind of move, Dupin was in no doubt about that.

They walked into a remarkably high-ceilinged room, large windows with a view of some woodland. Enormous, round, high-grade steel tanks—a good four meters tall—to their right and left and in front of the windows too, with a walkway down the middle. Around the tanks, also made from high-grade steel, there were steps and platforms to stand on, the highest ones level with the enormous tank lids. Imposing, strange structures. In the midst of all the round tanks there was a rather large rectangular machine and on the ground in front of it were beer bottles with blank labels. There was a pile of large sacks in between two of the tanks.

Right at the end of the room, Dupin caught sight of Brecan Priziac with two police officers. And the dead man. Jodoc Luzel. He was lying stretched out on the walkway.

"What on earth were you . . ." Dupin headed straight for the pharmacist.

Priziac immediately cut across the commissaire. "Jodoc—he asked me to meet him here. *That* is what on earth I was doing here."

This would make him the first person to have been confronted with the gruesome sight of his dead friend.

"He was already here when he asked me to come." Priziac looked around, seeming forlorn for a moment. "This is Jodoc's playground, his laboratory. Creating new beers is his great passion." Priziac paused for a moment. It was warm in the Espace

Création and the pharmacist was perspiring in his suit, the sweat running down his forehead. "Jodoc had been experimenting with new recipes and ingredients all week. I presume there was something he had to do today, that he had a new idea and didn't want anything going to waste."

"Your mutual friend and business partner is murdered, then shortly after that an attack is carried out on your company in which four men are injured, some critically, you receive a serious threat—and Monsieur Luzel is thinking about his new beer recipes?"

Priziac had taken a handkerchief out of his jacket and was wiping his forehead. "What can I say, monsieur?"

"Who called who to arrange to meet here? And when exactly?"

The pharmacist looked hard at Dupin. "When did you arrive at Héros Naval this morning? The phone call with Jodoc was right before that. So a little before half past eight. I called him from the communal office at the shipyard."

Dupin remembered. Priziac had made them wait because of a phone call.

"You called him?"

"Yes. We spoke about the attack again. And about insurance issues. Then at the end he asked me to come and see him at the brewery."

"And between that point and arriving here, you didn't hear anything else from him? No phone call, no text message, nothing?"

"No."

"The dead man," Nevou interjected in a grim voice, "doesn't have a cell phone on him. I've checked. But we'll get the phone records. Then we'll see."

"I take it"—Dupin was also starting to sweat in his polo shirt and jacket—"you two spoke on the phone several times after the incident, both yesterday evening and this morning, Monsieur Priziac?"

"Of course."

"Jodoc Luzel didn't feel the need to come in to the shipyard again this morning?"

"Well, he'd got the picture last night."

"When did you arrive at the shipyard?"

"Eight o'clock. There's a lot to do, as you can imagine."

"Did anyone see you, are there witnesses?"

"I was with our manager most of the time. Before he drove to the hospital."

"We left the office around nine thirty, you found the body around ten forty-five—what happened in between those two times? And when exactly did you arrive at the brewery?"

"Well, probably around quarter to eleven, then. Maybe a few minutes earlier. And before I left, I also made two phone calls to our insurance agents."

Dupin crouched down to take a closer look at the corpse.

Meanwhile Le Menn started questioning Priziac: "Did you see anyone at Héros Naval who could confirm the time you left?"

Priziac gave the young policewoman a withering look.

"I have no idea."

"It doesn't really matter anyway," Nevou said sharply, "just a few minutes would have been enough to kill your friend."

"The time of death," added Le Menn—they worked well as a team now—"cannot be determined to the exact minute anyway. If the phone records can back it up, Luzel died between eight thirty and ten forty-five."

Dupin studied the enormous hematoma on Luzel's right temple. Hideous discoloration, a nasty swelling the size of a fist; the skin had cracked open in one place and blood had run down his face, although there wasn't much of it. Luzel's head was turned to one side, blood had trickled into his eye too. It was gruesome. His arms and legs were totally straight, as if the muscles were still very tense. Luzel was wearing a long-sleeved Lacoste polo shirt in pale green with dark green slacks and leather loafers.

Dupin stood up again.

About two meters away from the body, at the edge of the central walkway, there was a broken bottle, a few large shards of glass, and lots of small shards. Beer had spread out across the concrete floor. Dupin had spotted the shards of glass earlier as he walked in.

Nevou saw Dupin's gaze.

"We're assuming the bottle didn't smash during the impact on Luzel's skull. The shards are too far away. The murderer probably dropped it after the crime. The shards are within a relatively limited radius. It's one of the bottles that was on the floor over there. With a blank label for the description. There are full bottles and empty ones. This was a full one."

"Where are Luzel's glasses?" Dupin had been looking for them but couldn't see them.

Nevou pointed to one of the high-grade steel structures. "Under that thing, maybe. Presumably the impact of the bottle made them fly off. Imagine someone using a full beer bottle to smash you in the skull with maximum force. And hitting you pretty squarely in the temple too . . ."

Dupin turned slowly on his heel and took another careful look around the room.

"We've already taken a look at everything," Nevou said. "Nothing of note yet."

Dupin noticed Priziac gazing at the lifeless body of his friend. Dupin watched him. He was well versed in the art of reading people, yet in that moment he couldn't have said what was going through Priziac's mind.

But he had noticed there was a thought bothering him. It was ridiculous, but not surprising either—with a case as strange as this one, you simply had a lot of strange ideas. But he couldn't allow himself to be distracted by crazy ideas, he needed to focus on Priziac.

"What do you think, monsieur?" Dupin came and stood close to the pharmacist, who was still looking at his dead friend. "Is this another crime by your shipbuilding rival? But what am I asking? Of course, you have no idea what could have happened here." The commissaire headed off another evasive answer from the pharmacist. "In any case, that's it for now. If we have any more questions, and I'm sure we will, then we'll be in touch."

The aggressive challenge in this was clear to Priziac.

"I hope you know what you're doing." The pharmacist tried to smile sadly but it turned into more of a grimace. He turned around and walked toward the exit.

Dupin swung around to the two policewomen. "I want us to get right onto—"

"So what treat have we got in store here?"

Dupin had not heard him coming.

René Reglas. The greatest medical examiner in human history.

His two assistants in tow, as well as the crime scene investigators. Dupin had been hoping for old Lafond, who had been on duty the day before.

"That looks really nasty." His tone of voice fake, his sympathy faked. It was all—as always—just for show.

"*Mesdames, messieurs*—if you could please clear this area? So that I can begin my work. And then maybe you can solve the case, Commissaire?" He set down his ostentatious aluminum case. "Let's see if we can track down this 'great stranger' everyone is talking about at the moment. If we do, it will have to be by scientific means, of course."

It took Dupin's utmost self-control not to react to any of the medical examiner's outrageous comments.

"I need the exact time of death, and I mean exact, not approximate. It probably happened between about eight thirty and ten forty-five."

"Dupin, I'm sure you'll be well aware—"

"And as quickly as possible."

Dupin hurried to follow Nevou and Le Menn, who were heading for the other end of the room and the exit. He was only half listening as Reglas unleashed a flood of curses. Turning to Nevou and Le Menn, Dupin said, "We need to know the whereabouts of the mayor during the relevant time period. That goes for Madame Chaboseau too, up until our meeting with her at least. And for her son"—he had, of course, only arrived at his mother's a little before ten—"and for Docteur Derien and Sieren Cléac."

Nevou didn't look convinced.

"With Derien and Cléac, it's hard to imagine a link to Héros Naval and the three friends' investments. Are you still considering other motives?"

"I'm considering everything." This was one of Dupin's sacred principles. "Check every last detail of everything. We need witnesses, evidence. I—"

"Boss!"

They were almost at the exit and Riwal was racing toward them.

"I need to speak to you. I have two pieces of news!" Riwal was in full flow, immediately diving in: "First, the experts have taken a look at the anonymous threatening email. As we suspected: it's impossible to trace it back. The author probably hid in the TOR network and accessed one of the many dubious VPN services from there and then in turn used a VPN tunnel to—"

"Move on, Riwal!"

The inspector had said there were two pieces of news.

"So, it wasn't easy on a Saturday and it took longer than we thought, but I've personally spoken to everyone on the phone. I spoke to Renan Budig, who is the man that Rêves Maritimes, the subsidiary firm of Héros Naval, wants to build the yacht for. And I also spoke to his brother, who had the Dauphin company build him a yacht a while ago. And finally I also spoke to the owner of Dauphin himself, who was in touch with Budig's brother."

An elaborate but skilled buildup of dramatic suspense. Riwal paused, looking like he needed to gather his thoughts.

"Renan Budig had *two* quotes drawn up for the yacht, one was from Dauphin in La Rochelle like we thought. His brother had recommended it to him. Although he didn't tell the people from Héros Naval, or rather Rêves Maritimes, about this. But he did tell the owner of Dauphin about the two quotes. Renan Budig had, as he describes it, started to have his doubts about whether it was a good idea to be the first person to have a luxury boat built by this company with no experience in the sector. But then he did choose our trio's company, after all. Their price was substantially lower than Dauphin's. That was how they were planning to buy their way into the market. Aggressive, but effective."

Riwal's calls had yielded a lot more than Dupin had dared hope.

"Which means," Le Menn reasoned, "that the owner of Dauphin might have been extremely angry."

The young policewoman was correct. Still—was that enough of a reason to commit murder? Maybe it was, of course—it did happen. But clearly it was also possible that there was a lot more to the story than they knew at this point.

Riwal was not done yet. "Nolwenn is investigating the company and its owner, Denis Malraux. She has spoken to our colleagues in La Rochelle too. And they're making extensive enquiries into the company and its owner now too."

"Great." Dupin was pleased. "Perhaps," he wondered, "you should drive to La Rochelle yourself, Riwal, and have a word with the man in person. Maybe we should even drive over there together." In theory, this was a good idea; it might even be necessary given the circumstances.

"Or we have him come here." This suggestion from Nolwenn would obviously be the easiest thing to do.

"If he doesn't come willingly, we have no leverage to force him to, though. And he'll probably be damned if he's going to . . ."

Le Menn was right again.

"How do we want to play this, boss?"

Dupin couldn't decide.

"One thing, Riwal." Something he had meant to mention earlier had crossed his mind again. "Priziac said that Jodoc Luzel probably had something to do in the brewery today. That he had been trying out new beer recipes all week and possibly came here because of that. So that nothing went to *waste*, or something. What could he have meant?"

No doubt Riwal was an expert on brewing beer too.

The inspector looked like he was having a think, then went over to an aluminum table to the right of the doorway with a dozen white plastic containers underneath it. There were a handful of potbellied glasses on the table. He picked one up and took it over to one of the tanks with a small tap on the side. With something bordering on a flourish—and Le Menn and Nevou looking on in fascination—he held the glass underneath and opened the tap.

Dupin, who had followed him over, could see mainly one thing: foam. Whitish-gray foam.

Riwal swirled the glass, eying the foam critically. There was some amber-colored liquid visible, but only at the very bottom. He calmly took a sip.

He still didn't say a word.

"What are you up to?"

Dupin was impatient. But it was his own fault, he had encouraged Riwal.

"Impressive! Very aromatic, a scent of malt, berries, and peach—perhaps apricot. Some unexpected caramel too. Exquisite on the palate, a hint of bitterness, pleasantly refreshing, with"—he seemed to be trying to pin down the taste—"notes of grapefruit, I would say. Wonderfully rich, a beautiful texture in the mouth."

Riwal abruptly put the beer down and strode purposefully toward something that looked like a chest freezer lying diagonally behind the aluminum table.

It was indeed a chest freezer. He took out one of the many pouches inside it.

"Brewing beer is an extremely creative process, almost an art form. And Bretons have perfected it! This is a special kind of hops from Alsace. Aramis, a very refined flavor. Hops are one of the few raw materials required." Riwal put the pouch back, closed the freezer, and went over to the large sacks between the tanks. "This malt is completely Breton, Yec'hed Malt, it's really good. You just mix it with water, yeast, and the hops. As ever, the most important thing is the savoir faire. Take Katell's brother, Erwann, for example! He's got the knack to it with his Storlok beer!"

Dupin needed to step in. "Do you see any plausible reason why Luzel needed to come back here for his beer experiments, or not?"

Instead of answering, Riwal inspected two more tanks, coming dangerously close to the area the medical examiner had marked out as his. Riwal opened and closed some of the flaps and doors on the tanks. It looked like a meticulous inspection. Then he gave his verdict:

"No. I don't see any compelling reason. This beer has finished brewing. And it's excellent. Otherwise, yes, there would have been a reason. Because when you're at a specific point in the brewing process, you've got to move on to the next step within a certain amount of time, otherwise the beer is ruined. But that is not the case here. Perhaps he just wanted to try it. Or take a few bottles home." Riwal pointed to the large rectangular machine with the beer bottles in front of it. "That's a bottling machine, maybe he wanted to test out his creation somewhere?"

"I see."

If it hadn't been to brew beer, then why had Luzel come here? It remained a mystery. But perhaps it really had been like the inspector had speculated just now: Jodoc Luzel wanted to try his new beer. Here at the site of his passion, a passion he was determined to pursue despite the violent death of Chaboseau and the attack on Héros Naval—this would, of course, entail a certain callousness on his part. Or perhaps it was to take his mind off things? All plausible. If—and this was a big if—Priziac had told them the truth in the first place.

"I'm not too sure." Nevou did not seem satisfied with this answer. "Anyway. I've got something too."

They were almost back at the exit again.

"There have now been a dozen more reports of the suspicious stranger and all of the places he has supposedly been seen." She made an effort to sound authoritative. "Some of the reports are surprisingly similar. A man. About one meter seventy. Dark hair, slim build. Likely dark trousers. For instance, three workers from the fish market hall say they saw a person matching this description get out of a white car yesterday evening, and he was noticeably nervous. He parked the car at the end of the fish market hall, near where the shipbuilding harbor begins."

Dupin studied her. "You're taking this seriously, I assume?"

Riwal rushed to his colleague's defense: "I do think we should take it seriously. For now it just means allowing for the possibility that a person we don't know yet could be involved." He was trying hard to make it sound less mysterious. "It could of course be the henchman of one of the people we've already come across."

Dupin had been on the point of immediately contradicting him, but he held back. Although this theory wasn't completely beyond the bounds of possibility, it seemed too far-fetched for him.

The commissaire turned away and strode over to the medical examiner.

René Reglas was in the middle of a conversation with his two assistants. He pretended not to see Dupin.

"Can you say anything about the time of death yet?"

"We're now going to take the corpse to—"

"Closer to eight thirty or closer to ten forty-five?"

It was clear that Reglas was torn between the impulse to make a sharp retort and the impulse to be pragmatic and give in. He decided—looking even grumpier than he had earlier as he did so—on the latter. He had clashed with Dupin too many times before. He gave a dramatic sigh.

"Around ten thirty. But—"

"And death was caused by the blow from the bottle?"

"Yes."

"Signs of a struggle?"

"No."

Without another word, Dupin left him standing there and turned to the head of the crime scene investigation team.

"Nothing to report so far!" he remarked before Dupin could ask a question. "We're going to take the shards of glass away and have a look at them in the lab."

Dupin nodded. "Thank you!"

There was nothing more to be learned here for now.

Riwal, Le Menn, Nevou, and Dupin were back in the brewery's modern foyer. Roi Gradlon's various beers were proudly displayed on floor-to-ceiling shelves made from lots of smart red plastic boxes.

"Denis Malraux, the head of that yacht-building firm, shall we ask him to come here, boss?" Riwal asked.

"Yes, get Nolwenn to have a go."

Riwal seemed weary all of a sudden, but then he had been up since five.

"And we'll handle the alibis now," said Le Menn.

Dupin nodded.

"You do that. And keep me up to speed."

Nevou and Le Menn set off straightaway.

Dupin hesitated for a moment, then went outside too. Riwal followed him.

The commissaire needed to think. To have peace and quiet to think. Nothing fit together so far. Nothing at all. On top of this, he realized that the thought that had come to him earlier was still playing on his mind.

Last but not least, and this had to be the case for Riwal too, he was starving. He desperately needed to eat something. He could already feel the irritability and tetchiness that always set in if he ignored his stomach for too long. And—another *petit café* certainly couldn't hurt.

Dupin stopped walking, breathing in the fresh air.

"How about a quick detour to La Corniche, Riwal?"

The best *sandwicherie* for miles around. An institution in

Concarneau. Both the shop and its owners. "Jean-Yves and Dame Nicole," as it said on an oar that hung on its wall. Just a stone's throw from Claire and Dupin's house. They made heavenly sandwiches. And perfect chips. The people of Concarneau met, chatted, and swapped stories in La Corniche. Jean-Yves and Nicole knew everyone and everyone knew them.

Riwal beamed in agreement.

"I also wanted . . ." Dupin hesitated, but then steeled himself; Riwal would be the last person to make fun of odd ideas. "To discuss something with you." He hesitated again. "A strange thought. Not even a thought, I . . ." Dupin broke off.

"Absolutely, boss."

The smile on Riwal's face never faltered.

"I drove my car here, boss. Shall we meet there?"

It wasn't far. Nothing in Concarneau was far. And yet you never felt hemmed in, quite the contrary.

"Let's do that."

They set off for their cars at the same time.

Exactly four minutes later, Dupin was switching off the engine. Riwal was sure to arrive soon too.

The *sandwicherie* was in a magnificent spot. It was on the coastal road to Sables Blancs, right on the sea. A dazzlingly white building, an Atlantic blue awning with *"bar à sandwich"* written on it in white script, and on the wall above it in large lettering it read: "La Corniche." A blue bicycle outside the door and flower boxes on either side of the doorway. To the right was a long bench painted turquoise, and from there you had a fantastic view of beaches, villas, and tall pine trees. To the left you could see the sailing club, the aquarium, the institute for marine biology, and diagonally opposite was where Dupin used to live. But the most spectacular view was of the sea and the long, narrow Quai Nul, another well-known spot in town. At the end of the nineteenth century, the Quartier de la Croix, which was right on the water, had been the famous cannery quarter. There had been more than ten factories there, with several hundred female workers in dark clothes and white caps, and they had written a significant chapter in the modern history of the town over the course of decades. At first the fishing boats that came in every day—several hundred of them, there were old photographs where the water was just a sea of boats—had landed on the beaches in front of the small factories. This was pretty risky during storms and high tides so they had built a quay out into the sea. There wasn't much luck or skill involved in building it though. It took twenty years to finish and it turned out really badly anyway. Incorrectly aligned, it wasn't able to offer any protection, which is why it had earned the grim name: *nul,* or zero. But for strolling along, or sitting and admiring the view from the quay, there was hardly a more beautiful or more atmospheric spot in town.

"Well?" Jean-Yves was nodding at him from behind the counter.

"A Loch for the inspector who is just about to arrive and the usual for me, the Mataff."

Dupin's standard sandwich: pork pâté, tomato, crunchy cornichons, and fresh salad.

"Sure."

Behind the counter hung a large painting of three fishermen painted in broad brushstrokes, and higher up the wall was a genuine fisherman's cap.

"And a portion of chips." Riwal's likes and dislikes were as familiar to Dupin as his own. "And three *petits cafés*. And a bottle of water." It was going to be a long day. Who knew when they would next get something to eat.

Dupin's gaze fell on the large sign: *Les Règles de la Plage,* "the Rules of the Beach." And unlike what you might have expected, they did not list what was forbidden, but the opposite: what you absolutely had to do. Strict guidelines. Among them was *"jouer avec les vagues,"* "play with the waves," as well as *"admirer les couchers du soleil,"* "admire the sunsets." All of those things seemed a long way off right now.

"Are you making progress?" Jean-Yves asked casually.

"Slowly," muttered Dupin.

"Well. It was on the radio just now. The wine merchant is dead."

He spread a generous amount of pâté onto Dupin's baguette.

"The mayor announced that all of the events since yesterday relate to a business matter involving a certain group of people—" There was a pause as he cut the cornichons. "—and that there's no cause for alarm for the general public. And also that the festival can go ahead as planned today."

"Excuse me?"

This was beyond belief. But—of course, it fit with Kireg and the philosophy he had revealed yesterday evening. The opening of the Été en Fête! They would celebrate no matter what.

"This was after the report about what happened in the brewery. The mayor addressed the people of the town directly."

He had two options: lose his temper and intervene or just put up with it.

"Do you have any solid leads yet?"

Jean-Yves put the lid on the sandwich.

"No."

"Are you eating here or shall I pack this up?"

"We're staying here." Riwal was sure to arrive any moment now.

Jean-Yves handed the sandwich to Dupin.

"And the great stranger?" Jean-Yves got out the *andouille* for Riwal's sandwich, a proper Breton sausage not for the faint-hearted that consisted mainly of offal. Then he spread salted butter on the sandwich and put ham, gherkins, and salad on top. "Just a ghost?"

"Here I am, boss."

Riwal spied his almost finished sandwich and his eyes gleamed.

"So he's not going to come to Concarneau. He just doesn't see the point." Riwal meant Malraux, the head of the company in La Rochelle. "During the phone call he was, shall we say, a lot less friendly than he was earlier. Three of our colleagues are on the spot now, grilling him. He's freaking out. I don't think he'll be—very cooperative anymore."

Jean-Yves handed Riwal the finished sandwich.

"Have a seat," he said, "I'll bring the rest over to you."

The commissaire and the inspector sat down on the idyllic bench in front of the *sandwicherie* straightaway.

"What do we do, boss?" Riwal was already chewing. "Shall we drive to La Rochelle? Shall I do it on my own? Or both of us?"

Dupin wasn't sure yet. A trip like that would take practically the whole day. "I should really pay the mayor a visit."

Because of the outrageous public statement he had made. But mainly because of the obvious bitterness to the clash over the brewery issue between himself on one side and Chaboseau and Luzel on the other. It was getting more and more complicated. The brewery dispute seemed to be more important than they had assumed. But shipbuilding still appeared to be involved. And maybe some other issue too, something that specifically related to Chaboseau.

So this meant: there were three issues. Could someone be infested with fleas, lice, and a third pest at the same time?

"No problem, I can question Monsieur Malraux on my own."

The inspector took another bite of his sandwich. Dupin was about to take another bite too but the piercing noise of his phone stopped him. He cast a reluctant glance at the screen.

Kadeg, his other inspector. Surely this couldn't be happening.

"Kadeg—what's wrong?" He had called just yesterday, after all.

"I've just heard about the death of the wine merchant. I'm sitting on the beach with the kids, Sables Blancs, where the slide—"

"What do you want, Kadeg?"

"If I can help in any way"—it sounded, and this was some comfort, genuinely desperate—"then just say."

"Is your wife back?"

"No, not yet, but I wanted to know how the investigation was going."

"Then let's talk again another time, Kadeg. *Au revoir.*"

A second later Dupin had hung up.

"He's not finding it easy," Riwal remarked drily. "I get it."

"There's something else I wanted to ask you, Riwal."

Like Kadeg, Dupin was not finding this easy.

"Yes?" His inspector looked inquisitively at him.

The commissaire got his notebook out.

"In this crime novel by Georges Simenon, *The Yellow Dog*—among the characters in it," Dupin wondered how to put this, "you said yesterday that there was a doctor, a pharmacist, and a wine merchant, right?"

"Right. But as I say, the pharmacist isn't a main character, the doctor is retired, and then there's also a journalist who writes for a paper in Brest. The pharmacist stays mainly on the sidelines. For example, he finds out on the first night of the investigation that the Pernod in the Amiral is poisoned with strychnine."

Even Dupin didn't know why he couldn't stop thinking about this.

"And the wine merchant," Riwal finished up his detailed report, "isn't one of the central characters either. He gets shot and wounded right at the beginning and then doesn't appear again."

Dupin had read a whole series of Maigret novels and really liked them. But that was many years ago now. And *The Yellow Dog* had not been one of them.

"Tell me a bit more, Riwal." He had his pen in his right hand, making notes every now and again. It took Riwal a moment to register what the commissaire had said. It wasn't every day that he quizzed him about crime novels.

"These three men, who are some of the notables, the wealthy, powerful families in town, form a kind of men's club. They meet in the Amiral in the evenings, they smoke, they drink. They call it 'The last spot left for jolly fellows from Concarneau.' And they do business there too." Riwal paused. "Are you thinking of something specific, boss?"

"No, no, just keep talking."

"But the real heroes are Emma, the waitress in the Amiral, and her lover, who is sent to his ruin by the three men."

"I see."

"Et voilà." Jean-Yves put down a tray with coffee, water, and a large portion of chips on the bench between them, and next to it some little bowls with different sauces: sauce Américaine, barbecue, and mayonnaise.

With a gesture, Dupin signaled to Riwal to help himself. Which he did without hesitation.

"And they're also on the hunt for some 'great stranger' in the crime novel, by the way."

Dupin took a few chips too.

"Do you believe there's a 'stranger' in our case?"

"No," replied the inspector with surprising confidence. "But strangers play a special role in Concarneau's stories and legends." Dupin was reminded of his bizarre dream.

"Hmmm. And in the end, who murdered who in this book?"

Riwal took a swig of coffee.

"There's no dead person at all. The wine merchant survives, the strychnine attack fails, and a supposed crime scene with blood in a car is just a stunt because the journalist fakes his own murder. A red herring. Incidentally, the mayor of the town also turns up in the book, and he's an utterly infuriating character who is constantly putting pressure on the commissaire. Which doesn't," Riwal seemed delighted by this, "bother Maigret in the slightest."

Dupin was silent for a while. He sighed. "Well, that is a little odd."

Riwal looked uncertainly at the commissaire.

"You mean the—parallels with our case?"

Dupin nodded.

"Well, yes. But every small town has these people. They're

permanent fixtures: the doctor, the pharmacist, the mayor . . . And of course, there's so much that's completely different in our case."

The tables had turned. Riwal gently telling Dupin that reality and fantasy were two different things.

"More importantly," Riwal added, "what would it mean? That someone is committing murder using the book as their guide? Reenacting *The Yellow Dog* in some sick way? Which wouldn't even really make sense, you could imitate it much better and more accurately. And what would the motive be?" Riwal was trying hard to sound matter-of-fact. "Are we dealing with a lunatic? A psychopath? A serial killer?"

Dupin didn't even attempt to give an answer. He didn't have one.

Riwal was right, right about everything. It was just that Dupin had noticed it playing on his mind ever since the gallery when Françoise had mentioned *The Yellow Dog* and the murder of the wine merchant.

Dupin reached for his second *petit café*.

"It's as if the three of them were struck by a curse."

"One moment, Riwal."

Dupin got to his feet—having finished his coffee—and ordered another one.

Then he sat next to the inspector again and they both fell to thinking.

"You know the story of the selkies, don't you? The ancient sea folk, the rulers of the depths who control the elements and live in profound harmony with the water and the winds . . . Perhaps what's happening here is like that story."

Now Riwal was drifting off into the fantastical, after all.

The story was part of the town's core repertoire, just like the story of Emilia and Siprian, the desperate lovers. It was about the ugly side of humans, about jealousy, resentment, greed, callousness, stupidity, rabble-rousing, violence, revenge. In the abridged version of the legend, the love between a young man called Pierre and a beautiful selkie called Mauve ended in a terrible catastrophe. A group of residents from the Ville Close, envious of their happiness, organized a dreadful hunt, and at the end Mauve was brutally speared by several harpoons. So the selkies took their revenge on the people responsible for the tragedy with tireless determination. They died one after another.

"The merciless curse was only broken when the last person responsible departed this life," Riwal finished. "At least then there wouldn't be any mystery about what's been happening anymore. If we had an old curse on our hands too, I mean. By the way, there really was a couple in the Old Town once called Mauve and Pierre, and their story ended tragically. The wife was brutally murdered."

Dupin was silent.

"So, boss," Riwal broke the silence after a while, "what do you think? It's more than three hours to La Rochelle."

"I . . ."

"Salut, Georges!"

Dupin looked up.

Claire. And her parents.

All wearing light summer clothes. Claire's father was wearing a straw hat with a black band, Claire's mother was wearing a wide-brimmed black hat with a flamboyant pink floral pattern. Along with sort of loose-fitting black linen dungarees and red espadrilles.

Before he knew what was happening, Dupin was being greeted with kisses and hugs.

"Ah, at last, it was about time!" Claire's mother rushed to clarify. "We're just on our way into town. Doing a bit of puttering and shopping. And then we wanted to have lunch. In that new restaurant at the fishing harbor."

Dupin was still too bewildered to say anything at all, but he had stood up, at any rate.

"I thought there was a murder case." Hélène's tone of voice turned stern and she took her hat off with a theatrical gesture. "Yet another person has just been killed. Shouldn't you be on your way there?"

"They're talking it over, Hélène!" said Claire's father, and he meant this as a genuine defense. "That's work too. Plus, even the police have to eat now and again."

"But . . ." Hélène started to retort.

Claire interrupted her just in case: "We'll leave you in peace now, Georges."

Claire's mother wasn't admitting defeat that easily. "But we'll have dinner together tonight. Otherwise we just won't see you at all, Georges."

"That's not up to Georges, unfortunately." Claire made a point of starting to move away and Dupin was extremely grateful to her.

"But we—"

Dupin's phone. A good moment to be interrupted.

It was Nolwenn.

With an astonishingly conciliatory "All right, I can see work is calling . . ." Claire's mother turned away now too and followed her daughter.

Riwal had been impassive this entire time, his expression not giving anything away.

"Nolwenn, we're just in the middle—"

"We've got it, Monsieur le Commissaire! I think this is the solution!"

Dupin couldn't believe his ears.

Nolwenn's words had echoed so loudly down the phone that Riwal could hear them clearly too.

"We're a good bit closer, at least. It's nothing like what we thought earlier."

Nolwenn was keeping them in suspense.

"Maybe it's very simple."

Dupin put her on speakerphone; this way he wouldn't have to repeat everything for Riwal in a moment.

"Just tell us, Nolwenn."

"I know Dorien Meheut through my husband. The hotshot lawyer from Rennes, he's an expert in commercial law."

She left a pause for Dupin to comment. He didn't. Dupin had never heard the name before.

"We have him to dinner now and again."

To this day, Dupin did not know exactly what Nolwenn's husband did for a living. It was clear that he constantly had dealings with all sorts of people, from oyster fishermen to beekeepers, and from pub landlords to fire chiefs, politicians and, as Dupin was now finding out, lawyers. Sometimes it sounded like he was in "import-export," sometimes like he was a consultant or business coach. At the beginning, over the first few years, Dupin had worried about this from time to time, but he had grown used to it.

"He has just reached out to me in confidence. With some

concern about his attorney-client privilege. I told him he needn't worry about that."

"And what . . . ?"

"Jodoc Luzel contacted him. Two months ago. He, Chaboseau, and Priziac had fallen out. There were serious disagreements. Luzel was considering suing them both. It was to do with the new yacht business, Rêves Maritimes. He would have preferred to set it up himself. Luzel claimed the whole thing was his idea. So he demanded the most shares, even more than at Héros Naval. The other two were being awkward. So it was the old story. Money. Greed. People always wanting more."

"Crazy."

Riwal's exclamation hit the nail on the head. Had the three men been at war with one another and then their war escalated drastically?

"So did the other two know that Luzel had contacted a lawyer and wanted to sue them?"

Riwal's question was crucial. If they hadn't known anything about it then this story would fall apart.

"Monsieur Meheut doesn't know."

"I'll need to speak to our pharmacist very soon."

"I think so too."

"When did the lawyer last speak to the wine merchant, Nolwenn?"

"Last week. But only briefly. They agreed to meet the following week or the week after that, to discuss legal action against Chaboseau and Priziac."

"Thanks, Nolwenn. I'll be in touch again."

"Just one more thing, very quickly: two of the shipyard workers have been released from the hospital. And the other two are also doing a lot better. But unfortunately they haven't thought of anything that might help solve the case."

Dupin was relieved to hear they were doing better.

"All right. Talk soon."

Nolwenn ended the call.

Dupin walked around the corner, paid, and said good-bye to Jean-Yves. A moment later he was back with Riwal.

"There's one thing I'm still not clear about." The inspector's brow was furrowed. "If this is because of a fight between the three of them—how do the attack on the shipyard and the threatening email fit into that? The two murders, fine. Maybe at a stretch the attack too . . . But the threatening email?"

"Come on."

Dupin crossed the street; he hadn't parked his car far away. He had the phone to his ear yet again.

It took a little while for the call to connect.

"Hello?"

The pharmacist sounded out of breath.

"Commissaire Dupin here—where are you at the moment, Monsieur Priziac?"

"I have errands to do."

"What kind of errands?"

"Private ones."

Dupin was gripped by a sense of unease. As if they needed to act swiftly.

"I'll ask you again, Monsieur Priziac: Where are you right now?"

"That's none of your business."

Dupin had reached his car, Riwal close behind him.

Dupin was frustrated; he should have given some thought

beforehand to how he was going to manage this conversation. They needed to be extremely cautious now. After what they had just learned, anything was possible. Even Priziac being on the run. Or at least planning to go on the run.

"Monsieur Priziac," Dupin started again, "we've still got lots of questions about your friend Luzel. Personal questions. As he has no family, you will probably be the person who can best answer them for us." Dupin was trying not to sound either too urgent or too vague, but the contrast with his tough approach at the beginning of the conversation must have looked suspicious.

"I've got things to do at my pharmacy in Le Cabellou. I'm just on my way there."

Clearly this had worked.

"Then let's meet there, Monsieur Priziac."

An uncertain silence. He couldn't hear any car noises. Or any noises that would have given away where Priziac was.

"Fine."

Dupin could tell how much effort it had taken him to agree to this.

"When will you be there?"

"In fifteen minutes, I'd say."

"See you soon."

The call ended.

"You're coming with me, Riwal."

"I'll take my car, I might head straight to La Rochelle from there."

"All right." Dupin opened the door of his Citroën.

As he was getting in, he paused suddenly.

"Wait, Riwal!" He got back out of the car. A thought had struck him. An extremely important thought.

Riwal had just got to his car.

"The wine merchant's house—it's in Le Cabellou, isn't it?"

"Right."

"Do we know where, exactly?"

"Avenue des Glénan, it's the big villa right by the Plage Cabellou. Why . . ."

Riwal paused—the penny had dropped, you could tell from his expression. "Of course! Well, yeah, it's possible."

"Are any of our team there yet?"

Dupin had already got back into his car. He started up the engine.

"Not yet, I don't think. The crime scene investigators were going to head there as soon as they were done in the brewery."

"See you there, Riwal."

"Speaking of crime scene investigators"—Riwal raised his eyebrows—"not only could they not find a cell phone on Luzel, they couldn't find any keys either, no key ring, nothing."

The commissaire pulled the door shut and reversed with his tires screeching.

"And you think he's at Luzel's house?"

Nolwenn's voice came rattling out of the hands-free car kit, loud and piercing.

"It's a possibility."

Maybe this was the place where Priziac had "errands to do." Perhaps he wanted to go and get something. Get rid of something. Papers, documents, any evidence. Dupin had had a strange feeling during their phone call. The pharmacist was determined not to say where he was; there had to be a reason for that. But of course, Dupin could be wrong.

"We need an arrest warrant, Nolwenn, just in case."

Dupin had reached the last roundabout before the long straight road that led to the Cabellou peninsula. It was once mainly the "well-to-do" who lived here—just like in the Sables Blancs and Corniche neighborhoods—but these days they owned holiday homes here. Magnificent villas among old pines, maritime pines, and palms, a life lived amidst lush vegetation and exquisite peace. Dreamy beaches with fine white sand among craggy granite boulders, not to mention one large picture-perfect beach with stylish old seaside resort charm. Steeped in tradition, you could picture the resort exactly the way it was when it sprang up at the end of the nineteenth century.

"No problem." Arrest warrants were one of Nolwenn's—many—specialties. "Do you really think it was Priziac who murdered Luzel?"

Dupin put his foot down again once he left the roundabout. He could see Riwal's car in the rearview mirror.

"Let's just say it's plausible."

"And that he carried out the attack on the shipyard too? Or arranged for it to be carried out? And wrote the supposed threatening email?"

"Possibly."

There were so many plausible scenarios right now.

Something else had just occurred to Dupin—the answer to the question Riwal had asked earlier but that Dupin hadn't replied to at the time. The pharmacist was the only one he and Riwal had spoken to about the threatening email. It was he who had shown it to them. Maybe Priziac had written it himself as a diversionary tactic, a kind of smokescreen.

"If so, Priziac is probably the one who murdered Docteur

Chaboseau too. Or"—Nolwenn was thinking through a different scenario—"it was Luzel who killed Chaboseau. And then today he became a victim himself . . . In any case"—she had to stop her thoughts running away with her—"I'll take care of the arrest warrant."

"I'll speak to you soon, Nolwenn. We need to fight our way to the heart of the matter at last . . ."

"You do know what prize you used to get for winning the traditional wrestling matches in the Ville Close, don't you, Monsieur le Commissaire?" She didn't wait for a response. "A whole pig! A big one!"

Pigs, Dupin knew this much, had been among the most valuable things in the impoverished lives of the locals over the centuries. There were plenty of old photos where people were taking pigs out for walks on leads through the alleyways of the old town, just like people do with dogs nowadays. Dupin was also aware that, historically, the Concarnese had a great passion for wrestling—but he had never heard how these two passions were linked before.

"So! To the pig!"

This was intended as some pithy encouragement from Nolwenn as she ended the phone call. One thing was for sure, anyway: this investigation really did feel like a wrestling match.

Dupin braked.

He had arrived at the peninsula, and to his right was the Belle-Étoile beach. He reached Avenue des Glénans. He knew which house he needed: a magnificent villa in the south of the peninsula, set right on the sea. A park-like plot of land enclosed by a stone wall, meter-high bushes, and trees. A simple white gate, no name on it.

Right next to the villa was a path to the wonderful Plage Cabellou—that's why Dupin knew it; he particularly liked this beach. There was a nostalgic feel to the place. The sea was riddled with dark rocks. A large, erratic boulder lay in the middle of the beach, shimmering, almost alien, as if it had come from outer space, tumbling straight out of the sky onto the sand.

Even from a distance, Dupin could see Priziac's car. A silver SUV—Dupin had noticed it at the pharmacist's house yesterday. His instinct had been correct.

"Damn it!" he blurted out. Priziac had probably come straight from the brewery. He would have had plenty of time alone if so. Why hadn't they thought of this earlier?

Dupin parked his Citroën right in front of the tall, closed gate. Riwal, still right behind him, stopped too, and they jumped out of their cars at the same time.

The gate was not locked.

A moment later they were inside the sprawling park. And practically bumping into the pharmacist, who had just come out of the house. He seemed to be in a hurry too.

Priziac froze, seeming momentarily thunderstruck. His expression was one of deep frustration. His hair, usually so carefully smoothed back, was tousled.

"What are you doing here?"

"You're clearly the one who needs to answer that." Dupin had planted himself menacingly close to Priziac. "What on earth are you doing at Luzel's house?"

Unadulterated rage flashed in the pharmacist's eyes.

"I've just lost a friend, I . . ."

"What were you doing in his house? What were you up to?"

Dupin had no time for games.

"I wanted to say my good-byes to . . ."

This was ridiculous. He was openly mocking them.

"How did you get into the house, Monsieur Priziac? With your friend's key, I presume."

"It was open. Jodoc rarely locked it, people generally don't here, you should really know that, Commissaire. It's still open now."

"Surely even you don't believe that."

Dupin was firmly focused on the most important things: "We know about the row between the three of you. We know Luzel had got himself a lawyer to take action against you."

Priziac flinched. But he composed himself again straightaway.

"Oh." A pointedly sarcastic tone. "You mean our little differences of opinion about the shares in Rêves Maritimes? That's just ridiculous, young man! We were business partners. Real business partners. It wasn't the first time we'd had different points of view."

"*Little differences of opinion?*" Now it was Riwal who was aghast. "That's what you call two murders and an attack that—"

A loud, fake sigh.

"Oh, so that's the way the wind is blowing, I see. So you think—"

"You're claiming you knew your friend and business partner wanted to take legal action against you?"

"He got himself a lawyer—so what? Jodoc wanted to do the deal by himself, we weren't inclined to agree to that. So yes, it was a genuine difference of opinion." He became serious. "That's just how it is sometimes. And sure, it could definitely have ended up in a legal dispute. But that would inevitably have been fol-

lowed by a settlement! We would all have known," this was the
height of cynicism, "how the law saw it. Yes, Jodoc told us that
he would go that far. He—"

Dupin interrupted him: "I'm going to ask this again: did
Jodoc Luzel openly tell you that he would be taking legal action
against you?"

"It wasn't a pleasant thought, of course, far from it—but it
wasn't the end of the world. If friends do business together, they
need to be capable of handling complex situations. And believe
me, we were! It was Jodoc himself who brought three excellent
bottles of Château Margaux 2005 when we met on the terrace
at my house the evening before last. We sat together for a long
time—does that sound like a falling-out, Commissaire?" It
was strange to think of it, but just yesterday Dupin had seen
the lounge chairs where the three men had relaxed. Three men,
of whom two were now dead. Priziac lowered his voice. "Don't
go getting the wrong idea: Pierre and I obviously consulted our
lawyers long before then."

If things really were the way he described them—and anything was possible with this trio—then the story that moments
ago had seemed explosive enough to explain everything would
now just go up in smoke.

"Can you prove any of this?"

"That he had told us?"

"Exactly."

"Didn't he tell his lawyer? That Meheut chap?" Priziac gave
a condescending snort. "If not, then yes, it will obviously be
tough for me. Now, since—" He stopped short as if something
had just occurred to him for the first time. "Seriously, though.
Believe me, Commissaire, when the three of us spoke, we came

very close to a solution to our problem. We didn't have it yet, I'll give you that, but we would have found it soon. Without any lawyers."

Why hadn't he just said this before? Did he think they were stupid?

"What would this solution have looked like?" Riwal asked sharply.

"We would have given in a little. Not much, though. You need to counter hard-line positions with hard-line positions, even with friends. And now and again," Priziac's eyes flashed, "you send a little signal."

"And I take it there are no witnesses, of course, to this claim that you came pretty close to reaching a solution to your dispute yesterday?"

Dupin didn't believe a word Priziac said.

"I obviously have no idea what Jodoc told his lawyer. Or whether they spoke on the phone again after our meeting."

Every sentence was just a taunt.

The hint of a nasty smile appeared on Priziac's face. "But let's turn the tables for a minute now, young man. If you keep up this ridiculous barrage of questions, how are you even going to find the time to do something about the attack on our company? And the murder of my two friends? Who sent us that anonymous email? That would at least be a start."

These last sentences were the final straw. Dupin's voice became quieter and quieter, colder and colder. "We'll just do it this way now, Monsieur Priziac: we will arrest you. Provisionally to begin with, but right this instant."

Dupin let his words sink in and then added, "You, Monsieur Brecan Priziac, are suspected of the murder of Jodoc Luzel."

The pharmacist gave an indignant laugh.

"Without an arrest warrant? This is an absolute farce—and you know it. I've heard about Commissaire Dupin's—*unconventional* methods before but I'd say that's going too far, even for you."

"Don't worry. The arrest warrant will be available any moment," Dupin bluffed. "And I wouldn't even need it. Not for a provisional arrest. For that, there just needs to be an acute suspicion and an acute flight risk, for example. And I hereby note both of these things are present in this case."

Priziac stared at him in disbelief.

"You're serious."

"You wouldn't believe how serious I am."

Several cars were approaching the villa. A moment later they were visible through the open gate: Nevou, Le Menn, and the crime scene investigators.

"I'm going to ask you one last time: What were you doing in Jodoc Luzel's house? It's over now, anyway—cooperate."

Priziac took a phone out of his trouser pocket. "I think from now on you'll only be speaking to my lawyer."

Without waiting for a response from Dupin, he walked a few meters away.

Nevou and Le Menn hurried over.

"Have the house and grounds scoured with a fine-tooth comb!" Dupin greeted them.

Riwal was keeping an eye on the pharmacist as he paced up and down the garden, speaking on the phone.

Le Menn looked at Dupin and for once she was at a loss. "And what exactly are we looking for in the grounds?"

"Maybe Priziac wanted to dispose of something. And took

it out of the house but hid it. He would have had enough time for that."

"All right."

The policewoman turned around and went over to her colleagues from the crime scene investigation team to pass on the instructions.

Dupin turned to Nevou. "What's the situation with the alibis?"

"Basically, none of them have a watertight alibi. Not a single one. I'll go through them. So, Docteur Derien—"

Priziac came over to them and aggressively cut the policewoman off: "My lawyer says not to be intimidated by you in any way, so I will be driving to my pharmacy now, Monsieur le Commissaire. He will be in touch. *Au revoir.*"

He was already heading for the gate.

Riwal was at the ready; Dupin gave him the nod. The inspector intercepted the pharmacist before he even reached the gate.

"You're coming with me to the station right now, that's all you're going to do, Monsieur Priziac," Riwal informed him, without batting an eyelid. "Feel free to call your lawyer again."

"Outrageous! You're committing false imprisonment . . ."

Dupin turned away. He didn't feel like hearing even a single word of the ensuing tirade.

The commissaire's mood darkened by the minute as he looked around Luzel's house.

They couldn't find anything unusual. While they had found a charger, they hadn't found a laptop—or any external hard drive or USB sticks—and no cell phone either. Again, there was just a charger for one. If it had been Priziac who wanted to dispose of a laptop and cell phone, he would have had plenty of time. The thing that made Dupin's mood darkest of all was that they needed at the very least to consider the possibility that Priziac had been telling the truth earlier. More or less. That the three friends had dealt with the conflict openly. If this were the case, maybe it really was all to do with rivalry from other companies in the yacht-building sector. If that was the case, the postponed meeting with Monsieur Malraux, the owner of Dauphin, would need to go right back to the top of his to-do list again. And putting this theory back on the table would mean—and this was much more devastating—being confronted yet again with the sense that nothing quite fit together. Even the order of events didn't make sense.

Dupin left the house and walked through the garden toward the sea. If Priziac had taken something out of the house to get rid of it, the sea would have been a good place for it.

The grounds were separated from the beach by a tall fence with a narrow gate in it. There were two options: stretches of the finest sandy beach or flat, light gray granite rocks that were just right for lying on.

Dupin walked up and down the beach once, keeping an eye out for craggy niches and crevasses. He didn't find anything, of course.

He stopped next to quite a large rock.

The view was phenomenal. You could see as far as the magical Glénan archipelago, which looked incredibly close today. You could see the individual islands, Penfret most clearly, as well as the lighthouse and the dazzlingly bright Caribbean-looking Saint-Nicolas Island. There were days when the sea created optical illusions like a telescope or telephoto lens. And days when things that were close seemed far away. When the sea worked in tandem with temperature, air pressure, humidity, and the incidence of light, it could make things disappear and reappear, just like a breathtaking magic trick.

"The crime scene investigation team are about to come down to the beach too."

Le Menn had come and stood next to Dupin; he hadn't heard her coming.

"They still haven't found anything of interest, unfortunately. They—"

Dupin's phone rang.

Nolwenn. Maybe she had good news at least.

"Yes?"

"We can't get it, Monsieur le Commissaire!" Nolwenn was beside herself. "It's hopeless."

"What do you mean?"

"The arrest warrant. For Priziac. The magistrate didn't think it was enough, not even I could change his mind. And his wife couldn't either, she's a good friend of mine. Like I say: it's hopeless."

In all his years of working with Nolwenn, he had very, very rarely heard these words coming from her mouth.

"Don't worry about it, Nolwenn. To be honest, I don't even know if . . ."

Dupin broke off. He couldn't think straight right now. He needed time to think. Peace and quiet.

"Do you not even think the pharmacist is the murderer anymore?"

Dupin sighed. "I don't know. I get the feeling we're right back to square one."

"Now is not the time to give up, Monsieur le Commissaire. We just need to keep thoroughly investigating the leads we already have."

Dupin had begun to circle the rock. The clear water a few meters away sparkled an emerald green.

"Just think of Six Cent Soixante-Deux! Think what that little seal has to overcome! And all by itself, too."

Nolwenn was bringing out the big guns.

"The next thing on the agenda"—her tone of voice became matter-of-fact—"is the meeting with the owner of Dauphin. I just spoke to our colleagues in La Rochelle again. Well, we know one thing at least: Malraux has a seriously bad temper. Apparently he made a real fuss. And he has called in his lawyer too. The lawyer would be at the meeting with Riwal now, no matter what happens. Is the inspector still going on his own?"

"Yes."

"Great. Then I'll arrange it all. And I'll tell Riwal that he needs to let Priziac go. Pity."

Nolwenn hung up.

Dupin was standing next to Le Menn again. They started walking along side by side. "So what were you saying about the alibis? You said nobody had a watertight alibi?"

"Evette Derien claims she had a lie-in till ten o'clock today, alone, then had breakfast till eleven, also alone."

Le Menn was reading out the notes from her phone.

"And what about . . ." Dupin didn't finish his sentence.

Something had struck him. He should have thought of it sooner! He reached for his phone without any further explanation.

"Yes, Monsieur le Commissaire?"

"Nolwenn, I want someone tailing the pharmacist. Following him everywhere he goes. It doesn't matter if he notices."

"The order has already been given, Nevou is going to do it. She's just leaving."

He really didn't know what he would do without Nolwenn.

"I . . . Thanks. Speak to you soon, then."

Le Menn continued her report.

"The mayor has lots of meetings today. Prestigious meetings. They're particularly important to him given the current situation. The first few events of Été en Fête have been very well attended, by the way. We Concarnese won't let our festivals be ruined that easily."

She was right.

"So." Le Menn focused on the alibis again: "The mayor was at the grand opening of the Édition 2018 des Vieilles Coques on time, at eight thirty." The annual parade of dozens of wonderful old wooden boats that came from all over Brittany and sailed into the harbor one after another to a rapturous welcome.

"Then at eleven he was at the Chants des Marins, the famous sailors' choir, and he also did a quick welcome there. He claims"—she gave an irritated roll of her eyes—"he was at the boat parade until exactly nine thirty-five, which we haven't been able to corroborate yet. All we know is that he was at the choir performance on time at eleven o'clock. Apparently he went home briefly between the two events to get changed, according to his own statement. The thing about getting changed is probably true, he was wearing different clothes at the second event."

It was a good thing she had checked that straightaway.

"Without witnesses, it's hard to find out how long he was really at home. His wife was out. In any case: he could have easily made it to the brewery and back again in the intervening time."

"Very true. I'd like to speak to him again anyway."

"One way you could do that is by going to the big Poissonnade in the car park in front of the fish market hall at two thirty this afternoon; he's going to give a speech there. The topic is 'Fishing: Concarneau's past, present, and future!'"

At this stage, Dupin knew all of the most important types of fish in the Blue Town. He had had to learn them off by heart under the watchful eye of both Nolwenn and Riwal: haddock, hake, sardines, monkfish, langoustines, and tuna.

"So that would be a good opportunity to catch the mayor," Le Menn added.

Dupin glanced at his watch. It was 1:35. That gave him another fifty-five minutes. That would work out quite well.

"Great. And the others?"

"Madame Chaboseau says she was home alone. The whole time. Until her son came over and then you came. She says there has been 'quite a lot to do' since the death of her husband."

That's the way it always was: death was followed by a lot of admin.

"And according to his own statement, Félix Chaboseau left home at nine twenty-five. His wife has confirmed this to us. Sieren Cléac has been at the cannery since seven o'clock this morning, half an hour before you got there. She has probably only just left her office. But it would have been possible for her to leave her office briefly without being noticed any time." A short pause. "And that's it. So they're all still in the running."

"I need to have a bit of a think, Le Menn, I need some time."

"Got it." The young policewoman was as unfazed as ever.

"I'll be at the Poissonnade at exactly two thirty."

"Shall I come with you?"

"I . . . Yes, please do."

"See you then."

"One more question, Le Menn." Dupin ran a hand through his hair. "Have you read *The Yellow Dog*?"

"Back at school. I was born here."

"Do you remember the plot?"

"Only vaguely, to be honest."

"What crimes did those three powerful men actually commit? Riwal said something about them being serious criminals."

"They ruined a young man's life. They had him sail to America with contraband, I think. It involved smuggling. Or drugs. I can't remember. In any case, he makes it back somehow and then it's about revenge or something. I'd need to read it again. It's been a long time."

Three men from the crime scene investigation team had turned up and were searching the beach, their eyes riveted on the ground.

Dupin set off. He would walk along the seafront and get back to his car via the beach path.

It was one of Dupin's favorite spots in Concarneau—and admittedly he had plenty. But he definitely didn't have so many favorites because of an indiscriminate, Dupinesque enthusiasm, it was just because of how many objectively extraordinary places there were in the area—in other words: the entirety of Brittany was extraordinary.

He came here whenever he was in this neck of the woods. He came here at lunchtime sometimes, with a sandwich from Jean-Yves or a bacon quiche from Maurite at the covered market. It was the ideal spot to think without being disturbed. Exactly what he needed right now. There was nobody for miles around, not even today, on this gorgeous Saturday in early summer. It had been a spontaneous decision to come here, to this rugged little beach that was just a few hundred meters from Luzel's house. It was between two headlands, the landscape was charming and beautiful, the scenery fit for a painter.

You could see the opposite shore, an old hamlet called Pouldohan, then out across the long untouched beach as far as Trévignon. In the shallow waters, the sunbeams made dancing patterns on the seabed that Dupin loved.

You could walk over the rocks at the edge to get to the next little beach, and if you kept going you got to the sandbanks at the mouth of the inlet.

Dupin had almost reached the first sandbank and was climbing over some particularly jagged rocks, almost stumbling a few times. Which was mainly because he was flipping through his notebook as he walked. He could have just sat on one of the rocks, but nothing helped him think quite like walking did. He had always been in his element while walking, especially since Claire had read about it in one of her science magazines and explained in great detail how time passed more slowly for something or someone in motion than it did for stationary things or people. So he was actually gaining time by going for a walk or jog. He couldn't remember the exact logic of this phenomenon anymore. But he remembered the gist of it.

His phone rang. It sounded even louder in the silence.

It was Riwal.

"I just wanted to say that I'm on my way. It's all been sorted out. Oh yes, and I let the pharmacist go, bloody annoying. He's on his way to one of his pharmacies now."

His split second of carelessness while answering the call had been long enough for Dupin to step in one of the many little rock pools. Dupin's right foot was instantly soaked.

"Anything else, Riwal?"

"No."

Well, that had really been worth it.

"When are you meeting Malraux?"

"Five o'clock. Let's see how I get on. By the way, they've just said on the radio that Six Cent Soixante-Deux is near Limerick. A bit beyond it actually, it—"

"Let's talk later, Riwal."

That couldn't be a coincidence—the seal, Nolwenn and Riwal had arranged it between them . . .

Dupin needed his peace and quiet now.

"All right, boss, speak soon then."

Dupin had reached the sandbank.

"Georges!"

He jumped. A voice. From off to one side.

"A relaxing little walk?"

Claire's mother had popped up from behind a rock and was now walking toward him across the sandbank. He could see Claire and her father now too and they were—deep in conversation—strolling along the rocks to his left.

This could not be happening.

"I've got to say"—she was standing in front of him now— "you've got it good with the police."

Her next words were shouted over at Claire and her husband: "Look who's going for a nice little walk!"

Claire and her father turned around and came toward them.

"Right over there"—Dupin pointed toward where Luzel's villa was—"we just searched a house—after another murder. We're in the middle of an operation here, Hélène, we . . ."

"I see. Hard graft." She winked at him.

"And what are you doing here?" Dupin tried to change the course of the conversation.

"Claire is showing us the most beautiful little spots in the area. Such a pity you can't be with us."

"And how are you liking it?"

"It's no Normandy, of course, but it's very pretty too."

By now Claire and her father had joined them.

If someone were to see them like this, the four of them standing here, they would think: here is a relaxed group of tourists enjoying early summer in Brittany and the breathtaking beauty of the landscape. They're enjoying the light, the feast of color that is the green and blue sea, and the temperature—it was twenty-seven or twenty-eight degrees at this stage.

"Were you at the murdered wine merchant's house?" Claire sounded serious. "We heard it on the radio."

"You hear all sorts of contradictory things: that you're just about to arrest the perpetrator and then that you don't actually have any leads," Claire's mother added.

"That sounds about right." Dupin did his best not to sound too dejected. "Both things are correct, I mean."

"Maybe taking fewer breaks would do the investigation some good."

It had sounded polite.

"But Hélène, we've been over this. He is thinking! A commissaire needs to think, it's important." Claire's father clumsily leaped to his aid once again.

Claire tried to save the situation: "We'll leave you here to keep . . ." A brief, totally unnecessary pause here, Dupin felt, ". . . working. Right, come on." She turned to her parents.

"See you later then, Georges. Catch the killer!" Hélène gave a cheery laugh. "I've always wanted to say that . . ."

With these words she turned around and caught up with her daughter and husband.

A moment later Dupin was standing by himself again on the majestic sandbank. He checked his watch. So much for his quiet thinking time. He needed to go.

The enticing smell of the tuna steaks, sardines, and mackerel cooking on the enormous charcoal grills was drifting all the way across the car park. Heavenly. The commissaire's mouth watered.

The enormous barbecue stalls on the Quai Carnot were arranged in an L shape. There were dozens of wooden tables and benches around them. And live music coming from several different directions.

The mayor's impassioned plea seemed to have had its effect: the Concarnese and the visitors from farther afield weren't letting anything spoil their festive mood. There was a real buzz about the place; people had come in droves.

It was 2:27. No sign of the mayor, the podium for his speech still empty—Dupin was standing just a few meters away. Le Menn had not turned up yet either.

Dupin hesitated. He had had an idea on the journey here from Le Cabellou. He had actually already dismissed the idea, but now the chance was right here in front of him. It was just a stone's throw away. He would—very quickly—drop in on Amélia and Alain at the newsagent's.

Just a short time later he was walking into the shop.

Alain waved to him from behind the cash register. Dupin hesitated for a moment, then strode up to the counter and reached for one of the paperbacks in the display. There was a picture of the sea on the cover, a quay wall, a smallish lighthouse, a bright sky with some clouds darkly looming. A moody photograph in black and white. On the right-hand side, almost in silhouette: a large, bright yellow dog. In enormous letters: "Georges Simenon. *Le chien jaune*."

"One of his best cases," Alain said appreciatively, apparently not finding the situation at all odd. He gave change in return for the ten euro that Dupin had held out to him. It was a thin volume.

"See you soon, Alain."

"*Bon courage*, Georges."

Dupin was outside the shop again. He slipped the paperback into the back pocket of his trousers.

The mayor's speech had started. Only a small number of the Poissonnade visitors were interested in the speech. Most of them were still single-mindedly focused on the culinary delicacies. Still, there were around twenty or thirty people crowded around the podium by now. Dupin spotted Le Menn standing next to the barbecue with the large tuna steaks.

"He won't speak for long, ten minutes, he reckoned. Then we can talk to him," she said by way of greeting.

Dupin nodded.

"Nevou got in touch. She's in position outside the pharmacy. Priziac hasn't turned up yet."

"If necessary, she can call him on some kind of pretext and find out where he is."

"I'll tell her."

The mayor had great poise, but his speech didn't avoid the usual platitudes. "Without fishing and our fishermen this town would not exist. It's our past, it's our present, and," a dramatic pause, "our future." But he got more specific: "Our fishermen here today are offering you just a small selection of the fish that come into our harbor every day. At the moment there are around seventy species handled here. That makes us the ninth-biggest fishing harbor in France. Eight thousand tons of fish are sold in the market hall every year, around a hundred fishing boats are registered here, around eight hundred fishermen. That's what I call a substantial fleet." What he neglected to mention was this: there used to be significantly more. "From nine-meter inshore fishing boats with nets to eighty-meter tuna-fishing boats"—he was going for the emotive angle—"every boat really matters for our town. As you know, sardines and tuna were, of course, very important historically! So I would particularly recommend you try them today. Tuna, *fleur de sel*, pepper, lemon, and olive oil. And grilled sardines with *piment du Léon*. Because of course, Brittany has its own *piment d'Espelette* now too." You could now get a Breton version of one of France's essential spices, the patented "*piment*" from the south of France. Kireg was doing a good job as a salesman too; Dupin's mouth was watering again. "Of course, I don't want to fail to draw your attention to the stalls of the six canneries based in Concarneau: our largest, Courtin, with its wonderful new building, then Gonidec and Goullien, as well as Délices de la Mer"—Chaboseau's investment—"Fête de la Mer, and JB Océane, which is owned by Jean Burel. Who is building a new factory right now that you absolutely must see sometime!"

Dupin was familiar with Jean Burel and his wonderful recipes, especially the *bisque de homard,* an exquisite lobster soup with vegetables, potatoes, exotic spices, and a shot of cognac; the head of the *conserverie* was a skilled cook and had sailed the seven seas for twenty years before finally setting up on his own in Concarneau.

A historical digression about the fish-canning factories followed. The speech would drag on for a little while yet—Dupin didn't believe the ten-minute estimate.

"Maybe we should go straight upstairs to Le Chantier with Kireg. One of the rooms there is still completely empty," Le Menn suggested.

Right next door to the present-day market hall—in the middle of the fishing harbor—a modern reconstruction of the old halls had been built, and it was superbly done, from an architectural point of view. There was an excellent fishmonger there and a new restaurant with a splendid view of the harbor and the Ville Close. Claire and her parents had eaten lunch there today. It had opened just a few weeks before; Claire and Dupin had "tested" it once—and liked it. Dupin remembered the restaurant had an empty side room on the first floor that he assumed would soon be a venue for big parties and receptions.

"All right." A festival was not the right place for this kind of discussion.

All of a sudden, Dupin turned to one of the men behind the grill; there was nothing else for it. "I'll take one of those, please."

Le Menn gave him a quizzical look.

"Do you want one too?"

She nodded.

"Two please, then!"

They promptly found themselves at one of the tall tables, a paper plate in front of each of them with a chunk of tuna on it. Dupin took a bite. It tasted as wonderful as it smelled. Seared on the outside, still red and raw inside, firm and tender at the same time, you could taste the sea, the *fleur de sel,* the lemon.

Le Menn nudged him in the side just as he was about to take another bite. "Look over there! Slightly to your right."

Dupin immediately saw what she meant. Whom she meant.

Evette Derien was in the crowd.

Dupin put down the plate and within moments he was standing next to her.

"Docteur Derien. What a surprise. A fan of the mayor?"

She smiled at him, that frank smile he knew from the day before. She was wearing a loose-fitting blue dress with a white collar and blue canvas shoes, both chic and casual.

"Monsieur le Commissaire—*bonjour.*"

It was clear she was not going to answer his question.

"You really do seem to have a lot in common with Kler Kireg: a love of local festivals and surfing, and now you share the chairmanship of this surf club. Which I'd imagine requires very regular meetings."

"With the fabulous waves it's got, Brittany could do so much more when it comes to surfing. So the commitment is worth it."

"Did you know about the bad blood between the mayor and Chaboseau?"

"Because of the brewery?"

"Yes."

Half listening to the mayor's speech, Dupin gathered he had somehow got onto the topic of art by this point. He was talking about how fishing had been a big motif for artists.

"I did hear about it once. But as I say, Docteur Chaboseau and I didn't"—she spoke in a friendly and solicitous way—"meet socially. To go back to the question you asked: so far, working as joint chairpeople hasn't meant Monsieur Kireg and I have met socially either. We were going to arrange to meet next week or the week after to discuss the most pressing club matters, but we haven't even managed that yet." She told him everything with disarming frankness.

There was one more point Dupin was interested in: "I've heard Madame Chaboseau was dead set against handing the entire practice over to you early."

One of Dupin's favorite techniques: just putting a statement out there. And letting it take effect. Very little made people as nervous as this did.

"I don't know anything about that. I've never had any personal dealings with her at all."

She was smiling as frankly and serenely as before.

Suddenly there came the sound of labored clapping, from just two young men, civil servants no doubt, who were trying hard to seem enthusiastic. And the mayor was leaving the podium.

Now was the moment to catch him.

"I'm afraid I've got to go, Madame Derien. Have a good day."

Even the unexpected end to the conversation couldn't throw the young doctor—her only response was another smile.

They had withdrawn to the empty room at Le Chantier, Le Menn having asked the owner whether they could use it for a little while. Charcoal-flecked carpeting, the walls painted blue and white, a balcony overhanging the harbor. They had positioned themselves in front of the large windows.

Dupin came straight to the point. "The dispute between yourself and the owners of Roi Gradlon was far more acrimonious than you let on, Monsieur Kireg. You even met Pierre Chaboseau specifically to talk about it. You didn't tell us anything about that either. At that meeting, Chaboseau threatened to move the brewery out of the town. And not just the brewery."

Kireg couldn't help it, his expression changed and he went pale. Anxious shock in his eyes, the man who so loved to come across as dynamic and poised. All the more reason for Dupin to redouble his efforts.

"Which makes you highly suspicious, of course. There are two people dead so far. Both of them were owners of the Roi Gradlon brewery." When it was put like that, it really did sound significant.

Kireg swallowed. The nonchalance he usually projected seemed to have vanished. Dupin hadn't reckoned on being able to break down his defenses this quickly.

"You'd better tell us the truth," Le Menn added.

Kireg looked back and forth between them both.

"Spit it out!"

The mayor was still hesitating, one final glance at Dupin. "I also met Pierre Chaboseau a second time, two days later. I," he faltered, "I reached an agreement with him."

As he said these last few words, Kireg tried hard to make his voice and posture a little firmer again.

"What does that mean?" Dupin asked sharply.

"Next week I'm going to present a proposal at the town council not to grant any more brewery licenses for the foreseeable future. And I think I've already got the majority required."

Dupin had been expecting something else; perhaps not an outright confession, but definitely something very different. He was at least expecting a story about the dispute becoming more acrimonious, not this one about a resolution.

"And why," asked Le Menn, "do you feel so uncomfortable about that? You made a deal, right?"

"I . . . It's—it's a question of absolutely crucial work that needs to be done to the walls and towers of the fortress in the Ville Close. The town can't raise that kind of money by itself. There's a society and Pierre Chaboseau promised to make a generous donation to the society."

"That's bribery," Le Menn shot back coolly.

Kireg gave her a filthy look.

"That's politics. All over the world. And perfectly legal, I . . ."

"Thank you, Monsieur Kireg, that's enough."

If what the mayor had just confessed was true, the brewery angle wouldn't give them a motive either.

"What is your relationship with Docteur Derien like?"

"My relationship with Docteur Derien?"

"What is the extent of your relationship?" Dupin was glad Le Menn was asking this question for him.

"You mean are we—having an affair?" asked the mayor, visibly stunned.

"That's right," confirmed the policewoman.

"No!" The mayor looked downright desperate now. "How do you make that out? We have no personal relationship whatsoever."

Dupin had to admit that right now there was nothing to suggest an affair. And even if there were? They would be two people who had each had a dispute with Chaboseau, yes, but would that really lead to the drama that had resulted in two murders?

"Fine. Then we'll let you get to your next engagement."

Le Menn—who had definitely been expecting Dupin to keep pursuing this angle—gave the commissaire a mystified look.

"Let's go."

Dupin was already on the stairs, and soon after that he was back in the hubbub of the Poissonnade.

"What are you planning?" Le Menn had caught up with him.

"I just want to check something quickly."

He had spotted the Fête de la Mer stall.

And also: Sieren Cléac.

Le Menn had noticed Dupin's searching gaze. Moments later they were at Sieren Cléac's stall. Chaboseau's company, Délices de la Mer, had its stall right next door. Although Dupin didn't know any of the staff.

Sieren Cléac was standing to one side, sorting through a pile of rather large sardine jars, and she was clearly focused on the task.

"Did you get all the sardines done?"

She spun around. She was wearing jeans and a loose-fitting black shirt, her dark blond hair tied back.

"Ah, Monsieur le Commissaire—we meet again. I've only just arrived. We're a long way from finishing all the sardines. But the festival is very important to us too, you can do good trade here." She smiled, then her expression grew serious. "So awful, there being another murder not long after we met. I've been thinking about it all day."

"Have—have you thought of anything else that might help us, Madame Cléac—since this morning, I mean?"

She looked at the commissaire, just as stunned as the young policewoman.

"Me?" She didn't seem to know what to say. "No." She shook her head firmly.

"Good luck, then. With the trade today, I mean. And with the rest of the sardines."

"I . . . you too—good luck to you too, Monsieur le Commissaire."

Dupin left the stall, Le Menn following close behind. Within the first few words of their conversation, the commissaire had been struck by the same depressing feeling he had had earlier with Derien and the mayor. He could speak to everyone a dozen more times and he still wouldn't find out anything that would help them make any progress. They had reached a dead end in the investigation.

"Damn it."

These words were charged with all of his frustration. Le Menn gave him a worried look.

Dupin wove his way through the crowd of people, bass

thudding in his ears; he didn't stop until just before the edge of the harbor.

"I've got to . . ." He broke off. Then started again. "I've got a few things to take care of. Phone calls and things."

"Of course." Le Menn understood. "I'll go to the station in the meantime and see Nolwenn."

"Great idea."

Maybe Nolwenn had found out something else, after all. It would be a while before they heard anything from Riwal about Dauphin. Dupin had an idea for how he could use this time.

"See you later then, Commissaire."

"See you later."

He was well aware of how strange it must have looked. He was an experienced commissaire in charge of urgently solving two brutal murders and an attack in which four people had been injured, so he was in the middle of an extremely demanding investigation. The entire town, probably even all of Brittany at this stage, had their eyes on the Concarneau police. And what was the chief commissaire doing?

He was sitting on a bench reading.

As a rule Dupin didn't care what other people thought of any potentially strange or unorthodox methods he used during his investigations. It just hadn't been easy to find the right spot. A spot with no people but that was still central enough for him to be on the scene quickly if there were any new developments.

The commissaire had ended up in the little park behind the church in the Ville Close, a hidden gem with a very special atmosphere, the perfect place for what he was planning. Even when the main street in the Ville Close, Rue Vauban, was mobbed all the way to where it ended at Place Saint-Guénolé—the place was deserted all of a sudden if you walked toward the church and the park. And the few people who did come to this part of the fortress were usually walking along on top of the enormous ramparts to get a glimpse of the sensational view of the town and bay.

Dupin had immediately set his eye on a particular bench, his favorite bench, so to speak, underneath large, elegant chestnut trees. It was a long time since the bench had last been painted, and the white was flaking off. This was a storied bank with history and soul. The trees' low-hanging branches and leaves almost covered it up completely. Next to the bench, a gorgeous rhododendron grew wild; it wouldn't be long before the bench would be almost totally invisible. From here you could see the Parc du Petit Château and beyond that, the revered old walls.

Of course it was absurd that a commissaire at a low point in his investigation was reading a crime novel in the hopes of coming up with an idea, but somehow he couldn't stop thinking about the parallels to their case.

Dupin had quickly realized he needed to skim-read, otherwise he would be sitting there long into the night. But the real problem with his reading was this: he didn't even know exactly what he was interested in, what exactly he was looking for. Some of the parallels really did seem astonishing. Some of the details of what happened back then seemed incredibly similar to the events of today. Some details were less similar and many were completely different. The problem was, and Dupin knew this: once your mind has fixated on something, you spot confirmation of your fixation everywhere. Dangerous, flawed logic. A trap.

There was one part of the novel where he almost couldn't help laughing out loud: "There is just one plausible hypothesis," some-body reasoned, "and that is that we are dealing with a lunatic . . . Although despite knowing the whole town as we do, we can't work out who can have lost their mind." Other parts gave him goose bumps. Like right at the beginning where the brasserie at the Amiral was described in detail. And then the description of the wealthy, powerful families who had ruled the town for gen-erations with absolute decadence.

But the problem was, every time the commissaire thought he had discovered another parallel, it raised the question of how this was meant to help him. What could it mean? Was some-body in town staging a cunning play imitating the criminal case? The "great stranger," perhaps? That was absolutely absurd. Still, Dupin caught himself briefly musing that they were deal-ing with a genuine lunatic. And it was impossible to deny that psychopaths did exist, of course. But the likelihood of that was very low. Perhaps it was just that a similar story was playing out in the present day as in the book. Someone had fallen victim to unscrupulous, cruel people and then plotted their revenge. And this was the only reason Dupin believed he could spot parallels.

His phone wrenched him away from his alarming thoughts. Nolwenn. Dupin was glad to hear her voice.

"Where are you, Monsieur le Commissaire?"

Dupin sighed.

"In the park in the Ville Close."

"On your favorite bench?"

"That's exactly where I am."

"We've now got a list of all the relevant businesses that sell customized luxury motor yachts on the European market. There are quite a lot of them, twenty-seven; there are nine in France alone. We're looking for an extremely brutal, aggressive competitor. And it must have something specifically against Rêves Maritimes entering the market. But we don't have any leads yet. The whole thing is going to be a Sisyphean task."

This was definitely true.

"Priziac still hasn't turned up, by the way. Nevou tried to call him but no luck. His lawyer has credibly stated that he doesn't know where he is. Our pharmacist seems to have vanished into thin air."

"Like in the book," Dupin blurted out. Moments later, he felt embarrassed. But it was true: a person had just disappeared in the crime novel too. The journalist. It was meant to look like he was murdered. This would later, as Dupin already knew, turn out to be a hoax.

"Are you still looking into *The Yellow Dog*?"

It wasn't clear whether this question had been meant as encouragement or criticism. He didn't want to know. The wind made the leaves of the chestnut tree rustle; a pleasant breeze had sprung up.

Nolwenn came back to the issue of Priziac. "There are three possibilities: Priziac is guilty and has done a runner. Or he isn't and just wants to be left alone for a while to mourn the deaths of his friends. The third option: he is going to be the next victim. Because the perpetrator has it in for the whole trio. If that's the case, it would be an extremely bad sign that he is nowhere to be found."

She was right.

Dupin had been so fixated on the first possibility, in part because of his strong feelings about Priziac, that he had badly neglected the third possibility. But then again: if the pharmacist had just allowed himself to be placed under arrest, he would at least have been safe by now.

"We need to put out a search for him, Monsieur le Commissaire. I'll see to it straightaway."

"Great."

"One more thing. We've got access to Luzel's bank accounts. Nevou is going through them. She has such good instincts on that." Nolwenn's voice brimmed with undisguised pride.

"All right."

"Speak to you later then, Monsieur le Commissaire."

Dupin glanced at the time, quarter to five. He became absorbed in his reading again.

From the corner of one eye he noticed a group of people approaching. Just a few minutes before, a few lost walkers had wandered in and, without looking up, Dupin had—pretty pointedly—placed the book flat on his knees so that there was no way anyone could make out the author and title. Luckily they had disappeared again quickly. He had just decided to do the same thing again this time around when he paused. This could not be, it was absolutely impossible.

Here came Claire—and her parents.

In a panic, he tried to think. Then he slid to the other end of the bench, half in the rhododendron. And stayed there, motionless.

"Georges!"

They had spotted him. Claire's mother sounded about as dumbfounded as he felt.

"Claire was just telling us how much you love this place. And that you like to spend your breaks here. How lovely! Another one of your favorite spots."

Dupin lifted his head with ostentatious surprise, slid out of the rhododendron, and got to his feet. Claire and her father were standing a few paces behind Hélène. While they had both defended him the last time they met, it seemed they couldn't think of anything more to say this time.

He had to admit, it must have looked extremely odd: Dupin with a sandwich by the sea, taking a stroll in breathtaking coastal scenery, having a cozy read in the idyllic park of the Ville Close. And they only knew about these three moments, of course, nothing about everything in between.

Even Claire, who knew how important moments of quiet and focus were for Dupin during investigations, seemed unable to dream up any more explanations.

"Well, this is the wonderful little park." She turned to her parents. "And—and now we really need to get going, there are still quite a lot of places on the list."

"And I," Dupin said quickly, "am going to continue making my phone calls." He pointed to his cell phone on the bench. "Pretty long calls." The book was clearly visible in his hand, so to be on the safe side he added, "This book is probably related to the case."

It was clear from Claire's mother's face that a snide comment was now brewing, after all, but Claire headed her off.

"So, let's go up onto the ramparts now." She took her mother forcefully by the arm. "You'll get an amazing view from there."

Claire's father threw Dupin a friendly look and hurried after the two women.

"See you at dinner later then, Georges," Hélène called over her shoulder. It sounded like a threat.

Dupin sat back down on the bench, took a few deep breaths—

and began to read once more. He wanted to know how the case turned out now.

He snapped the book shut in one swift movement. He had been able to read the ending in peace. Yet the unease inside him had grown. His thoughts kept drifting back to Priziac. What else could they do apart from searching for him?

At least he now knew more details about the crimes committed by the three powerful men in the crime novel. The story was tragic, not unlike the fable of the desperate lovers from the Ville Close. Emma's boyfriend, young Léon Le Glérec, had bought a boat and called it *La Belle Emma*. He used to use it to transport fruit and vegetables to cold old England. A lucrative business, which was entirely in keeping with historical fact, as Dupin knew: a considerable number of the Breton fishermen had turned to this after the shoals of sardines stopped appearing. One day Léon was asked by three men whether he was interested in a great deal: twenty thousand francs for one or two months of work. A trip across the Atlantic to a little port not far from New York. They didn't mention the cargo. Léon wanted to marry Emma, to be able to provide for her, and he risked it. The three men smuggled a huge consignment of cocaine into the cargo on his boat; the profit at stake was several million. Later it emerged that Léon was not the only person they had taken advantage of. They had ruined the lives of a whole series of young men in this way. Léon was arrested and things got even more despicable: the three men reported him to the police during the investigation so that they could—due to a new law designed to curb smuggling—still pocket a third of the estimated value of the smuggled goods. A million-franc deal. Léon ended up in an American prison, where he was tortured and subjected to starvation. He only just survived this period and returned to Concarneau years later, a broken man. He and Emma plotted their revenge.

Although the commissaire had been engrossed as he read the ending, he was still left with the same question as before: What was he meant to do with this information? Did their case revolve around smuggling too, perhaps, or drugs or other illegal goods? In shipbuilding or in the brewery trade? And, if so, who was the victim?

Dupin got up, reaching for his phone. He would talk it over with Nolwenn.

"Monsieur le Commissaire?"

"Is there any news on Priziac?"

"No signs of life yet."

This offhand phrase touched on the very thing Dupin was worried about. He had a bad feeling. Right now, this case could be costing a third person their life. And what had he been doing this entire time? Reading. Following a hunch, a trail that ultimately led back to a ridiculous and untenable copycat theory.

"The entire police force and gendarmerie of Finistère have been informed as well as the public, we—"

"Great." Dupin hesitated. "I'm going to drive to the pharmacist's house."

"One of our cars is already there. They would have noticed Priziac."

Of course.

"Still. I want to take a bit of a look around."

"Good. Do what you've got to do. By the way, Riwal got caught in terrible traffic, he has only just arrived in La Rochelle.

He'll be in touch straight after the interview. Le Menn and I will do a bit more research. There are new tips from the public too. Who knows, there could actually be something of interest among them."

Dupin parked his car right next to the patrol car belonging to the two gendarmes from Fouesnant. Still no sign of Priziac. Not at his pharmacy and not here at his house either.

Dupin walked into the garden above the beach and went over to the three lounge chairs where he had spoken to Priziac the day before. It seemed like much longer ago. Dupin leaned on the stone wall. His gaze swept across the majestic bay. A wind had sprung up here too, salt and iodine blowing inshore from the open sea. The sky was still a pristine blue.

For a moment the commissaire felt like he was standing at a dead man's house. Dupin pulled himself together and walked up to the front door. It was locked.

There were sure to be several doors. That was standard for houses of this kind and size. Maybe there would be another door on the other side. Or at the back.

Less than a minute later Dupin had discovered a plain wooden door on the side facing the parking spaces, covered up by camellia bushes. This was locked too.

During his recon mission he had noticed a window open on the raised ground floor. The commissaire fetched one of the chairs from the veranda. Obviously he had no warrant for entering the house. But desperate times called for desperate measures.

Just a few moments later Dupin found himself inside the villa. He was standing in an enormous room with a panoramic view of the sea. A sitting room cum dining room. A semi-partitioned-off kitchen that must have been renovated in the last few years. Very modern and chic. It looked unused. In the fridge there was some cheese, a few salami sausages, butter, and milk. An expensive espresso machine on the counter.

Dupin headed for the hallway. There was no cellar door; the house was built right into the cliffs. A wide wooden staircase led to the upper floors.

There were three large rooms on the first floor. A study with an old bureau and a designer desk chair in front of it, a computer in standby mode but password-protected. Dupin had tried it immediately. Then there was a television room: a sofa and a large, modern screen. Finally, a sparsely decorated guest room.

On the floor above was a spacious bedroom that faced onto the Atlantic. On the opposite side was a large, turquoise-tiled bathroom with a dressing room off it. While there had been just a handful of oil paintings on the white-painted walls in the other rooms, the walls of the bedroom were covered in old framed photos. There must have been dozens of them. They reminded Dupin of his mother's drawing room in Paris. Perhaps Madame Priziac had put them up. It occurred to Dupin that he didn't know how long she had been dead. Some photos even seemed to be from the last century. There were old pharmacies in some of them. Among them was a framed newspaper clipping with a photo from 1924: a stylish new building, with a sign reading "Pharmacie" above it, three men laughing in front of the door. Names he didn't recognize underneath. Madame Priziac's family, perhaps; it looked like they had been pharmacists too. Various portraits from the thirties, presumably all relatives. And a wedding photo. Next to it was a newspaper article about the wedding. They had been important people, that much was clear. Another photo showed people in front of a restaurant. Dupin stopped: he wasn't sure, but it could have been the Amiral. The building was much closer to the water, though.

Dupin looked at his watch. It was 6:30 P.M. Claire and her parents would be eating at the Amiral in half an hour. And would be expecting him.

There was nothing more he could do here.

He realized he could kill two birds with one stone by leaving now: first of all he could speak to Madame Chaboseau again. Perhaps she was the secret core of this case after all? He didn't know why this suddenly crossed his mind. Maybe just because he'd had the feeling all along that she was hiding something from them; secondly, this way he could at least briefly join Claire and her parents. He wouldn't be able to stay for the whole meal, of course, but maybe for the starters. As an olive branch for the family's Pentecost weekend.

Dupin hurried down the stairs.

"There you are, Georges! Just in time, we're discussing the starters! And where we're going to go tomorrow evening. I'm all for Chez Émile, which you rave about so much," said Claire's mother as Dupin greeted Claire with a kiss and sat down next to her. "Claire reckoned you wouldn't make it but I was sure you'd manage." A short, dramatic pause, then, "It was time for your next break, right?"

She laughed.

Claire shot Dupin a meaningful look.

"It's so lovely to have you here!" She beamed at him.

They were sitting at their favorite table, at the back on the right-hand side. The table was underneath a large picture of a fine-liveried, venerable old waiter standing next to an empty chair, the embodiment of his career's grace and style. There was a certain melancholy in his face and posture, perhaps because the great, elegant era of his once highly respected profession had come to an end.

"I won't be able to stay for the whole meal. But I really wanted to see you briefly."

"Don't worry," said Claire's father with a warm smile. "It's lovely you've managed to get here at all."

Dupin had tried to call Madame Chaboseau on the journey, but he couldn't get through to her. He had rung her doorbell. No answer. He had seen two rooms with lights on, the library and the drawing room. Either she had left the lights on or she was at home and purposefully not opening the door. Dupin felt uneasy. He had no idea what this case had in store next. Perhaps he should have put her under surveillance too?

He had spoken to Nolwenn on the phone again just now. Riwal was still in the—apparently complicated—conversation with the owner of the yacht company and the man's lawyer; the interview was taking place at the headquarters of Dauphin.

"So, what do you think, Georges," asked Hélène, "what should I have? The classic *terrine de foie gras*? Or the lobster cocktail with pomelo?"

"You can't go wrong either way, Hélène. I'm having the *palourdes farcies des Glénan*. And a coffee to start."

The pink *palourdes* from the Glénan Islands were the best. Grilled with herb butter and cayenne pepper on top. Absolutely delicious—just thinking about it filled Dupin with joy.

"But what about the salmon tartare and the artichoke and

mussel salad? The poached oysters with ginger butter and kat-suobushi sound amazing too."

This was what Hélène had meant by "discussing the starters." Some people felt the need to talk through the menu in detail, and then ended up having exactly what they had secretly chosen at the beginning.

"All equally delicious." This was true. But his choice was made. He wanted the *palourdes*. And quickly.

"I don't know. The poached oysters sound really delicious. Maybe there's a starter of the day too. And you're definitely having the *palourdes,* Georges?"

"Hélène, just let Georges eat what he likes," Claire's father intervened.

"So—how about Chez Émile, Georges? We'll book this evening for tomorrow, all right?"

It was a small restaurant with an incredibly cozy feel to it in picturesque Pont-Aven, run by their friends, Marie and Lionel. Dupin and Claire absolutely loved it. "I . . ."

"But first of all you've got to tell us about your big case. We've just spoken to Bernard about it," she said, referring to the excellent head waiter at the Amiral. "Apparently it's a bit like in that crime novel from the thirties"—she shook her head in disbelief—"as if we were living through that time ourselves."

It hit Dupin.

He leaped up suddenly, his chair tipping over with an almighty crash.

That was it!

"Of course!" He hadn't meant to say this out loud; he couldn't help blurting it out. If this was true, then it was absolutely unbelievable.

All of the customers had turned around to look at him. The commissaire was completely oblivious.

This had to be it. Even though it all seemed rather fantastical. He had been turning things over in his mind for so long. Going around in circles for so long—and it was nothing like he thought! Their case wasn't about the present at all.

"Georges." Claire sounded alarmed. "What is . . ."

"I've got to go, Claire."

He was already dashing to the door.

"I'll be in touch," he called over his shoulder as he wrenched the door open.

He ran across the road and through the car park to the edge of the quay. He was standing right by the water now, a stone's throw from the Ville Close.

His thoughts were racing, his mind went into overdrive. He needed help. He had his phone in his hand.

"Monsieur le Comm—"

"You've got to think with me, Nolwenn." He could explain in detail later. "*The Yellow Dog* by Simenon was published in 1931, if I recall correctly. Written the winter before. While Simenon was here in Concarneau, right?"

Nolwenn was immediately on the ball. "Wait, just a moment, I'll check again."

He could hear Nolwenn typing.

"Here, I've got it: that's exactly right. In April."

There might have been several possibilities, but this was the first one that occurred to Dupin: "I've got to go to the town hall, Nolwenn. Now. Immediately."

"Got it, let me think." It was Saturday evening, Pentecost weekend.

"The mayor! He must have a key!" Dupin realized.

"Right, then . . ."

"I'll call him myself, Nolwenn. And send Le Menn. We'll meet there in three minutes. Oh yes, and tell Nevou to drive to Priziac's house in Beg Meil. It's locked, but there's a window open onto the garden, on the raised ground floor, she can get in using a chair."

"Got it."

"She needs to go to the second floor. To the bedroom."

"The bedroom?"

"There are old photographs and newspaper clippings on the walls. She needs to take photos and send them to you and to me. Photos of the newspaper clippings too. You need to be able to read the names in the captions."

"All right. What will we do about Riwal? He has just . . ."

"Later. I'll be in touch again."

Dupin hung up.

He had already started walking again. He was looking for Kireg's number on his phone. While crossing the road he almost ran out in front of a car. The driver braked hard and beeped. Dupin raised his hand in apology.

A noticeably terse "Hello?" from the other end of the line.

"Commissaire Dupin here. Have you got the key to the *mairie* on you, Monsieur Kireg?"

"Why—"

"Have you got the key on you or not?"

"Yes."

"Where are you?"

"At the big crêpes banquet for the Association des—"

"The town hall in five minutes. We'll meet there."

"I can't just leave, I—"

"There in five minutes."

No answer.

"Otherwise I'll send someone to pick you up."

"Fine. I'll be there."

Dupin reached the town hall first. Powerful gusts of wind were sweeping through the streets now, making loose objects clatter and rattle. The town's decorative blue-and-white bunting was dancing about wildly. The light from the low-hanging sun lent the world and its colors a particular intensity. A deep, golden shimmer, a magical spell that enveloped everything.

The town hall was a functional building. Large lettering above the entrance read "Hôtel de Ville." Hanging close together in a concrete arch were the Breton flag, the town flag, and the regional flag. Next to them, set slightly apart: the French and European flags. Above them was another French one. A bit bigger than the others.

Le Menn got there not long after Dupin. The commissaire was walking restlessly up and down. When she asked what needed to be done so urgently, the policewoman received nothing but an unintelligible growl in response.

"What's this about, Commissaire?" the mayor also asked as he joined them soon afterward. He already had the key in his hand.

"Open it up."

"First I'd like to—"

"Open it!"

The mayor gave in.

Dupin went over to the reception area, where a detailed plan

of the building hung. He immediately found what he was looking for.

"Thank you, Monsieur Kireg." Le Menn took charge, having
walked in with the mayor. "If you could leave the key with us
now. We'll bring it back as soon as we're done here."

The mayor hesitated. It was clear he was torn. Eventually he
held out the key to Dupin.

"Speak to you later, Monsieur Kireg."

Dupin went over to the stairs and motioned for Le Menn
to follow him. They went past the town hall chamber where the
brewery licenses had been debated, among other issues. On the
first floor they ran down incredibly long corridors and then took
the stairs to the second floor. They ran down more hallways until
Dupin came to an abrupt stop in front of a door and Le Menn
almost ran into him.

A sign next to the room number read "Archive." Dupin
opened the door.

The air inside the archive was stuffy; it smelled of old files
and dust. On the left were simple wooden floor-to-ceiling
shelves full of black document binders with white stickers. A
practical desk, one chair behind it and two in front.

"Can I help in any way?" Le Menn had come and stood next
to Dupin and was looking at the shelves.

"I need the archive folders from . . ." Dupin thought about
it. ". . . 1928 to 1930." He changed his mind: "Maybe from the
years before that too. From the early or mid-twenties, maybe."
Those photos in the pharmacist's bedroom—there had been several names there, but just one name was missing: Priziac.

The municipal archive's files seemed to be arranged by topic
and geographical area. One shelf was labeled "Series J Police.

Public Hygiene and Justice." A second said "Series 1J Local Police." Within the shelves, the archive folders were arranged chronologically. The oldest were right at the bottom. Dupin crouched down and Le Menn did the same. Dupin pulled out the first file from the bottom shelf. There were layers of dust on the pages; nobody had leafed through this in many years.

Dupin couldn't make head nor tail of the files' labels.

"1J1 Local Police 1800–1900."

"1J2 Local Police 1800–1900."

This was too early; they needed a file with later documents. Dupin put it back and reached for the next one. "1J3 Beuzec-Conq 1875–1955" read the label. A little better.

Dupin put it on the desk. It was a standard folder for office use. He opened it to the first page straightaway. A table of contents with a system that was difficult for the uninitiated to understand. But this was the relevant time period. It seemed to cover various topics.

Entertainment tax: 1877

Hunting: 1884–1933

Miscellaneous Events: 1871–1931

Criminals: 1934

Municipal Police—Territorial Powers: 1881–1929

Some terms were hard to make sense of. Dupin flicked through the file. A huge number of documents. The category "Miscellaneous Events" contained by far the most documents.

"What are we looking for?" asked Le Menn eagerly.

"I won't know until I find it."

"We—"

His phone rang.

Nolwenn.

He answered it immediately.

"Nevou has taken care of everything. She's still upstairs in Priziac's bedroom and wants to know if there's anything else she should be documenting."

"Has she sent me all of it?"

"Yes, she has."

"Good. That's it for the moment."

"You need to explain . . ."

"Soon, Nolwenn. Soon."

"All right."

She hung up without saying another word.

Dupin sat down and began to read. Minutes went by as he flicked through the folder. One document was followed by another. He became more and more discouraged with each one.

Twenty minutes later, he was turning over the last page. He had found nothing.

"Bloody hell."

He stood up.

"Here—another folder from the late nineteenth century and early twentieth century." Le Menn had gone back over to the shelf while Dupin was looking through the last few documents. She placed another folder on the desk.

She opened it to the contents page. Mystifying clues again, and it went even further back in time. But it went back to the period Dupin was interested in. And there was also the following:

General political affairs: 1807–1929
Fishing police: 1921

English corsair: 1812
Seditious writings: 1818–1853
Miscellaneous events: 1807–1924
Demonstrations, riots: 1849–1922

And:

Refugees from the Spanish Civil War: 1937–1956
Miscellaneous events: 1900–1941
Surveillance of foreigners: 1851–1931
Surveillance of dangerous individuals: 1851–1852 and 1911–1937
Trade union organizations: 1897–1962

Dupin started to flick through again.

The minutes ticked by once more. Le Menn was watching him carefully.

Then suddenly—Dupin had already given up hope—something caught his eye.

It was in one of the four cases listed under the heading "Surveillance of dangerous individuals: 1851–1852 and 1911–1937." A "sinister vagrant," it read, had "haunted the town and intimidated the people." There was "public panic." There were two typewritten documents too, from February and April 1927. Then another document. It noted the arrest of the "dangerous party" on May 29, 1927. His name was Michel Penhut. The last document dated from the end of July. It was a handwritten note winding up the file on the "individual."

Dupin read it.

He leaped to his feet as if thunderstruck. He felt goose bumps on his arms and he was dizzy.

He quickly made a note of something: "I—I'm coming right back," he said to Le Menn, who shot him a quizzical look. Before she could say a word, he had bolted out of the room.

Dupin was walking up and down outside the town hall. The story was so unbelievable that his thoughts were in a tailspin. Perhaps more so than on any of his previous cases. They had only been scratching the surface of the great tragedy this entire time. It was exactly the way Françoise in the gallery had predicted with those sinister words: "You'll delve deep into the history of the town." And he was struck again by how disturbing it was that it had been about *The Yellow Dog,* even then.

There had been multiple clues. He should have seen it sooner. It really was about the past, about a story that must have played out more or less the way the story from Simenon's crime novel did. That legendary novel—it was not pure fiction. It was based on *true* events. Incidents that really happened before Simenon's stay in Concarneau. That was the crucial point. Like with the legend Riwal had talked about.

Dupin needed to get his head around this whole thing first. There had been a real crime that obviously had not played out exactly as it was portrayed in the novel—but it had happened. In reality. In the handwritten note in the file from 1927, it had been summarized—with bureaucratic concision. The "dangerous individual"—a former fisherman—who had been the topic of the two earlier documents, had been cross-examined in a hasty trial after his arrest. And he had revealed an outrageous story. A story about "three wealthy businesspeople from respected families." More specifically: a doctor and a pharmacist. Even at this Dupin had felt uneasy—the third person was not described—and they had treated him in the most contemptible way and ruined him. In fact, three wealthy businesspeople from Concarneau had given a large boat to the young man. "Michel Penhut, engaged to a certain Emma Mataut" for a trip to England "under the false pretext" that this was an important vegetable delivery. Though in reality there were enormous amounts of alcohol and drugs involved. The man eked out a miserable existence in prison for years and fell critically ill. The man "claimed"—for some reason the word had been underlined—that there had, in fact, been several similar cases. The last sentence read: "The man originally on trial will soon be a witness in court himself. Outcome unknown at the time of writing."

Dupin needed to keep a cool head now. They were still a long way from where they needed to get to. In a way, this was just the first half.

So: if this real crime from the past, involving three men from wealthy, long-established families in Concarneau, if this real crime from back then was really behind what had happened over the last few days, then who was the murderer here? And why? Who was so badly affected by a real story from 1927 that had then found its way into a crime novel three years later?

Dupin stood still. Something had occurred to him. Something that could potentially be very helpful.

There were two things he needed to check.

Just a short time later, he was back at the archive. Le Menn, who was standing at the window, turned around and gave Dupin her full attention.

"I need to compare some things."

Dupin pulled out his phone and opened Nevou's email with the photos. He quickly went through each of them in turn. There were fourteen in total.

He was looking for something very specific.

It was the seventh attachment. The newspaper clipping from 1924 with the old photo of the *pharmacie,* the photo of the three men. The man in the middle, who looked like he was in charge, was a certain Fabien Dupois.

Dupin turned to the archive folder, which was still on the table and open at the handwritten memo about the "dangerous individual." Le Menn didn't seem to have touched anything while he was gone.

He was looking for the names, having only skimmed through them earlier. Paul Viché was the name of one of the real businessmen; he was the doctor. The pharmacist was called Fabien Dupois. *Dupois!* It was the same name as the one under the old photo in the newspaper clipping. Which hung in a frame in Priziac's bedroom!

Was this proof? At the very least, it was solid circumstantial evidence that he was thinking along the right lines. Another piece to add to the puzzle. A coincidence was out of the question now. Priziac or his late wife—they were members of the Dupois family, an old family of pharmacists. From the *exact* family of pharmacists that had been involved in the crime decades ago.

A triumphant smile spread across Dupin's face.

The commissaire was running along the Quai Peneroff. The leisure harbor unfolded to his left. Dozens of boats were bobbing in the wind, the bells on their masts ringing wildly like a warning.

Dupin breathed deeply in and out. It had turned a little colder; the fresh air and the wind were doing him good.

He had tried to explain some things to Le Menn as concisely as he could. Then he had quickly said good-bye. Le Menn left to go back to the police station.

His thoughts were still too jumbled, or rather, they kept branching off in different directions. And strangely this progress was twofold: with every new thought, the events seemed at once clearer and more confused.

The sound of his cell phone was almost drowned out by the loud ringing of the mast bells.

"Nolwenn, I . . ."

"Come on, tell me, Monsieur le Commissaire!"

He obviously had to let Nolwenn in on it. Even though on principle he was reluctant to show his hand too early.

"There has been a—shall we say—shocking twist." He started with the file.

Four minutes later he had, he felt, summarized the most important things. Much more clearly than he had to poor Le Menn. This was followed by an unusually long pause from Nolwenn's side. Then:

"Not bad. You've outdone yourself again."

It was not clear whether she meant his powers of deduction or whether she meant it as a criticism in the sense of "What on earth have you come up with this time?"

"So we're dealing with one of the oldest stories in the book, then: a story of revenge. It's about retribution." It was clear she was, in fact, deeply emotional now. "Somebody is out to get even!"

She put it in a dramatic way—but it was true. It was a similar scenario to the one Riwal had contemplated earlier that day, although that was in the context of the legend of the crime committed against the mermaid. Somebody wouldn't rest until the crime was "atoned for."

Dupin had reached the end of the quay and turned right onto the coast road's long promenade. This was also the way to Docteur Chaboseau's surgery.

"Somebody . . ." Nolwenn seemed to be thinking things over. "So somebody is avenging that terrible business from years ago. On the families . . ." She broke off again. "On descendants of the families from that time." She paused again. "These are people who still have a lot of money, power, and influence. They feel superior and do business at the expense of others. Like the Dupois family, for instance. An empire of pharmacies that has survived for a hundred years. Their wealth and status today were founded on the wealth and status they had back then." There was a mixture of disgust and sadness audible in her voice now. "And perhaps the same is true of the Chaboseaus? Pierre Chaboseau comes from one of the old medical families. They were art collectors and shrewd businesspeople. The only one who doesn't come from a family like that is Jodoc Luzel. Which clearly hasn't," a brief pause, "done him any good anyway."

This was the sort of thought that had also crossed Dupin's mind since making his discovery in the files. But was this really the most plausible conclusion to draw? Weren't there other alternatives? Other possibilities that bridged the gaps between the past and present? Theoretically, there was one possibility: that the trio from the present were crooks themselves, had committed crimes themselves—or were still doing so. Possibly even similar crimes. But that the police just hadn't found any evidence for it yet.

"That's how it is: *An arc'hant danzeet fall a ya da fall*—'Ill-gotten gains only bring ill,'" Nolwenn said, and sighed.

This was the first time Dupin had heard this idiom, but it was true.

"This also means there must be potentially one or more direct descendants of the victims from the past. Today . . . In our town, I mean." Her tone was somber. "Potentially somebody who has long since changed their surname."

It was possible. Exactly that. It was entirely plausible.

"If so, then it must be someone from the grandchildren's generation."

"I think—"

Nolwenn interrupted him. "I'll research potential descendants of Michel Penhut. And of his fiancée, Emma Mataut. Was there any record of them having had children?"

"No, nothing like that."

"That's another crazy detail: that there really was an Emma. In the real story, not just in Simenon's novel."

"So crazy."

It had been bothering Dupin too. Maybe the author had wanted to create a defiant memorial to the real person. When you read it, there was no other character from the novel you felt for and empathized with as much as Emma, the waitress.

"Is there no postscript, Monsieur le Commissaire? In the archive file, I mean? A note giving an update on developments?"

"No. Nothing."

"Another question is why this is all coming up again at this exact moment? Why now?"

"Absolutely."

Dupin still didn't have the slightest idea.

"What about the mayor, Monsieur le Commissaire?"

"You mean he could be a descendant of Penhut?"

Right now they didn't even know if Penhut had any descendants.

"Absolutely. Or—a descendant of Emma, who knows. Kireg is adopted. We've got to find out more about his origins. About his biological parents."

"Do it."

Nolwenn was—as always—right. And it made sense to work systematically through everyone now anyway.

"The same goes for Evette Derien's origins. And Sieren Cléac's."

"Definitely."

"All of this also means that our assumption that the pharmacist's life is in danger is even more time-critical now. Do you think the perpetrator has him? There's absolutely no sign of him anywhere."

"Or it could be the other way around, Nolwenn. Priziac"—Dupin's voice turned grim—"could be the one on the hunt."

By now the commissaire had reached the promenade by the sea. It was just another few hundred meters to his house.

Nolwenn was silent for a moment. Then she said firmly, "I'll get Riwal to come back, in any case. Apparently the conversation with Malraux from Dauphin was fraught and there was nothing of interest."

Dupin had completely forgotten.

"Absolutely. And we need to know where Cléac and Derien are right now."

"Let's get right on it."

"Great."

Dupin had reached the Quai Nul, right in front of the *sand-wicherie*.

"Right, Commissaire, I'll handle the past now."

She hung up.

Dupin had walked to the end of the quay. To the place where there was a gap in the stone wall and an alarmingly rusty ladder down to the sea. A favorite spot for children; they jumped into the water from here and climbed back up the ladder. Depending on the tides, these were daring jumps of a good eight or nine meters.

He looked out across the bay. The Glénan Islands were lit up by the low-hanging sun, the lighter colors standing out, especially the white. Like the lighthouse on Penfret. And the Caribbean-looking beaches.

Dupin froze. Something had suddenly crossed his mind.

Of course. It was possible!

"Damn it."

It would be the most despicable of all the possibilities. And thus—in this awful story—perhaps the most obvious. After all, she had told him: "My mother is Breton." That would fit perfectly. If this was true, a little shudder ran down his spine, she wouldn't have come to Concarneau "by chance." She—she would have planned it all. Meticulously, in cold blood and far in advance. Perhaps over the course of many years. It would have been the only reason she joined the practice. To get as close to him as she possibly could. Only to reveal who she was one day. And strike.

Dupin immediately looked up her number and called it.

The voicemail kicked in.

"This is the voicemail of Docteur Evette Derien. Unfortunately I'm not available right now, but you can reach me—"

Dupin hung up.

He dialed Nolwenn's number.

"Mons—"

"Evette Derien. Send a car to her house straightaway. And one to the surgery . . ." Dupin thought it over. Where else? Where could she be? "And send one down to the beach at La Torche." She loved surfing at sunset.

"Got it." Nolwenn remained perfectly calm. "I'll send the cars right away. By the way, I've spoken to Kireg about the adoption. He claims not to know his biological parents. I'll keep looking into it anyway."

"Absolutely."

"Talk soon, then."

Dupin was standing directly above the ladder now. It was still low tide but the water was slowly rising again. Sand clung to the soles of his shoes. Large waves had washed it onto the quay.

Was Evette Derien at the center of all this? With her odd mix of gentleness and ruthless determination? Might she and Priziac be together right now? Was another tragedy happening? Had she followed him somewhere? Or had he followed her? To kill her? To get rid of her, and with her, the only person who knew everything?

Part of the building where Derien and Chaboseau had their practice was visible from here. It was Saturday, the practice was closed. You wouldn't be disturbed there.

Dupin was already running. He would get there quicker than a car from the station.

The exterior of the villa was freshly painted, a radiant white, with natural stone around the windows and a peaked slate roof. The gate to the property was locked but not tall. It didn't take Dupin long to get over it.

He ran down the concrete path that led to the side door. Elegant old granite steps. An aluminum sign with both of their names: "Docteur Pierre Chaboseau. *Médecin généraliste*," and underneath "Docteur Evette Derien. *Médecin généraliste*." There was a doorbell on the other side of the door.

The door was locked. Dupin went around the corner. There was a wide wooden veranda with steps leading into a lush garden. A glass door through which the chic waiting room was visible: a dozen fancy chairs, steel frames, black leather.

Dupin kept walking around to the other side of the building. There were some large pink rhododendrons but no more ways in. He couldn't get a glimpse inside the other rooms here either, the windows were too high up.

Dupin walked back to the door. Rang the bell. He would really have preferred not to make his presence known. He rang the bell again. No response. He heard the sound of a car braking hard behind him. Probably the officers that Nolwenn had sent.

What should he do?

He walked back to the raised veranda.

"Docteur Derien?" he called as loudly as he could. A second and then a third time.

His phone rang.

It was Le Menn.

"Yes?"

"They've found Priziac's car. At the edge of the L'Atlantide car park."

A large thalassotherapy center—it was called Aquapark now—not far from the Plage Porzou. By the sea, next to a little wood, a quiet, secluded area.

Dupin dashed toward the gate. "I'm on my way. Send all available cars."

A moment later he swung himself nimbly over the gate, landing right in front of two bewildered police officers who looked like they had just been wondering how to get into the property.

"The operation is taking place in the L'Atlantide car park. We're searching for Priziac."

He shouted this to the—now even more baffled—police officers as he ran past them. It took him a few minutes to get to his car. And that was running fast.

The agonizing squeal of the brakes in Dupin's Citroën was audible throughout the sprawling car park of the swimming pool.

Three police cars had already arrived; Le Menn was in one of them. Nevou was back from Beg Meil too; only Riwal would be missing for the operation.

Priziac's car was parked at the other end of the car park, right by the meadow in front of the wood. A hundred meters away from the swimming pool building. Beyond the wood lay the sea. The rocky coastline was rugged here and a handful of winding paths ran through the wood.

The place was deserted, not a soul to be seen, the swimming pool long since shut.

Le Menn and Nevou came running up to Dupin.

"We've got our people searching the woods and the shore. They haven't found anyone yet." Nevou gestured to the two-way radio in her hand. "Priziac's car is locked. We've forced open one door and the trunk. There was nothing significant in the car."

Dupin walked away—he wanted to take a look at the car for himself. Before he had even got there, his phone rang.

Nolwenn.

"We are—"

"It's a little complicated," Nolwenn interrupted him. "It's Saturday, Saturday night!" A complaint she seemed to be directing at the situation itself. "Even I can't get hold of everyone on a Saturday. In any case: as regards the doctor, I can't find anything about her during the time before her studies, that's as far back as I can go. She studied at the UFR de Médecine in Paris, the best faculty. Excellent finals results, a doctoral thesis about new therapeutic approaches to cardiac arrythmias. There must be a few documents about her in Chaboseau's files too. Although if it is her we're looking for, she'll have planned exactly what information to keep from him."

Nolwenn seemed more and more frustrated.

"The only thing that would really clear it up would be the birth certificate. But for that I'd need to know where she was born. At the moment, all we've got, if I'm not mistaken, is her statement that her mother is from Brittany, nothing else. That's not enough. Kler Kireg's parents have confirmed that he doesn't know the identities of his biological parents, by the way. He appears to have been telling the truth on that point."

"I see." He was impressed by all of the information Nolwenn had found.

"I haven't been able to find out anything at all about Michel Penhut yet, at least not on my initial search. Or anything about Emma Mataut either. The same goes for information about court proceedings against a pharmacist called Dupois—nothing! Nothing about any of that business." She sounded downright indignant now.

That "business" was a long time ago. And presumably every effort had been made to cover up the evidence of it as much as possible at the time.

"The name Dupois does crop up a few times though—that was them, all right—the great family of pharmacists from the twenties and thirties here in Concarneau. Oh yes, one other thing."

"Yes?"

"The most powerful medical family before the war were actually the Vichés. Unfortunately I haven't been able to find out anything more about them yet. The situation is a little simpler with Sieren Cléac, as far her origins go, at least. She was born in Audierne. Someone there is getting me the birth certificate."

Dupin had long since reached Priziac's car. The chic silver SUV was in pretty bad shape, the driver's door and boot having been forced open.

"The problem is, of course"—Nolwenn was not done yet— "even if we assume that the people involved changed their names, we obviously still don't have a clue when they might have changed it. If the name Penhut is not on the birth certificate of our suspect, it's possible that the name was changed even earlier than that."

She had worded this in a slightly complicated way, but Dupin understood exactly what she meant. This was how it always was on a case: shortly before you found the solution, it usually got a little bit more complicated.

"We need to try anyway. I'll talk to you later, Nolwenn."

He had walked around the car twice during the phone call and nothing had caught his eye. Nothing inside either.

He gave up on the car and looked around.

A moment later he was walking toward the little wood. Where on earth was Priziac? He had to be somewhere nearby. Unless he had gotten into a different car. Either voluntarily or under threat of violence.

They needed to be vigilant, go over everything, think through every possibility, and if possible, think ahead.

Dupin quickened his pace through the close-set, strangely overgrown trees covered in mistletoe and ivy. Another great pair of lovers from Concarnese legend had fled here. Riwal had told him the story many times, spellbound: Fanch and the beautiful Gaëlle, whose father, a cold-hearted, tyrannical king, had been opposed to their love. Here, in the Porzou Wood, they had met a friendly dwarf called Clet and they helped him find a lost vial containing a magical potion in a grotto. To thank them, he gave them a few drops of the magical potion and they put it in the king's wine. The drink turned a person's personality into its opposite. Which meant the king became a charitable person, generous and selfless. And allowed the two of them to wed on the spot. One of the few love stories with a happy ending.

Dupin rounded one last bend and came upon the sea, at the farthest tip of the rocky headland. To the right was the harbor and opposite was the Le Cabellou peninsula that stretched almost as far as the harbor. To the west, you could see as far as the famous fortress. The ruins of the old fortress tower were visible from here in the evening light.

Dupin stopped for a moment. He looked around. To his left, a path ran along the coast for about three hundred meters, then there was a little bay. The low tide had exposed the seabed here too. Dozens of colorful boats lay on their sides, looking like they were resting until the next demanding high tide.

Had Priziac taken a boat out, perhaps? If so, it didn't matter how long they searched on land . . .

Dupin took his phone out of his trouser pocket. It rang at that exact moment.

Nolwenn. She was excited. "Kireg! He filed an application for information on his biological parents with the relevant agency in Quimper—and had it granted. Kireg lied—he knows who his birth parents are! I tracked down the director, he lives close to the agency and looked it up on the system for us especially."

Dupin froze, motionless.

"This—this could be it."

Maybe this really was the solution.

"Why else would Kireg have lied? In these critical circumstances?" There was triumph in her voice. "It's the mayor we're after!"

"We've got to find him straight—"

"I've sent out the last two officers we have available. They should be at his house soon."

"Excellent."

"Then they'll bring him into the station."

It wouldn't have been Dupin's first choice, but that didn't matter right now. He had already set off.

"By the way, I've applied all the pressure I could to find out the names of the birth parents, but it's not going to be easy. It's very strictly regulated, legally. But for now, come to the police station."

"Will do. Speak soon, Nolwenn."

It was a rare sight: Commissaire Dupin walking through the door of the police station during a case.

In no time at all, Dupin was on the first floor, where Nolwenn was waiting for him.

"We haven't said anything to Kireg so far. He has turned out to be surprisingly cooperative, he came with us after a quick discussion." Nolwenn was walking ahead of Dupin down the corridor to the interrogation room—they were dodging buckets of paint and ladders, and this wing of the building still stank.

"Great."

"I asked the head of the adoption agency to scan and send me the document about the process, it should be here very soon."

They had reached the interrogation room. Dupin wrenched the door open and walked in. Nolwenn went back to her office.

"You lied, Monsieur le Maire." Dupin strode over to Kireg, who had leaped out of his chair in shock. A bewildered look on his face, but Dupin had seen his fair share of those.

"You know who your birth parents are. You met them. And they told you everything. Everything that was done to your family."

Dupin paused. It made sense not to get too specific. Besides, he didn't know enough, not even if Kireg's biological parents were still alive or had died in the last few years.

The mayor seemed extremely confused.

"What are you talking about?"

Dupin kept a cool head.

"I'm talking about the fact you are well aware of the identity of your birth parents and that you lied to us."

"I . . ." The mayor started to stammer. "I have been considering, ever since my eighteenth birthday, since I found out I was adopted, I mean, whether I would like to know who they are. My 'real parents.' I couldn't decide. I . . . Then one day"—he looked the picture of misery now—"I decided, yes, I do want to know. And filed an application. I didn't tell my adopted parents anything about it. I didn't tell a soul! And then I was given these two names. Names that were totally alien to me. Suddenly it felt all wrong again. Once I knew the names, I didn't want to do it anymore." He breathed out hard. "I've never contacted them. Although I still think about it now. I have an address in Dinard. I . . ."

Kireg didn't finish his sentence, sinking into the chair in exhaustion.

Dupin was momentarily disconcerted. They had not thought of this possibility. Unfortunately it sounded very credible. And would ruin everything yet again. But maybe Kireg was just a good actor.

"Give us the names right now, we need to check this."

"I'm not going to do that." Kireg sounded combative now.

"Oh yes you will."

A harsh tone of voice—Dupin knew by now how the mayor needed to be handled.

"Write them down, right now."

Dupin ripped a page out of his notebook and held it out to Kireg with a pen.

The mayor hesitated briefly, then did as he was told.

The door flew open.

Nolwenn was holding a piece of A4 paper.

"Monsieur le Commissaire," her voice shook, "this has just come in. You need to take a look."

She was standing in front of him, holding it out.

"Here! Look at the middle name. That cannot be a coincidence."

Dupin skimmed the document. It was a birth certificate. From Audierne.

"There."

Nolwenn pointed to the place—Dupin had seen it now too.

It said "Emma."

The four letters were in the space for middle names.

Emma. The waitress from *The Yellow Dog*. And, most important, the—real—fiancée of the—real—fisherman from the twenties. Who was ruined by the three men. Michel Penhut.

Her full name was Sieren Emma Cléac.

Dupin stood rooted to the spot. Time seemed to stretch out in a strange way.

Kireg was staring at him, a puzzled look on his face.

Incapable of saying another word, Dupin was on his way to the door within seconds.

Nolwenn ran after him.

"Where are you going? I mean, where are you going to search for her? Where should I send the squad cars?"

That was the crucial question.

"The *conserverie* is not that far from the swimming pool. It's low tide, you can easily walk across the bay to it now."

Of course! Nolwenn was right. At this hour all of the staff were sure to have left, and it was a secluded area.

Dupin ran across the street to his car, which he had parked right in the middle of the pavement. Nolwenn was right behind him.

"I'll try there."

Dupin opened the car door, the key to the ignition already in his hand.

"I'll send a car to her house then," said Nolwenn, out of breath. "And we'll keep the search operation at the car park going too. Just in case."

"Call in boats from the harbor police too. They need to keep an eye out for small boats coming in close to the shore."

"I'll pass it on."

He almost lost control of his car twice on one roundabout, he had driven onto it so fast. He only slowed down slightly after it happened the second time.

It took him nine minutes.

The sun had already set. In a spectacular, ever-changing display of red shades this evening.

Up ahead, Dupin could see the old barn that had been converted into the *conserverie*. Was this where it was all going to end?

The world seemed infinitely peaceful here. Perfectly silent. Not even any crickets to be heard.

Dupin had parked a small distance away, behind a bend in the road. And had walked the rest of the way.

He approached the building cautiously. There were no cars anywhere. No lights either. The *conserverie* seemed deserted. He took a circuitous route to approach Sieren's office annex unnoticed.

Everything was dark here too. He peered through the window. Nothing caught his eye. Dupin walked back around to the front.

He strained his ears. There was no sound from the building. Nobody was here.

"Bloody . . ."

He paused in the middle of cursing. He had thought of something. A place that would work just as well. Even better, maybe. In some ways, it actually made perfect sense.

Dupin ran back to the car as quickly as he could. He had tossed Simenon's crime novel onto the back seat earlier. He opened the car door and found the book on the floor behind the passenger seat. It must have slid off one of the times he had braked hard. Dupin frantically tapped the flashlight function on his phone and turned to the final pages. It was here somewhere.

There! There it was! This was where the place was mentioned.

There had been nothing about it in the brief report about Michel Penhut in the archive file, but given how faithfully Simenon had obviously borrowed several details of the real incident, it was possible that he had—as with so much else—known this too.

It was not easy, read Dupin, *to get those three scumbags locked up. But I was determined to do it. I crashed on board a grounded ship with my dog, then for a long time I lived in the old guard post at the fortress on the Pointe du Cabellou.*

"Crashed" was playing it down—Léon De Glérec had eked out a miserable, solitary existence there. The character in the novel. Michel Penhut, the real man, might have done the same thing. Besides, at low tide, it wasn't far from the car park where the pharmacist's car was parked to the Pointe du Cabellou.

As he had done quite a few times in the last few hours, Dupin jumped into his car and sped away with his tires screeching.

The commissaire pulled over hard. On the peninsula he had turned off the relatively large Avenue des Glénan onto the Allée du Fort, a cul-de-sac with a small car park at the end of it. You could get to the fortress from here. And to the old guard post.

He would make his approach via the rocks. The tide was coming in, but that wouldn't be a problem yet. This way, he wouldn't be able to see if there was a car in the car park, but he would have the element of surprise on his side.

Night had fallen, there was just one last glowing ball of light visible in the west, the last blue tones resisting the dying of the light. Suddenly the wind dropped completely. Dupin got his torch out of the boot, grabbed his gun, and put his phone on vibrate.

He started running. His torch trained on the ground, the light focused into a narrow cone of light to draw as little attention to himself as possible.

He reached the sand quickly, then flat rocks. He needed to keep to the left. It was about another two hundred meters to the fort. He moved swiftly but cautiously across the stony ground. If it were daylight, the trees would shortly give way, revealing his first view of the semicircular fort complex. He should reach the footpath that led up to the fort soon.

There were only a few parts of the once massive fortress complex from the eighteenth century left, but they had been carefully restored. Before Brittany had had lighthouses, fires had been lit here to guide ships.

Dupin was coming from the northwest and the old guard

post was on the southeastern edge of the semicircle. Everything was dark and silent here too. There was nothing more than a gentle plashing from the rising tide to be heard tonight. No sign of waves or surf. It was noticeably cooler now; you could tell it was only May.

Dupin had reached the footpath. And was running toward the fortress complex. It was on a headland, surrounded by rocks and sea. No one could escape that way. If anyone was even here.

Dupin cautiously approached the stone wall surrounding the complex on the land side. He switched off the torch and headed for a narrow passageway—the "official" entrance—then darted through it, keeping close to the wall. He waited awhile, until his eyes grew accustomed to the dark.

The outline of the guard post was visible—roughly five meters by three.

The complex he was standing in was deserted. Dupin moved toward the little guard hut as silently as possible. There were two doors on this side.

Slowly, very slowly, Dupin clasped the cool handle of the first door. His right hand on his gun.

He waited a moment, then tried to push the handle down in one swift, firm movement. A strange, resounding noise rang out. He almost groaned out loud, he had pushed so hard. The door handle moved two or three centimeters, but then it got stuck. The door was locked. He tried the second one—and got the same result.

For a moment, nothing happened. The noises faded into the night.

Then suddenly there was a sound. Not from the guard hut; it was coming from the sea. Below the complex.

"H—o—he—llo?"

Faint, indistinct. Unintelligible. The voice sounded strained. Or rather, muffled.

Somebody was here.

Another strained call. It sounded desperate.

Dupin left the complex as quickly as he could and headed for the rocks.

Suddenly he heard muffled noises, words he couldn't make out. This time it sounded as though the person was shouting through a scarf, as if their mouth was gagged.

The commissaire approached silently.

If he was judging things correctly, the person was about twenty meters away from him. Dupin had been here several times before and he remembered some ruins of an old tower, just a few stones really, roughly at the spot where the calls were coming from. At high tide, these rocks were underwater. And it would be high tide very soon.

All at once he saw them: the last remaining ruins of the stone tower. And next to them he could now also see the outline of a man lying on the rocks. A large, heavyset man. He was lying on his side. His arms bent, bound with a rope, as were his legs. The rope was tied to one of the metal rings for mooring boats that could be found all along the coast. The figure on the rocks wasn't moving.

Brecan Priziac. No doubt about it. It was him.

The pharmacist didn't seem to have noticed Dupin. A shiver ran down Dupin's spine: the water had almost reached the top of the rock already, it would be up to the pharmacist's neck in half an hour at the most. Then he would drown horribly.

Dupin stopped.

"Don't worry, Commissaire. It's only for him."

Dupin flinched. A clear, high voice. He instinctively reached for his gun again as he slowly turned to face in the direction this strange sentence had come from.

"You don't need that."

Now he saw her.

A female figure sitting on a high rock. Five or six meters away.

Relaxed, apparently, one leg bent, the other outstretched. Her torso bolt upright. She was propping herself up with one hand, the other hand lying on her thigh. Her ponytail was clearly visible.

Sieren Cléac. Sieren Emma Cléac.

Dupin kept his weapon drawn for a moment longer, then lowered it a little.

"Is he injured? Seriously injured?"

He wondered if he needed to call an ambulance straightaway. The wretched human mound moved as it lay there, the pharmacist raising his head, trying to say something.

"No. He's not hurt. Monsieur Dupois and I have just been talking," Cléac said quietly. She sounded almost cheerful. It was creepy.

"Monsieur Priziac," Dupin corrected her, almost offhand.

"He was only called that later, after the war. You know everything, I take it."

"The most important parts."

Dupin was walking toward her calmly. He moved slowly, very slowly. And spoke very evenly.

"The fictitious case in the novel, *The Yellow Dog*—it's not fictitious at all." Dupin hesitated briefly. "There is a true story behind it. Maybe the author heard about it during one of his stays here." Dupin was standing directly in front of her now. She was sitting up high, still only visible in outline, her facial features in the shadows. "And it's not just any story, no. It's *your* story. *Your* family's, your grandmother's and your grandfather's."

It was just as he, no, as Nolwenn—and this was the only way to phrase it—had dreamed it.

Sieren Cléac remained silent for some time. The silence was not oppressive in any way.

"He didn't need to explain himself. Or apologize. Not exactly. I just wanted Monsieur Chaboseau to know that I knew. His father—he was the ringleader of the three back in the day. I didn't want much at all. Not empathy or even sympathy. I just didn't want it to remain erased, or as good as. As if nothing had ever happened. Because that's the way they had spun it."

She paused. Dupin was silent too.

"My mother"—for the first time, she was finding it difficult to speak—"died three weeks ago. She told me everything shortly before she died." Sieren Cléac was barely intelligible now. "She—she had known about it all her life. Carried it with her. My grandmother told her when she was fourteen. She, the real Emma, grew to be very old. She only died in 1998, she was ninety-one then. When it happened, she had just turned twenty. Michel Penhut was her great love. Her one true love. My grandmother was the most wonderful person you can imagine, Commissaire. I looked up to her so much."

Sieren Cléac looked at the sky for a moment. Into the east. Into the absolute blackness.

"Emma Mataut, then Emma Penhut, the wife of Michel Pen-

hut. My grandmother never said a word to me. She wanted"—
Sieren Cléac's voice had grown warm and soft—"to love life in
spite of it all, she tried as best she possibly could, but there was
a deep sadness that never left her, right up to the end. A sadness
that debilitated her more and more, even though she fought it. It
even"—the words were clearly difficult for her to say—"made me
sad as a child, although I would never have known that."

They had come very close to the true story of their investigation.

"Do you know," she turned to Dupin now, "the lie they told
my grandfather? What he was supposed to be transporting in his
boat and what it really was?"

"More or less," Dupin responded.

"My grandfather fell sick with malaria in prison, he suffered
terribly with it, the illness tormented him. Tore him to pieces.
Even after he came back. He died of it a year later, while the trial
was still happening. It was dragging on, new lawyers kept turning up. They knowingly ruined my grandfather out of unadulterated greed, the doctor, the pharmacist, and the lawyer." Her
voice grew louder: "And it's not just my grandfather they have
on their consciences, they had already ruined two other young
men using the same trick. Both of them died, there was nobody
to tell their story. The three businessmen pocketed the profits, it
boosted their fortunes. And their descendants still own it, nobody has ever called it into question."

She stopped briefly. Priziac wasn't making any noise.

"My grandfather managed to escape from hell. He successfully broke out of prison after three years. He came back from
England at the beginning of 1927. He wanted to bring the three

men to justice. But the chief of police was friends with the men, he simply had the 'vagrant' locked up. Claimed my grandfather was a 'criminal character.' My grandmother, who worked in a cannery, then told the story to a reporter. Who started to do some research, secretly at first. My grandfather was dead by the time the doctor was sentenced to prison. Seven years, actually, but he got out after a year on good behavior; his family was friends with the judge's family. The pharmacist went to prison for three years and got out after seven months, the lawyer only got a fine." Sieren Cléac betrayed no emotion as she uttered these last few sentences. "All the same, it turned into a scandal. All three came from respectable old families—the Vichés had been doctors for three generations, the Dupoises were pharmacists for two generations, they were in the process of setting up the empire that Monsieur Priziac owns today."

All of what she was telling him had happened many decades before—but in this moment it seemed very close.

"They needed to come up with something to protect the families' reputations and status. And their fortunes, of course. The Dupoises and the Vichés decided to leave town first, and headed north. They went to Roscoff, it's only a hundred and twenty kilometers away, but back then the north was farther away than Paris is today. They left 'trustees' behind who ran their businesses. Then some family members used the Second World War, the Occupation, and the confusion after it, to come back to Concarneau. As people did everywhere at the time, people in town had bigger worries than the 'mistakes' of a few old men at the end of the twenties. Old Viché was dead, but his young son was brought back by his mother, with the name Pierre Chaboseau. Just as the son of the pharmacist came back, also under a different name: the family was not called Dupois anymore, they were the Priziacs. The family of lawyers was the only one that stayed in Roscoff. They fell on hard times and retreated from the spotlight. My grandmother was six months pregnant when Michel died. She went to Audierne all by herself before she gave birth. To start a new life there. She worked in another cannery."

All of this—and much more, the entire, protracted story— would be examined in the coming weeks and months, in every last detail. It was overdue. All of the minutiae needed to come to light. At long last. That was the least that should happen. It wouldn't make anything better, not for anyone, not for Sieren Cléac, not for the living, not for the dead. Still—it was all that was left to do. It was essential.

"I didn't know where to turn when I found out about everything. All I knew was that I needed to tell Docteur Chaboseau. That I knew what his father did. That I knew the truth. That's why I was at his house on Tuesday." She hesitated. "He said it was too late to properly judge something that happened in the past, apparently they were 'different times' and 'different circumstances.' He played it down. At first I was speechless, almost numb."

She fell silent. Dupin took another careful step toward her.

"Even that first time, I—I met him upstairs in his study, just like yesterday . . . And I just left that first meeting without saying a word. But I couldn't stop thinking about it. Then I went to his house again yesterday. Still not really knowing what I wanted." She was breathing hard. "He threatened me. Seriously. Coldly, without batting an eyelid. He said they would take legal action against me. He and Priziac. That he was going to do anything it took to protect his reputation and his family's reputation. Anything. That they would destroy me, if necessary. Just like—like the whole story of what his father did to my family."

There was a brief noise, as if Priziac had moved strenuously. Almost reluctantly, Dupin glanced at him. The water was clearly rising. It rose quickly at this point of the incoming tide.

Sieren Cléac was still sitting in the same pose as she had been at the beginning.

"I didn't intend to do anything to him when I went to his house. But then," another deep breath, "I just did it. When he started talking like that. Threatening me. I was standing at the window." Dupin could picture the scene only too well. "He was coming toward me threateningly, closer and closer. It all came to a head in that moment. I pushed him. As hard as I could. He didn't see it coming. And yes—I was aware that he might crash into the windowpane. That it might break." She broke off.

Dupin looked back to Priziac. He could still breathe safely. But not for much longer.

"The murder of the wine merchant. I've got nothing to do with that, Commissaire."

Dupin believed her.

"That was Priziac. He"—she turned to him for the first time—"told me everything, we've been sitting here for a while." She betrayed no emotion. "He became tearful eventually, he knew the water would be coming soon." Her voice was expressionless. "He knew I would have just stood up at some point and left." She must have known that saying this would get her in serious trouble; she didn't care.

She was silent for a while.

"Monsieur Priziac told me everything, right down to the last detail. Until I couldn't stand his pitiful voice anymore."

Priziac let out a noise of despair.

"He came up with the idea of the attack and the threatening email. As a diversionary tactic. To direct your attention elsewhere after the," a little hesitation, "death of Docteur Chaboseau. So that you'd be concentrating on that and eventually it would all fizzle out." It could have happened just like that. "Priziac knew exactly how the attack would work, he knows the shipyard very well. He didn't care that someone might be hurt. No, that's not it: it wouldn't have occurred to him, that's how he put it. And even he was shocked—those were his own words. I had to laugh, Commissaire."

Dupin felt his loathing of Priziac growing even more.

"Monsieur Luzel probably didn't know anything about the past, the dirty family secrets. But at some point yesterday he grew suspicious that something strange was going on. He was suspicious once the attack happened, if not before. Especially after he saw the threatening email that he didn't think was credible at all."

So Jodoc Luzel had seen the email, after all.

"Luzel sent Monsieur Priziac a message. Last night. Saying they urgently needed to speak."

That could have been why Priziac went to Luzel's house. Presumably he really did steal his laptop and the cell phone.

"They had been fighting anyway about some business issue. Maybe, I didn't know Monsieur Luzel, maybe he saw his chance. In the event that Priziac was going to be exposed as a crook or something. I don't know. Maybe he was just a harmless man who was exploited by the other two and got scared. Or his conscience got to him. In any case, this was exactly what he said to Monsieur Priziac this morning in the brewery: that he knew something didn't add up, he didn't believe the threatening email was genuine, and that he was going to go to the police. And Monsieur Priziac knew how to stop him doing that."

They had considered this exact cold-blooded possibility today: that it was Priziac himself who had killed Luzel, only to then claim that he had found him dead.

Sieren Cléac changed position. She stretched both her legs out, placing her hands in her lap now.

"That is the entire story, Commissaire. It's actually very simple."

Everything important had been said; the rest would be cleared up later.

But there was one thing Dupin was still curious about.

"After he returned to Concarneau many years ago, after his escape from prison, I take it your grandfather really did hide in the ruins of the old fort here? Like the character in the book."

It felt odd to realize that he had grown quite close to the characters from the novel. Like people he really knew or had known.

"Yes. My grandmother had thought he was long since dead."

Sieren Cléac tilted her head back for a moment.

"Monsieur Priziac was looking for me yesterday. Everywhere. I saw his car outside the cannery a few times today. He knew I was there. But I was surrounded by my colleagues the whole time. We drove to the festival as a group too, everyone went in my car. And you saw me there."

She pointed to something next to her, something dark on the rock that Dupin hadn't noticed before.

"I contacted him and told him to meet me here. Priziac brought a gun with him. He thought he was cleverer than me. I had thought carefully about where I would hide, where I would lie in wait for him. Just past the entrance, at the guard post, there's a blind corner. I got him with a wrench from my car. I didn't want to kill him. If I didn't, then the sea was going to do it. He was only unconscious briefly. I . . ."

"Boss? Hello, boss? Are you here somewhere?"

Dupin had forgotten everything around him in the last few minutes, because he was so completely immersed in the story that Sieren Cléac was telling.

With something approaching shock, he spun around.

A moment later, Riwal's torch was casting a bright cone of light on the odd scene. Nevou and Le Menn were following a few meters behind the inspector.

"It's all okay." Dupin gave the all clear, having suddenly snapped back to reality. "There's no danger. Come over here."

A moment later, he turned back to Sieren Cléac.

"We will have to arrest you," he said quietly.

"I know."

There was absolute clarity in her voice.

"I'm sorry."

Dupin hadn't meant to say this. Luckily he only said it softly.

She got to her feet. She nimbly climbed down from the high rock and a moment later was standing next to Dupin. Looking him right in the eye. He could see her long, delicate nose, the almond-shaped eyes, the intense gaze, the pride in the way she held herself. She seemed almost glad, buoyant. For a brief moment, Dupin even thought he spotted a kind of smile on her face, but maybe he was just imagining that.

Riwal and the two policewomen were there within seconds. Nevou and Le Menn were also equipped with torches. Cléac and Dupin stood there in silence, less than half a meter between them.

Riwal's gaze darted back and forth between them. Then it fell on Priziac.

"I'll tell you the whole story, Riwal," Dupin promised. "But not now. First of all, let's get him out of here. Straight to the station in Quimper. And call a doctor too."

Dupin gestured discreetly at Priziac with his head. "He's guilty of murder. Oh yes, and the gun he used to threaten Madame Cléac is on the rock."

In an instant, Le Menn and Nevou were next to Priziac, grabbing hold of him. They began to loosen the ropes and help him up.

Dupin set off. "I'm bringing Madame Cléac to the station myself."

The pharmacist looked dazed, but he seemed relatively steady on his feet. His suit was already soaked through with cold seawater. He was shivering hard now.

Dupin left the scene without turning around again, Sieren Cléac close by his side.

The Third Day

They were silent the whole way to the police station. Sieren Cléac sat in the passenger seat, looking out the window into the night. Dupin was mulling over how to approach the interrogation. Most important, what questions he should ask. What should the questions focus on? Or to put it the other way around, what would he make her say and in how much detail? And—what would he not make her say?

As always, it all depended on his word choice.

Was Sieren Cléac a cold-blooded executioner, had she planned her revenge, her retaliation? It was possible to interpret her actions as premeditated murder and attempted murder. Or just as actions taken in the heat of the moment. Both men had threatened her. Would it not, in fact, be understandable to have acted in the heat of those moments? It would all depend on who described it and how.

Dupin had brought Cléac to the custody cell at the police

station. It had a narrow bed for the night. He opened the door, Sieren Cléac walked in and said *"Bonne nuit"* like her mind was elsewhere. She seemed completely calm, perfectly composed.

Dupin had replied, "I'll see you tomorrow morning," and wished her a good night too, then closed the door and turned the key in the lock.

He would be there very early the next morning. For the official interrogation. And he wanted to do it himself. He would leave Priziac to his colleagues in Quimper.

He had brought Nolwenn, Riwal, and the two policewomen up to speed quickly.

Then he had—this was a very rare occurrence—called the prefect from his office. The prefect had been fast asleep after the many strenuous official speeches he had given that day, so the conversation had not ended up taking too long.

It was quarter to one when Dupin stepped out of the station and onto the street. Into the wonderfully fresh air of the early summer's night. The hubbub in the town had died down or moved on to bars and pubs where it would continue late into the night.

Dupin stopped and took a few deep breaths. He walked to the harbor and pulled his cell out of his trouser pocket.

Claire answered straightaway.

"Georges, where are you?"

"I'm just coming out of the station. We—we're done. With the case, I mean. I solved it. And you?"

"I brought my parents back to our house at eleven."

"And now?"

"Right now I'm sitting here—waiting for you."

"Where?"

"Very close by."

It only took him a moment to realize what she meant. He quickened his step, and there was a spring in it all of a sudden.

Less than two minutes later, he was opening the door to the Amiral.

Paul Girard had set a table for them on the first floor—this had been Claire's idea; the downstairs of the restaurant was still pretty busy. The table was in the gorgeous room that was usually reserved for groups. Not just any table—it was the nicest one. Right by the little balcony with the view over the town and the harbor. An enormous, fascinating painting that Dupin loved hung on the wall. It depicted a storm-tossed sea; the peaked waves and the foam looked like towering, craggy mountain chains, some dramatically lit by sunbeams, others in almost black shade. A quay, mostly awash with seawater, with a fisherman standing bravely on it. On the right, a fishing boat with the wind in its sails. Dry land in the background, a few houses. Between the clouds in the sky, scraps of pale blue. When you looked at it, you didn't know if a violent storm was about to break or the sun was about to shine. You could be equally sure of either one, if you wanted.

They had complete privacy up here and Dupin was glad of it. He had had enough of people and their complicated stories for one day.

"Are you sticking with your choice from earlier?" Claire smiled at him.

It took Dupin a moment to understand. The "earlier" she meant—when he had been sitting with Claire and her parents in the Amiral—seemed like so long ago. So much had happened since then.

"*Palourdes farcies?*"

"Absolutely." His mouth was watering.

The table was beautifully set. Claire had ordered a bottle of his favorite wine. A Châteauneuf-du-Pape, Vieux Télégraphe. The glasses were already filled.

"And then I really need a large entrecôte. And cheese. And a dessert." He really had barely eaten anything today.

"To you!"

Claire raised her glass to him.

"No," Dupin protested, "to you—to us!"

He took a very big mouthful. He loved this wine: full-bodied, flavorsome yet velvety.

Dupin closed his eyes briefly, then opened them again and gazed out over the Place Jean Jaurès. From up here you could see as far as the Galerie Gloux at the edge of the beautiful square. His gaze drifted across the water and the leisure harbor with its dozens of boats as far as the bridge into the Old Town, the Ville Close. Finally, he looked at the vast fortress tower, the Tour du Gouverneur.

"A little something to start." Paul had appeared next to them. "You must be very hungry, Georges. An artichoke and avocado salad with crabmeat."

He put two little plates down on the table. It looked tempting.

Dupin had his fork in hand.

Claire raised her glass again to toast to life: *"À la vie!"*

Dupin felt very moved. Claire had no way of knowing how appropriate her words were this evening. He was reminded of Sieren Cléac. Of Emma. Of what he would say tomorrow. Or wouldn't. He didn't know yet. Not quite. But this much was clear: he would talk about the three men. About the criminals from the past.

"Yes." Dupin raised his glass. *"À la vie,* Claire!"

Acknowledgments

My heartfelt thanks to John Simenon for his help.

**Turn the page for a sneak peek at
Jean-Luc Bannalec's new novel**

Available Spring 2024

The First Day

A piece of the Brillat-Savarin, please."

For a fraction of a second, he had hesitated. But Commissaire Georges Dupin from the Commissariat de Police Concarneau couldn't help it. He was salivating. It was one of his favorite cheeses. A rare, heavenly soft cheese. *Triple crème*. It tasted best on a fresh, crusty baguette, still warm from the oven.

To Dupin, cheese was a basic foodstuff—he could forgo many things, if it really came down to it, but not cheese. It probably ranked straight after coffee. And was followed by other unrelinquishable things, like baguettes and wine. Good charcuterie. And entrecôte, of course. Langoustines. On closer consideration, there was honestly so much that it made the definition of "unrelinquishable" seem absurd.

Dupin wandered up and down in front of the cheese stall in

the phenomenal market halls of Saint-Servan, a neighborhood to the west of Saint-Malo: "And a piece of the Langres too, please."

The market was lively but not hectic. It had that particular atmosphere of a week just beginning: the people had energy, and what lay ahead seemed conquerable. The Langres was another of Dupin's favorite cheeses, an orange-red-toned soft variety made from the raw milk of Champagne-Ardenne cows. It was refined with Calvados for several weeks and had an intense, spicily piquant taste.

"And also," he feigned hesitation, "a piece of the Rouelle du Tarn," a goat cheese from the south, aromatically well-balanced, with subtle notes of hazelnut.

Dozens of cheese varieties were displayed here, piled alongside and on top of one another. Cheese from goat, sheep, or cow milk, with a multitude of sizes, shapes, surfaces, and colors. Pure happiness.

The sign above the stand read "*Les Fromages de Sophie.*" All kinds of cheese aromas hung in the air, mingling with the promising scents from the surrounding stands: fresh herbs, local and exotic spices, hard-cured sausage and pâtés, thick-bellied *cœur-de-bœuf* tomatoes, raspberries and strawberries, dried and candied fruits, irresistible pastries. An aromatic orchestra of savory and sweet. It made one hungry—for everything.

"Try some of this, monsieur: the Ferme de la Moltais, a Breton Tomme. It's from the Rennes region, also a cow milk cheese, with astonishingly fruity nuances. It has a slightly firmer, gorgeous texture. You'll see."

The friendly young woman with short dark hair, glasses, and a sky-blue scarf knotted around her neck proffered a piece of the cheese. Dupin had wanted to try it even before the cheesemonger's persuasive efforts—the sight of it alone was enough—but her description made it all the more enticing.

"Take it," commanded an elderly, impressively white-haired woman who stood behind him in the queue, raising her eyebrows. "You're standing at one of the best cheese stands in town, young man! And we have a lot of them! Obviously you're not from around here." It sounded like an accusation.

The woman had accurately identified Dupin as an outsider, even though the commissaire didn't have the faintest idea why. Admittedly he was "far up north" here, to the east of the Canal d'Ille-et-Rance, not far from the Normandy border; but Saint-Malo in its entirety belonged to Brittany. However, he had already noted from Nolwenn's and Riwal's initial reaction to the news he would be attending a police seminar in Saint-Malo for a few days that the matter was apparently more complicated. The city must have some kind of special status, because both of them—his wonderful assistant and his first inspector—had only visited once, while they'd been to every other place in Brittany, or so it seemed to Dupin, countless times.

In addition, and this was also rather suspicious, the encyclopedic instructions they usually inflicted on him as soon as he had to leave Concarneau for any other location in Brittany had never appeared. Instead, Nolwenn and Riwal had instantly begun to talk about the Creed of Saint-Malo, which had shaped the self-assured city for centuries. *Ni Français, ni Breton: Malouin suis!* Neither Frenchman nor Breton; inhabitant of Saint-Malo am I!

Malouin. Riwal had briefly explained that the city had been bestowed with fairy-tale wealth between the sixteenth and nineteenth centuries, initially through the textile trade, and then predominantly through piracy—the corsairs, who were legalized by the French kings. Rich, powerful, and independent. The small city had become a bold maritime power that acted on an equal footing with the other maritime powers of the era. And so the *malouinière* character had formed: victory-assured, sovereign, proud. To some—like Nolwenn and Riwal—it was more like: arrogant, superior, cocky. What's more, the willful—scandalous, even—claim of not being Breton was deeply provocative. And yet the flip side, not belonging to the French, prompted the warmest Breton sympathies. The rebellion against all "foreign rule," the unconditional love of freedom and the defiant will to risk life and limb protecting it, all of this was, of course, deeply ingrained in the Breton spirit, with the result that Riwal, by the end of his uncharacteristically short explanation, had arrived at a bold paradox: that Saint-Malo, precisely because it didn't want to be Breton, was a "uniquely Breton, downright ur-Breton city." He had even expressed considerable praise: that the region was—"one has to give it fair recognition"—the culinary heart of Brittany. "A singular epicurean feast! The whole region, that is, including Dinard and Cancale, not just Saint-Malo."

"This Tomme is aged for ten weeks with secret ingredients!" The cheesemonger interrupted Dupin's train of thought. "Breton cheese has swiftly gained popularity over the last few years, monsieur. The young *affineurs* in particular are producing some fantastic creations."

Dupin really liked trying the offerings at market stands. It was an essential part of visiting the market. By the time he left the Concarneau halls on Saturday mornings, he was always full. Dupin loved markets in general—culinary paradises, which, through the sheer variety of their offerings, the abundance and overabundance, were capable of unleashing a sweet rapture.

Stands with kitchen utensils, especially pots and knives, were also an integral component of the rich market culture; Dupin had a penchant for good knives.

The Marché de Saint-Servan in Saint-Malo was a particularly noteworthy market. Not just for its location in the heart of this atmospheric part of the town, but also the exceptionally beautiful building. Dating from the 1920s, Dupin presumed. The floor was laid with large beige tiles, the walkways lined with rust-colored columns. The most impressive feature was that glass had been integrated wherever possible, letting light flood in from all around. The window and door frames were a maritime turquoise green, and there were decorative metal arches in the aisles, including above Sophie's cheese stall.

"I'll take a big piece, please." Dupin was blown away by it.

"Anything else, monsieur?" The saleswoman smiled expectantly. "I also have a . . ."

Now it was time for the voice of reason.

"No, thank you. That's it for today."

She weighed the pieces at an impressive speed and packed them, no less swiftly, into a light blue paper bag with the inscription *"Les Fromages de Sophie,"* which Dupin took from her contentedly.

He was fully aware it hadn't been a good idea to buy so much cheese, or to buy any cheese at all, for that matter. They would undoubtedly be given plenty to eat over the coming days. The packed seminar schedule—four pages in landscape format—included a restaurant visit every evening.

Dupin's mood had brightened significantly while he was in the market; he had begun with two *petits cafés* in the Café du Théâtre, on the corner of the tree-lined square in front of the market halls. On his arrival at the police school campus at 7:58 that morning, his mood had seemed low, only to sink even further, all the way through to lunch. Still: it was a beautiful summer's day. Everyone in Concarneau had warned the commissaire of the cold and rain "up north," even now, in early June, but currently it was twenty-eight degrees, the sun was blazing, and the sky a brilliant, shining blue.

His good mood unfortunately wouldn't last long. In twenty minutes, he had to be back in the police school. While conferences of this kind were essentially a nightmare for Dupin, this one was sure to be even worse than any that had preceded it. A month before, the prefect had turned up unannounced in Concarneau, and with a beaming smile, had declared to Dupin: "I have news, a great honor for you, Commissaire." Dupin hadn't been able to imagine—hadn't *wanted* to imagine—what the prefect meant, but had instantly feared the worst. And of course, he'd been right to. In the first week of June, at the École de Police de Saint-Malo, one of the most revered police schools in the country, there would be a "unique seminar." Every prefect from the four Breton *départements*—three women and one man—had been asked to select a commissaire to participate alongside them. It really couldn't get any worse. The unbearable thought of he and Locmariaquer, together, for four whole days, Monday morning to Thursday evening. That was many, many hours. Longer than ever before. Dupin usually managed to keep his encounters with the prefect drastically short. The comfortable special status that Dupin had commanded for a long time, due to an attractive job offer from Paris, had been forfeited last autumn when he'd definitively turned it down—ending, in the process, the prefect's moratorium on attacks. Their exhausting feud had long since resumed. Locmariaquer's final sentence sealed the deal: "You should know that this extraordinary seminar is also a recognition of your team's untiring engagement. Our colleagues in Saint-Malo have created an incredibly appealing accompanying program, you'll see."

For the purposes of "intensive teambuilding," the idea had been to have shared accommodation in the police school. A horror scenario had shot into Dupin's mind: prefects and commissaires in double rooms or dormitories, certainly with shared bathrooms. After first pondering falling victim to a severe flu-like infection in the coming month—which would have meant house arrest—he had taken immediate action, searching online for a nice, small hotel. It hadn't taken him long to find one: the Villa Saint Raphaël, a pretty *maison d'hôtes* in the center of Saint-Servan. Sure, Locmariaquer had been far from happy when he got wind of it, but Dupin accepted that.

He had arrived in Saint-Malo the previous evening, after a relaxing drive through the deserted Breton inland, and had established he couldn't have chosen better lodgings; his room—directly below the roof—was wonderful, just like the entire Villa Saint Raphaël and its expansive garden. Dupin still wasn't sure what the "unique seminar" was actually about. Neither the documents sent out in advance nor the truly impassioned introductory words from the host prefect of Départements Ile-et-Vilaine that morning had been able to shed any light. The prefect had said something about "improving operative, practical working alliances" between the four *départements*, adding with a smile that "the most important thing, however, was to get to know one another better in the relaxed atmosphere of Saint-Malo" and to "spend a few enjoyable and constructive days together." She had meant it seriously. And it fit the genuinely impressive accompanying program, from which Nolwenn and Riwal had surmised that a large part of this, for the proud Malouins, was self-promotion. "They even make a police seminar into a PR show . . ." A malicious interpretation, in Dupin's opinion. If Concarneau were the host location, they too would call upon everything the region had to offer. The eternal battle of the Breton tribes: Who was the best, the most Breton of them all? An ancient tradition.

Either way, it was a curious concept: all the prefects and commissaires crowded together in one place. Dupin couldn't help but think of the Druids' gathering in *Asterix and Obelix*.

Sighing deeply, Dupin made his way toward the market exit. "We'll recommence at two o'clock on the dot!" Locmariaquer had warned him as he left the seminar room. At least it wasn't far to the police school, whose grounds were as sprawling as a small village. Four hectares, the prefect had explained, in the best of locations, not far from the world-famous old town of Saint-Malo—*intra muros*—and its equally famous beach.

Dupin's gaze rested on a stall selling delectable-looking sausage meats. Breton sausages, entire hams, raw, cooked, smoked.

"How can I help you?" asked the tall stall owner.

"I . . ."

Dupin was interrupted by high, shrill screaming.

It came from nearby, perhaps just a few meters away.

Terrible screams. Screams of pain. Dupin whipped around to look. To his right was an imposing spice stall.

Something was happening toward the back of the stall, next to one of the columns.

The screams of pain stopped suddenly, but were replaced by different ones, of panic. And agitated voices.

Dupin darted toward the scene, ready to intervene. His muscles tensed.

The panicked cries came from two women who had terror etched on their faces. Other market visitors backed away in shock or began to run. Chaos broke out.

All at once, the screams stopped.

On the sparkling tiles—Dupin only saw her now—a woman lay on her right side, contorted, unmoving. Her white linen shirt was stained a deep red at chest height. There were several punctures in the fabric. And the most macabre detail: plunged right into where her heart was, there was a knife.

Dupin was beside her in a flash, crouching down, putting his ear to her mouth, checking her wrist, then her neck, for a pulse.

He pulled his cell phone out of his jeans pocket.

"Commissaire Dupin. I need an ambulance right away, Marché de Saint-Servan, by the big spice stall, close to the exit. A woman's been stabbed, she's unresponsive," he said professionally, "stabbed in the heart." He glanced around and noticed the stand selling knives, which he had just walked past, right next to the spice stall. "A kitchen knife, it's still in her body. And," he hesitated briefly, "send the police."

JEAN-LUC BANNALEC lives in Germany and the southerly region of the French department of Finistère. In 2016 he was given the award Mécène de Bretagne. Since 2018 he has been an honorary member of the Académie Littéraire de Bretagne. He is also the author of *Death in Brittany, Murder on Brittany Shores, The Fleur de Sel Murders, The Missing Corpse, The Killing Tide, The Granite Coast Murders, The King Arthur Case,* and *Death of a Master Chef.*

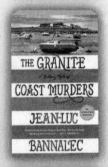